CON CODE

AFTEN BROOK SZYMANSKI

Appropriate for Teens, Intriguing to Adults

Immortal Works LLC
1505 Glenrose Drive
Salt Lake City, Utah 84104
Tel: (385) 202-0116

ISBN 978-1-7339085-1-1 (Paperback)
AISN B07Q36V4XV (Kindle Edition)

1

Four stories below, marchers demonstrate contempt for my existence, kept at bay by armed security. Picket signs with red-lettered protests tangle amongst the gathered crowd. People press toward the 'Do Not Cross' line marked with yellow caution tape. Not exactly the welcome parade I was once promised.

NuvoMundo TeleFormacion films both the crowd and my window at regular intervals. Even though the Mexico facility where I uploaded speaks English, the major world powers—in the form of the Intercontinents between the Tropics borders—control news outlet stations and get to name them what they choose. The constant attention keeps my mind off everyone I left behind inside the game.

It's been weeks since I uploaded to the mortal human realm, where second chances don't code themselves through the air and rematerialize with full health scores. There are no hacks for appeasing the masses of donors' families juggling emotions of mourning and vengeance or whatever drives their apparent loathing of a gamble that didn't pay off with an everlasting relative.

I drag one finger down the plastic ribs of the window blinds that conceal me from view. They're not unlike my non-human bone ribs structure. Except mine are metallic and supposedly have holes throughout to lighten the weight of my steel frame and allow for life-supporting liquid to connect my joint movements to my brain function. It's not my bones that feel hollow, it's something else. Like I'm missing the battery pack to my soul.

I can't help but feel like I've been constructed out of rusted left-overs instead of highly scientific alloys designed for efficiency. I guess that fits with all aspects of my existence—spare parts. Every motion feels poorly balanced while I navigate this gravity ruled world.

"Move back." A white coat robed tech slaps my hand away from the strips of plastic I've pulled so low fingers from the exterior crowd begin to indicate my position. The angle of the camera shifts to include the now covered window.

A large screen TV covers half the wall, ceiling to chair rail. On screen, cast by clear electronic lighting, a sharp-jawed man with a high part and excited hands continues to point toward the building behind him, assuring the raging crowd that the "first successful human intelligence transplant will soon be ready to greet the public, reuniting a donor with their no longer grieving family members." Even though no one below had the appearance of grieving, they look ready to fight each other for who gets to take my longest leg to the salvage yard.

"I told you to stay away from the windows." The tech speaks to me as if I'm a toddler learning language and unable to interpret directions. It works to my advantage. I tilt my head to one side as if I'm trying to force my computer language brain to translate his words.

Producing language proves harder. Like it only goes one way for my brain. Maybe some part of my computer brain isn't translating as it should like the output got dinged during the body transplant process. There are three main languages globally—Spanish, which dominates the Western Intercontinent band, and Mandarin and Arabic in the Eastern Intercontinent band.

English stubbornly lingers outside the Tropics. In Mexico, pretty much everything clings to powers of the pre-war past. We of the Outercontintents lost. Which means the English language we speak, lost. Here, they hold onto things after they're dead. Evident by the fact there are still people living here in a city incapable of producing edible vegetation, and whose only export is labor.

A low thud draws my attention back to the television screen. A reporter lunges out of the path of a flaming ball as it's lobbed toward the building. I brace like I'm going to feel the impact.

Nothing shifts below my feet. Then I realize the earlier thud was the impact, the television has a slight delay from the action outside. Slowly, I turn back toward the window, aching to pluck the blinds and fire back.

How long does Dr. Spaulding intend to keep me here? It won't take long for the protesters to learn how to make a more effective bomb. Not that they'd stand a chance against me if I had a green light to defend myself. My greatest strength in the game happened to be my brutality in survival. Why design a game with violent ambition embedded in progress, if it's not to be applied to the result?

Where I fail is movement. Dr. Spaulding can't show me off if I don't give the appearance of humanity. I've never been inside a human body before, real or otherwise. I've been in an image of one inside the game. But this monstrosity of a shell with its weak location of metal joints and thin tubes of lubricants running below the synthetic skin is all drag and cockeyed. Not like in the game where, even with half my body dragging after an explosion, I could push on.

I can't even sit correctly. I don't know which muscles to fire first. It should be first nature for a human, but I can't get the sequence right. Every motion is choppy. I try to skip muscle groups and ligament connections to achieve large motions. In my head, I can think, 'sit down' and it's one motion from standing to sitting. It happens that fast. I program the action in my brain—sit. The second I bend in half for sitting, the entire world falls on its side. Me with it.

The tech leads me in a soldier-walking motion back to the white-papered doctor's bench. Not because that's how they want me to walk, it's just the best I can manage. The more I think about how to move, the worse I am at it.

Three more white-coated wearing techs enter the room, each holding manila file folders in the air as if the thickness of paper stacks matter. "This one can be ruled out," the first tech announces and slaps his folder against his free-hand. I can't tell if he's beating it for not being the one or high fiving the fact that the donor information it holds is off the hook of having to claim me as 'itself'.

These techs have a thing for blank canvases. The more I familiarize myself with them, little details stand out like glitches in a document that's been copied and pasted too many times. I notice the inconsistencies first. Like with Gordon, his thin blue tie and crisp vest and white shirt are consistent. The buttons at his wrist cuff aren't. His right cuff is made up, but his left is undone. Stalagmite hair frozen in place with product in a manner meant to look messy. This leads my curiosity to the rest of his appearance—crisp attention to detail at every seam and corner except for the soft turns of his face and what I suspect is dark liner drawn around his eyes. I imagine he'd be a fem in the game. Where he lacks height, he makes up for in style.

The subsequent techs announce their failure files as well, all waving them, fanning them, thumbing through the thick pages of a life that didn't 'make it' like all of this is going to spur my memory and I'll announce, "Oh yes! Now I remember who I am—gamer number oh-three-nine." Announcing distinct personalities is less overt.

I could claim GenE247, as I did during my time inside the game, but GenE has a real file associated with her real name. And a real family who really knew her and her real personality. GenE knows how to sit and what face to make if she were pretending to not understand someone. And her real family would recognize someone posing as her and claim fraudulent upload.

All I can do is go slack in the cheeks. I've been told I hold my cheeks too rigid and high. But that can't be my fault. I've never had real cheeks. These are mechanical pads attached to a metal skull frame made to look the way I described myself after I woke up, being careful to mix features in hopes of not matching any profile pictures they might have on file.

I don't really know if there's a 'right' or 'wrong' way to 'hold' cheeks. Are they something you hold? That's one of those human phrases I mess up. I'm not used to idioms outside the game.

I only know the useless crap Ace uploaded into my personality, which makes me wonder. Ace programmed me to assassinate his competition within the game. Except he accidentally set me to the 'murder all the things' mode, and I shot, ripped apart, and otherwise dismembered my way through the system.

Nice programming.

The sound of breaking glass precedes another low thud from outside. Next comes a small ball of fire, popping and dripping flame trails. Sprinklers in a ceiling cough and sputter.

"Get down!" I shove Gordon aside and launch myself under a table. Gordon looks shaken and is moving far too slow to outrun the rain. "What are you doing?" I scream into the room. "Take cover."

"The sprinklers will put out the fire. It's not that big of a threat," Abby says. "Just some stupid protestor trying to intimidate us."

How can she be so stupid? "The rain." I pull tight so that no part of me will fall prey to acid rain. "It'll melt your skin."

"Dude, was there no water in the game?" Gordon pushes himself to his knees from where he crumpled after I pushed him with all my steel force. "She doesn't understand indoor sprinkler systems at all."

Ben shrugs, making no effort to help Gordon up. Like the others, Ben stands in the open, unconcerned with the sputtering ceiling rain spouts. All of them interchangeable in my mind—lacking personality and weight. Like paper. The techs are nothing more than paper to be stacked aside—out of my way until I know what to do with them.

Water drenches the tech files. "Move the files," Gordon says. It's too late. Countless lives of donors documented on the pages, lost. Gordon stacks the soggy files, cursing and shaking water off his arms, despite the fact it keeps spraying.

I stay where I am, under the table. No one screams out in pain, or horror, from the falling rain. It's weird. A drop splashes at my foot. I pull my mechanical legs in closer. The hundreds of tiny splashes static morph through my audio tubing into more of a sizzling sound. The yellow glow of the lighting tinges with memories of inside the game. Skin melting, code corroding, I tuck myself as tightly as I can, imagine I'm a ball of tin. I compact so tight, I can feel the gears flipping binary inside my head. Binary is familiar, I can work with it, manipulate it, change it. That's not a human way to think though. I need to be human here. What's the programming at the core of human thought? Can I work with it? Is there no changing human programming?

The sizzling drips fade. I uncurl and move so I can glimpse the culprit, desperate to analyze the expression behind the action. Beyond the dirtied glass are narrowed eyes and hands to shield the sun. I can't read humans like code. They're chaotic and don't follow logic. I narrow my eyes, focusing my sight to better study the crowd outside.

Someone from the mob below caused me to feel back inside the game and I want to spit acid in their face. I realize it's extreme, but I said, 'want to' not "I've devised a three-step plan to spit acid in their face." In my head, every image of melting skin, disintegrating players, and faces twisted in terror and agony play on repeat. I move toward the blinds looking for the culprit. Ready to eliminate the inconvenient source from causing any more disruption to my 'how to move like a real human' lessons. Security on the street pushes clear plastic shields against anyone standing close enough to touch the yellow tape. I'd do better than push them back.

"What's your Gen?!" Abby tech shouts at my side. The words reform to the setting as a tech moves around me to rush the soaked files to a dry location. "Watch it, Jen!"

I don't move. The tech must go out of her way to get around me. I'm in a paperweight shell and have yet to be given an objective. I can't shake the feeling that I'm still playing a game. Everyone in this room is either an obstacle or competition. Abby, the female tech, might be both.

She has a tight ponytail that pulls at the edges of her eyes. Everything about her is tight. She wears a white coat like the other techs, but hers is size extra small even though Abby is solidly a regular small. Her wrists extend beyond the cuffs by more than an inch. Her pants suction against her legs, which are peg-like anyway. I don't know about Abby's need for oxygen. She doesn't seem to be into breathing, at least not based on her apparel choices. Her facial expressions follow suit—tight, darting, and often pulled and squeezed at the edges.

"Jennie, come on," Gordon announces near the doorway. "We're moving rooms."

I step back in a stumble, realizing I'm targeting shots in the crowd, despite not having a weapon in hand. I turn quickly to see if anyone notices. The workers in the room all stare together at the television reporter. How easy would it be to pick them off in order to act on my personal directive to terminate outside threats?

Too easy.

Did the vulnerable and fragile human race, in their attempt to protect themselves while still furthering technology, accidentally upload an immortal, unbreakable, serial killer into their midst?

Water drips from my synthetic skin at a faster rate than it pours off Gordon's white coat. No matter how much liquid the fabric absorbs, it won't protect what it covers if, in fact, the humans have erred in their efforts to protect human interests.

2

Our new room is one floor higher than the previous location because somehow one additional flight of stairs defends against fire grenades.

Humans are stupid.

The entire level is a duplicate of the fourth floor. Same diamond-patterned tight woven carpet with the same path worn at the center of the hallway. Apparently, these people prefer to walk dead center in an open hall, not to one side or the other.

The room we enter houses less equipment than my previous quarters. One thing it has in common with my room from level four is a large screen television taking up nearly the entire upper half of one wall. Ben finds the remote and flips to the same channel as below —NuvoMundo news channel.

Abby, closes one eye then rapidly opens it again toward Ben. It's less than a second of movement, without the other eye mimicking the gesture. Ben is tall with broad shoulders and a broad stomach to match. He has a sharp jaw and dull eyes with heavy eyelids. His tight hair only grows on the top of his head and neatly over each eye. He has the stance of a person uncomfortable with the fact his gut extends beyond his waistband.

Ben strains a laugh, his head bobs slightly as if the gesture Abby made is some kind of code between them. I copy her actions in no direction in particular. I don't get it.

Repeating the gesture in Gordon's direction, I realize I've just sighted him in like I would with a weapon. When I blink, my fingers squeeze the same as if I'm pulling a trigger against the butt of a gun.

A familiar voice, high and sweet, full of life and lies, causes me to unclench and turn. She can't be here. She'll ruin my cover. But...

She can't be here. She can't.

"Welcome Donors, to the game of life. Humanity's best and brightest have ensured a safe and fulfilling environment for persons suffering terminal diagnosis." Purple hair bounces around GenE's perfect features. No liquid-red smears the image.

She's not dead. Can this be real? I look to her arm, her code visible on screen. Instinctively, I slap my right hand over my left forearm.

"Diagnosis is not the end. It's the beginning of a transplant process where donors will be challenged to solve problems, work as teams, overcome fears, encourage the best of human qualities in a variety of settings, while converting human brainwaves to computer circuitry so that donors can be uploaded into artificial intelligence housing..."

"What is this?" I ask.

GenE spins, her grace and poise evident in high contrast to everything I am even post player. "Don't believe me? See for yourself." The screen transforms. Teams build sparkling castles of blocky brilliance. It's nothing like how I remember it. No glitches. All softness and perfect alignment with each block placed.

Gordon responds, "It's an ad."

"A right now ad?" I don't take my hand off my arm. "Now, now?" GenE might be in the game still. Maybe she was right to choose ads all along. Her dramatic death was nothing more than a production.

"It's old, I think." Gordon waves me off like this isn't a conversation worth his investment. "Been running a while." He looks up, maybe noticing my interest, or maybe he can see deeper. I worry about the second possibility and adjust which areas of my face I'm engaging. Hopefully, it's enough to sluff the dial on his attention. "I think this ad tested as the most effective with the outside population. Something to do with being delivered by an actual player."

"She's not a player." It comes out of my mouth before I can take it back.

Gordon narrows his dagger eyes on me. I look away but know it's too late. "You know her?"

I stall with the motion of swallowing. I've seen Gordon do this. I have nothing to swallow, however. But humans respond best when I behave in biological responses similar to their own. They train me to do this just by their proximity. It's also their job to produce it in me as a perfect and non-robotically threatening 'Product of the Game.'

"No." I look at the wall then back at Gordon because the wall offers me nothing in way of help. "Ads are a different track."

Gordon's mouth opens, his eyes remain narrow, like he's confused by this. He doesn't voice anything though.

"Ads don't play the game," I say, keeping my right hand tight against my left forearm and out of eyeline from the screen where GenE247 describes idealistic challenges to enhance service and team-work. Like I need to hide my lies from her, even though she's not really here. I have no idea who wrote the script. They must have been in ads, too. No one who plays the game smiles that much.

Gordon's eyes shift focus again. I need to be cautious around that one. Keep him close and distracted with the tasks he's supposed to teach me, so I can learn what he's not supposed to teach me.

The commercial ends and a reporter continues about threats against programmers and investors. "The crowds can't be held back much longer. The Pierson Corporation must address the concerns of the families and associates of the donors within their facility..."

"We should consider going mobile," Gordon suggests. "Keeping our files from falling into terrorist hands."

"They're not terrorists," Ben says. "Everyone out there is afraid or mourning the loss of a loved one who became a donor."

Fame and celebrity have not been a part of life after the game. I hide behind double paned windows covered with blinds. I don't leave the building, much less the physical therapy room where they keep me. No bed because I don't sleep. I power down and charge but remain fully alert at all times. There are no personal or comfort items in my space, only things to improve my humanness. Walking obstacle courses and setting tables where I'm supposed to practice sitting without drawing too much attention to the fact I'm not eating while the others eat. Speech pattern samples to listen to repeatedly, and posture and gesture demonstration centers. I analyze the meanings of idioms and body language, which are unrelated topics, as it turns out.

But no one asks me if there is something they can add to comfort me in this place. If I was their sister, daughter, friend, would they realize I need an 'item from home' to ground me to this world, this place, these people? If they offered to get me something, what would I ask for? A gun? That would comfort me in this finite world.

Or perhaps I'd want to be reset. Like they can flip a switch and return me to the factory settings of the metal puppet, which has my brain shoved up its ass. The problem is, I remember everything. And according to my internal clock, I'm gaining time while humanity is losing it.

"My file's gone isn't it?" I have no file, but it appears to reassure the humans if I blame them for the fact there's no record of me. I'm good with this tactic.

The tech closest to me, the file slapper named Ben, rolls his head on his neck. His eyes also loop as though he's checking the grid pattern holding the tiles in place along the ceiling.

"She's so dumb." He angles his voice toward Abby. I notice how the two of them think the other one matters in their world. I suppose it's not my place to inform them that they're nothing more than repeats of the same boy-girl thing over and over throughout history. "How many times have I told her?" Ben adds.

Abby shakes her head indicating 'no' as far as I can tell, yet laughs, making it impossible to know if she's agreeing with Ben, mocking him, mocking me, or going insane.

Ben continues, "We'll find it."

"Did anyone anticipate this kind of reaction to the transplant?" Gordon asks. There doesn't seem to be a partner match for him in this group. I wonder if there is one for him in this world. He has the shifty eyes of someone who tallies my response patterns. Also, he's wearing one blue and one tan sock. It's not the sort of mismatch that can be excused by 'both being dark tones'.

The techs vary in size, shape, gender, and yet they all look the same. They all take on the same appearance—a bunch of zeros. TECH-chick would have bent these colorless gophers in two just for claiming her TECH Gen without any personality or swagger.

My attention shifts when Miller walks into the room. He and Spaulding were among the first humans I met when I woke up. Doctors of science and medicine, they both run the psychological and physiological wing of the Mexico donor facility. Miller has gray streaks in his hair.

Dr. Miller smiles at me first whenever he walks into a location where I am. Originally, I didn't know to return the gesture. I don't think about it now. I smile instinctively when I see him. He goes to the window to part the blinds. He studies the crowd below but doesn't grimace the way Spaulding usually does. A wrinkle between his brows forms then smooths, as though he doesn't want to burden the rest of us with even the appearance of his worries.

"Ten was the youngest age allowed to apply to the donor list, but even then, it was frowned upon." Miller lets the blinds go so they bite the small gap away. "Have we checked juvenile records?"

"Most juvenile donors flatlined in the dome," Abby offers.

Did they send kids into that warped hourglass of sand and water? It had to be horrifying. How could they? How could they do something like that to their own kind? The image of looking out in the sky at other domes, top half air and sand, bottom half water, moving at a slow but deadly rotation. The bodies not lucky enough to load into the air half of the dome floated lifelessly in the water beneath several of the domes outside my own. That's how I knew what was coming. Seriously, whoever programmed the donor games is sick.

I prefer Miller to Spaulding. Spaulding is a scientist first and a human second. The doctor part of him definitely resides in the secondary human section. Most people refer to him as *Dr.* Spaulding. I try not to refer to him at all.

Miller turns to the rest of the room. Some of the techs working in the office have family on the donor list. Their family members being the first ones they checked against my stats. "It's inhumane to condemn a child to never-aging immortality, just to ease themselves from suffering their child's loss." He doesn't wag his finger, but the room responds as though they've all been chastised by a parent. "This program is no game and can't be toyed with." Not that any of the techs have any influence over who makes the donor list or advances to be uploaded into the game.

Ben's face reddens before he can turn out of my view, but he's watching Abby more than listening to Miller. Distraction is a human weakness. I make a note not to be contaminated with it. If there's one trait I hope to avoid imitating, that's it.

Abby doesn't notice Ben, neither does she seem too terribly shamed by Miller's reprimand. Her tight ponytail pulls all the way to the sides of her smile. She stares at Miller like she's waiting for him to say more and the longer it takes him to spit it out, the more agitated she becomes. I keep my eyes on her until her gaze twitches in my direction. Upon noticing me noticing her, she startles, shifts her attention to Ben, and turns to leave the room, taking the water-warped file she carries with her.

Miller doesn't address the dip in emotion within the room. He closes the gap between him and me even further, forcing Gordon to move aside. "We will not cheat you, my dear." His hands rest on the edge of the bench where the paper tries and fails to curve around the edge, exposing a section of rubber-coated cushion.

Miller moves to adjust my features as I copy the facial expressions he demonstrates to me. He teaches me in this way. He's one of the only workers here who is unafraid and unangry to touch my invented covering. It's weird to appreciate someone for their lack of restraint and also want to slap his hands off his wrists for touching me without permission.

While showing me the correct human expression, however, his skin sticks to the surface where the bench isn't covered by paper, causing a falter in his reach and a slide of one finger along the paper's edge. A bright line materializes from the surface of his skin and a small bubble of red liquid forms at one end of the break of cells holding his blood inside.

Miller puts his finger in his mouth instinctively, then shakes his hand as if this motion will heal the weakness inherent in humanity—weak coverings and blood too close to the surface. "A room dedicated to healing, and no one has a band-aid they can offer me?" As Miller turns his back, searching his pockets for a small slip of sticky paper to cover the break of his skin, I slide my own finger over the papers edge.

The paper bunches and tears where it catches my finger. Wrinkles pucker and tiny rips curl away from the now tattered-edge-result from my imitation. It's impossible to understand how this material damages Miller so easily. I stare at the ragged paper's edge, then lift my eyes to the room of white-coat techs, seeing them now as tattered papers curling away from my touch when it falls on them to work with me.

"Maybe we missed something in the initiation logs?" Gordon thumbs the pages in the file he's holding. A thwick accompanies each pass of his thumb. "I mean, I know we've been through all the clips…"

Miller rests a hand over the file, silencing the thwick. "We've been over this. Donors create their own Avatars. How you see Jennie now may not be how she looked as a Donor." Everyone looks at me with a little more pout in their lips. It could mean they have emotional tenderness to my amnesiac plight or they are tired of the deadline to figure out who I am before the publicity tour once spoken of turns into a terror attack emergency escape. "Transitioning from a two-dimensional existence into this gravity-laden world again, it's a lot to require from the mind."

The difference is, this time, I do remember. I'm not an amnesiac, though I remember what that felt like, too. I remember waking up in the game, walking forward without any memory of what was before. Feeling like I had to fake every reaction, so I didn't give away the fact I didn't belong.

Now I'm pretending to not remember. This time, instead of hiding my ignorance with fake reactions, I'm hiding my reactions with fake ignorance. It turns out, I prefer it this way. I learn a lot by playing dumb and staying separate, much more than I learned from pretending to fit in.

3

Abby leads the techs into my room along with a widescreen tablet. "We haven't tried showing Jennie the video logs."

"Well, now." Miller smiles at her. "That's an idea." His hands rest on the padded portion of his hips, above his tailbone as he leans back. The way he shows pride, it's the closest thing to 'fatherly' I know. "Sometimes you've got to use your eyes, not just look at the numbers, ID, and code." He taps the wrinkles at the corner of his left eye. I watch Abby more closely, taking notes on how she lowers her eyes when smiling in the shining ray of Miller's compliment.

A crash outside, inches from our new fifth-floor window, causes everyone in the room to stir. They're accustomed to the sounds of close threats. It has no impact on their nervous system. My mechanical nervous system is set to alarm, but not from the increasing din from outside, which is now accompanied by glass-bottle-bursts and high-pitched wailing.

No. My internal workings are losing it because the humans are even less concerned with their created threat to human life, those inside the game. Is it human nature to accept the loss of life so easily? So long as it's not their own, or within inches of their own?

"There are three years of Donor footage," Gordon says.

Abby has her hair pulled so tight, not a strand could spring out. If it tries, it's sure to spring free from its roots being pulled out.

Miller walks near. He puts a hand on my shoulder. Abby has her eyes on the tablet, but her lashes flutter when Miller touches me, like dust lands in her eye, as she disapproves. I narrow my synthetic eyelids in her direction. I suspect it's me she disapproves of. My hearing is excellent, and though the techs like to keep their opinion-ated conversations outside my room, I hear the words they use. It's only a matter of time until I narrow down whose voices go with whom. I'm confident I've singled out the owner of the opinion 'it's unnatural, is what it is.' And I'm also fairly confident she refers to me as 'it'.

"Start at the beginning of the donor entries," Miller directs.

"There's no time to go through all the footage." Gordon doesn't whine. He states the information factually. I wish to correct Gordon with, "There is no human time." But suspect this will draw unfavorable attention to me, as I've yet to master the imitation of 'human-ness', and pointing out human limitation, which doesn't apply to me emphasizes my lack of mastery. It's frustrating to have to abide made up confines, simply because it makes humans comfortable.

Humans are limited by time in a way that is difficult to remember feeling constrained by. Time ran the game, the program. If you didn't level up 'in time' your game ended. Your chance of becoming a donor match ceased.

Humans run all their things by this 'time's up' philosophy. There is only so much time for humans and then it's over. Maybe that's the biggest mistake they made in creating the donor program. By taking away humanity's main limitation—time—they've eliminated 'humanity' in their creation.

"Set it to fast forward while viewing it." Miller removes the tablet from Abby's hand and places it in my hands. "Let's see how far we can get."

It feels like a precious gift. My friends from inside the game hide on this screen, even I don't know what they look like in real life. There's no way to know if I can recognize the donor face that matches the gamer avatar.

Not that it really matters. I pat my pocket for a small flash drive. Miller listened to me when I asked him not to reboot the system, not to flush the others from the program. He saved a copy of every file inside the game onto a small stick drive and gave it to me as a show of 'good faith.' He'd said that he was there to help me transition and wished to cause me no undue stress, and if having those files in my pocket helped me trust him, then that was what he would do.

The drive remains in my pocket. Spaulding, who greeted me first upon waking from the game, came back into the room shortly after Miller copied the program and flushed living codes into data purgatory. Miller didn't tell him he'd made a copy and given it to me. He also didn't mention that he'd dropped something into Spaulding's cup, which had increased his urgency to get to the bathroom.

Glass shatters just below our new window. Instead of jumping, I take the tablet and cover my arm across the screen protectively.

"Give it here," Gordon commands. "We need to move rooms. They know we're in here. They're targeting us. Maybe we need to go without lights and television." Ben and Abby moan at the suggestion.

Miller motions for everyone to stay back from the window while he leans to get a better look at what's happening outside. He slides the window open less than an inch to listen. Sounds of the crowd pressing against the security line travel across the sectioned off parking area. They're speaking inside a cardboard tube, amplified.

"Shut it down!"

"Release the codes!" is an increasing chant, which I imagine means make the list of codes and the list of donors public. From my own research in trying to figure out who was who in real life, the security measures to protect donor identities make it almost impossible to identify donors post game.

Before any of us make it out of the room, a flaming glass container sails into the room. The second it connects with curtain and wall, the flames spread. Whatever is in the bottle this time is an accelerant. More effective than the last bomb.

"Out!" Miller pushes Gordon ahead of him. Abby wastes no time and pulls people back so she can exit first. This reaction seems more appropriate. The immediate threat to personal well-being magnifies as the flames deepen from yellow to red with yellow smoke thickening greenly by the second.

I hobble out of the room, following the procession of workers up flights of stairs, because apparently, the best thing to do under threat of fire is to avoid all escape routes and dig in deeper. Higher.

Miller may be a doctor, but I question his intelligence when he announces, "We're safer up here on the seventh floor." Safer. Despite how we left the fifth floor a raging inferno. Right.

Every television on the seventh floor shows the same thing. Fire-hose spraying into the crowd outside, until the front lines of attack are pushed back behind the line of yellow caution tape once again.

Sputtering crackling noises proceed sprinklers kicking on throughout the building. Gordon has time to stow his device inside his jacket before the deluge. Televisions broadcast firemen turning their hoses to the building until the fire popping from the fourth and fifth-floor windows is nothing more than a smoking hole in a wall. The indoor rain douses my concern about being trapped in a human toaster oven. I need to get my hands on those video files. Once the water sputters to an end, I turn up my mouth in what I hope is a convincing smile. "Gordon, may I take a look at the footage you mentioned?"

Gordon makes eye contact with Miller before reaching inside his jacket to retrieve the device. I want to look at Miller too, to see what look these two idiot humans just exchanged, but I also don't want to take my eyes off Gordon. Stupid human heads only have visual receptors in the front plane of their face. How is that efficient? It's not. Gordon holds the tablet firm, even after letting me tug it toward myself. I have to stop and stare and him, waiting to see what game of wills we're playing, holding my face in the smile I practice constantly.

Gordon releases his grip. The tablet rushes my face, but I regain control. I don't want Abby or Gordon watching my reactions, but no one looks away while I push play. I have no idea what is expected of me here. Am I to sit comfortably? There is no way to sit comfortably for a metal shell being.

I risk a look toward Miller, hoping he'll understand I need privacy without my having to say anything. I mean, surely looking at Miller will benefit me here. Human thoughts are not computer thoughts. Thanks to Wi-Fi, I can connect with other electronic devices, whose passwords I can hack. Human beings are not so simple. I suspect it's still possible to hack a human brain across airwaves. I have yet to figure out how.

Miller's face isn't without reaction. I simply have no idea how to interpret what he's doing with his head. His eyebrows move in a barely perceptible lift, and his mouth parts less than a centimeter. I wouldn't even say it's enough to be considering talking, or even enough to inhale properly.

"May I have some privacy?" I ask.

Abby's ponytail swings like a pendulum at her back as she stands in reaction to my request then catches herself in a weird half-up, half-down position. "How are we to know if something jogs her memory if we're not here?"

Below the surface of my skin—way down deep on the inside, where the program runs—I smile because ponytail is exactly right. It's a tight smile reserved for emergency gloating, not currently beneficial for show. With an artificial steady expression, I look to Miller to await his verdict to my request. Abby slowly returns to a sitting position. My internal gloating grows to the brink of my ability to hold it in.

He blinks more times than his average. I know this. I know all their averages if I want to. It doesn't take long to get an average of someone. Humans are all so full of average it's overwhelming.

He blinks again. "You'll let us know. Won't you, Jennie?" Miller is one of the only people who call me by my name.

"Yes, Doctor," I say.

He claps his hands in front of his gut. "Well, then. I think we've all earned a break today." He takes the remote for the wall screen and silences the interior replay of what's taking place outside. I say replay because the screen is point zero seven seconds delayed from the action happening outside.

I try to ignore the voices and vehicles outside the window and wait for the room to clear. Gordon trudges out of the room first. I want to like him, but also want him to fix his cuff button. I can't decide if that's mutually exclusive.

Abby waits where she sits. My arms stay tight across the screen, even though it's black, I don't want to share it with her.

"Let's go, Abby." Miller waits for her to exit in front of him, then turns to provide me an expression I haven't deciphered yet. It could be 'don't let me down' or 'that Abby, what a pill huh?' or 'don't worry, I'll take care of this one, you get some rest.' Then again, humans don't murder and rampage one another—tallying take outs and kills like trophies in this version of their existence. Perhaps this sort of thinking is a byproduct of my programming coming into question again. Born a murderous zombie, always a murderous zombie. Or at least I hope not.

Once I'm alone in the new white-walled room with cream-colored blinds between me and the low roar of protestors hoping I'm their kin, I activate the tablet. It holds file after file of video footage with titles like 'donor files'. I slap my forehead. It doesn't hurt because no one programmed my fake skin to register sensation as pain. I can feel, but it doesn't hurt exactly. I could stab myself in the forehead with the same resulting sensation.

"No wonder I couldn't find video footage," I say aloud. I've spent every night after the techs and doctors and scientists leave riffling through every database I could conjure a password for searching for pictures or footage of fellow gamers. I passed these titled 'file' a thousand times without considering it. It's a different file code than the more updated sources. Something called an imobi file. "I can't believe I didn't at least check these."

It had occurred to me that there were an awful lot of imobi files, but I also thought, 'there is no way this old technology holds anything of importance.' Now I wonder what else I've overlooked because I'm being snobbish about outdated materials. I hate conversion corruption when updating information. It makes my insides crawl. If I have a sensation of pain, it's that. The raw sores from having to rewrite holes to fit something into better code. It's stabby.

I don't bother upgrading the images. I let the grainy footage stay fuzzy where it could be sharp. Searching source codes again, I look for profile pictures associated with players. The company overseeing intelligence donors maintains an anonymous identity once a donor receives their code in order to identify their intelligence as its true-perceived self.

I have no way of knowing what my friends look like. Their codes are easy enough to locate. With the codes comes address, next of kin, and other information that I have no way of utilizing. Ace never told me his address, nor the names of his parents. For all I know, Ed could have been a ninety-year-old woman with twenty-three grandbabies and twice that of great-grandbabies. Or Tony…

No. I'm pretty sure that kid's in the mob one way or the other.

It turns out, none of the admit names were entered as Ace. Even if they were, they cleanly sever admit names from code associations. There are three Edgars admits fourteen Edwards, and even one person listed as Edge. But, there is no way of knowing if the Ed I knew was actually named Ed on this side of the game, or if he chose the name because he associated more with being an Education Gen source code than he did his given name of anything.

I stare at the screen as hosts in white coats greet people in wheel-chairs, family members of coma patients, bald and sickly-looking individuals by the dozens. All looking like copy-pasted human illness entering double doors over and over. I can't tell them apart. None of them have hair, making it that much harder to distinguish one from another. In the game, there were persons lacking hair, but it was a choice, and those players had well-shaped heads. The persons on the screen of the tablet have lumpy, crusted, picked at, and rashy scalps. Some wear scarves. Others ball caps.

I notice families with multiple persons in military clothing. Armed services appear to be a family tradition for most humans. Ace likely hails from one of these. I digitally tag the files I see with mili-tary markings so I can return to them in order to analyze them further.

I don't know how far I get before the doors swing in. I expect one of the techs has come to teach me how to blink while staring, or that I must fidget my hands and not be too still both at the same time.

Humans are not still, but I am. It's in the stillness that I can observe their movements around me, but they don't like it when I do that. I'm supposed to imitate them in every fashion. I didn't have to think of this in the game. I was programmed flawed and glitchy. Apparently, those are desired human qualities on this side. Over there, it almost got me killed.

A tech turns on the large screen monitor on the wall again. I expect to see more of the shouting and hollering from the streets, but the channel is different. Everyone I know follows the tech, then a bunch of people I don't know. The room fills quickly. I tilt the device I'm using up to my chest to cover the screen.

"What is this about?" Spaulding asks, naseled and inconvenienced—probably more by the fact he's grouped with the grunt workers. Spaulding is the type who likes separation and height in addition to status. He straightens his tie below his coat and smooths his hair as though he's the one on the television screen being seen by the public on the opposite side.

"Announcement coming in from Ecuador," the tech says with a hand to shush the scientist.

"Ecuador? Like, the country?"

A nod and repeat hand gesture from the tech is the only response he receives.

A news reporter speaks Spanish, with a string of delayed English translation crawling across the bottom of the screen. "We are thrilled to announce that our very own donor program has resulted in a successful human intelligence transplant."

4

Spaulding lets go of his uber straight tie and rushes for the TV controls shouting, "Turn it up!"

Movement near the back of the room distracts me from the Spaulding spectacle. Miller shuffles the opposite direction from Spaulding. Instead of moving closer to the announcement, he puts people between him and the screen, like the bodies in front of him will absorb whatever toxic information radiates from the announcement. I'm unsure what all of the fuss on the screen means, but the energy in the room feels on the verge of jumping from human to human like a massive electron conducting cloud, ready to pulse from its host television prison and attack electronics at any moment. Maybe that energy can be harnessed in order to read their thought patterns. Human Wi-Fi could simply be manipulating anxiety.

"Unlike our Mexican counterparts, who seem unable to get their paperwork in order..." The television continues to speak, but I can't understand the Spanish over the conversation in the room around me and I can't read the screen due to all the people crowding my view. Everything muddles.

"That's a jab at us," Gordon says. "We're the only Mexican facility."

"No duh, Gordo. We all got that." Abby pushes Gordon from behind. With him being much shorter than the other techs, she looks to be backhanding a child.

".... We will reunite our upload with his family..."

"He doesn't have a name?" Miller asks, standing straighter and pushing one shoulder off the door frame where he was resting—all semblance of 'at ease' gone. "Why doesn't he have a name?" He signals Abby and Ben who both respond by tucking their heads over a tablet and scrolling information regarding Ecuador donors.

"We haven't announced Jennie's name," Spaulding adds.

"That's only because we can't verify her intake papers yet," Miller says. "If they're going to reunite their upload with his family, that would mean they have his intake papers."

"Maybe they're dealing with the same problem," Ben says. "But they want to beat us to the punch, so they're moving forward on their public appearances."

"Seems premature, don't you think?" Abby says. "To parade around a robot, they haven't tested or checked against failsafes?"

Robot? Failsafes? What failsafes? My imitation heart increases the rate of pumping like it's throbbing out a warning code I can't decipher.

"...In Ecuador's long history of being the go-to source in documented evolution, we will soon open a conference center and teaching lab for intelligence transplants..." the reporter continues over the theory surmising in the room.

"Long history?" Miller scoffs. "Just because they have those islands, is that it?"

"Darwin, screwing us again?" Ben slaps the table this time.

"No, he's not." Spaulding stands, walks to the window and parts the blinds, unabashedly drawing attention from the crowd seven floors below. I don't know how well the tear gas quelled the crowd, but just in case, I duck. "Because we're going to be the first to sign up to go down there."

"Pretty sure that's us proving their point. Like 'hey, teach us, we lost our paper trail and can't figure out who to contact regarding their family member because our upload's memory got wiped as a transfer side effect. Our bad." Gordon doesn't cover his head in time. Three techs smack him from three distinct sides.

"I'm sure they're dealing with side effects too," Spaulding says.

"They wouldn't just invite the entire transplant and engineering community to their front door if they had something to hide," Abby says.

Miller steps closer to the television. "But maybe they would."

"Yes." Spaulding nods like there is some language they're beaming to one another's brains the rest of us aren't privy to. I scan the room for a signal to be sure there isn't anything I'm missing between them. Of course, there's not.

"Maybe, just maybe... they want everyone with progress to meet. Like a debriefing."

"Debug the system."

"Or sabotage other companies' progress," Ben adds. That thought doesn't sit well with me. I'm their progress. I have no interest in being sabotaged. "No one in the Resource Ring wants the Outercontintents in control of a commodity." Ben looks at me. "There might be glitches, but we still produce results."

"Side effects may vary," Miller says. "It's likely everyone working toward an upload, even those without success, have dealt with certain side effects this type of program creates. Things we hadn't anticipated."

"Like how valuing individual privacy could cost us our funding?" Gordon adds. "Every precaution we've taken to protect donors and donor rights has backfired post upload. We can't trace anyone."

Blinds slap closed as Spaulding turns to face the majority and I jump. "We leave in two days."

"What? All of us?" Gordon asks.

"All of us," Miller answers before Spaulding.

"But..." I stammer. The occupants of the room remember me again. "The people outside."

"What about them?" Spaulding asks in a very huffy, not at all genuine-in-asking, tone.

I can't believe I have to explain the dilemma to them. "What do we tell them? They're waiting for their family member." We can't just run away in the night and hope they won't notice. They'll burn the building to the ground given the opportunity.

"It's common sense that you can't be all of their family members."

He paces in front of the window with his finger marked streaks cutting through years of dust. "We'll need to conjure a history in the meantime. To avoid any..." He straightens his tie like this is going to erase his crooked nature. "...anything we need to avoid."

"If we invent a background and then find Jennie's real relations, what are we supposed to say?" Gordon obviously doesn't know when to keep his red-flag questions to himself.

"You'll think of something."

The screen is still speaking Spanish behind the techs, who now scramble to come up with convincing orphan stories, or tragedies to explain how an experimental transplant donor could lose an entire family and not the other way around.

Spaulding holds up both hands as if he's silencing the environment, but nothing goes quiet. "Have any donor families suffered tragic accidents? Like, like, like they got in a plane crash or..."

"Or are any of them poor?" Abby chimes in. "Maybe we could pay someone off to claim her."

"No way. No way are we bribing some poor suffering family." Gordon doesn't gain a lot of support from his outburst. "Besides, where would we get that kind of money? The IRS is still a thing."

"What if we told someone that Jennie is theirs?" Ben gets his two-cents in.

"And why not?" Spaulding walks over to me and gives me an up-down nod. "She's got to belong to someone. Why not just match up a near approximation?"

"Because it's wrong." Miller steps in to argue. "Until we know who she is, we can't say she's someone else." He stands in front of the TV, blocking anyone trying to avoid the topic at hand by pretending they're invested in the news. "Eventually people would figure it out." He points a finger to me. "Or her memory will come back."

I can't exactly tell him that sudden memory recovery isn't a concern, so I stand and walk to the window to peek out at the crowds below. The doctors and techs continue to debate how to pass me off while maintaining their reputation. Or pride. Dignity is so far gone, I doubt they're worried about such attributes.

At ground level, families chat with one another. I imagine they're sharing stories about their loved ones on the donor list. What kinds of skills their family member brought to the game and how they'd make a great candidate for the brains inside artificial intelligence. What a noble idea.

"...Someone get on the phone with Ecuador..." Plans get made behind me, about me, without me. "...No... Someone who speaks Spanish, and won't say something idiotic..."

That rules out the techs. Those guys can make microwave popcorn sound like a fail-fail outcome is the only solution. I turn back to the window. The crowd, as a whole, is usually what I see. Like a forest, there is so much sameness below. Faces pivot around shades of angry, pained, sad, and vengeance for a new kind of loss, which carries guilt at having signed paperwork for loved ones to be plugged into a lie. I have to concentrate to pick out differences in each set of tightly drawn eyes.

I need to pay attention to differences and start adopting some of my own if I'm going to pull off being human. One woman scratches the back of her neck over and over. I try it. Not for me. It's uncomfortable and I don't see the use in the nervous habit.

Another man taps his heel. I could do that. It could serve as keeping rhythm and patterns around me, something I like to do anyway, and could hide my data collections behind a nervous habit. I try it. At first, I tap too hard and draw some attention at the sound of my bare, heavy metal-framed feet against the cold hospital tile. I try it softer, which requires more effort and attention. I'd rather pound indents in the flooring than bother controlling my strength. But I keep working at it because I need something to help me blend in.

"Whose turn is it to take Jennie for a walk?" Spaulding asks like my heel tapping is the signal that the dog needs to be let out. I know he's concerned about my ability to move naturally, seeing as I lack the ability to move naturally at the moment. And he wants to move forward on my public appearance since Ecuador announced more success and, what I assume, is a five-year plan ensuring grant money, endorsements, and investors. We've got nothing because my team has been waiting for me to show signs of success before seeking funding.

Ecuador changed everything in a matter of seconds.

"I'll take her," Gordon says. He doesn't lower his head, or huff, or anything that would indicate he's above the task at hand. Thanks, Gordon. I make a note that he's either a great faker or someone to keep around.

I turn from the window reluctantly but know I need help with how knees work for my own sake and follow Gordon out of the room.

"Let's focus on a smooth motion and gait that matches your height," he says as we exit.

I've seen footage of crisp blocky moving soldiers who walk as though they are made of wood and being propelled by motors. It's the closest to natural human movement I can accomplish at this point, but I've been told it's not natural enough.

I take large steps, matching my height by my stride.

"No, no." Gordon stops me in the hall. No one else watches us. The windows that flank the hall are unobstructed. The crowd outside are all on the other side of the building. Now we're in this hall with windows lining an atrium at the heart of the building. Natural light must have been the design theme of this structure since it's rich with windows and sunlight. "Look at how I walk."

Gordon saunters up and down the hall in front of the windows, silhouetted by the light coming in from the atrium. His arms swing gently at his sides. He takes little half steps compared to his short frame. I try smaller steps, still a bit unsure how to manage with the weird ball-joint in my knee. Such an unstable frame they gave me. Inside the game, none of this was a problem. I moved and knew how and there was no gravity or rotation of the earth. I didn't feel the degree of imbalance in the foundations of buildings, which I can now.

As a matter of fact, if I set a marble in this hall, it'd roll slowly into the window across from me. I walk toward the windows and turn on my heel like a soldier. Then return with a slightly less prominent heel clap on my return.

Gordon puts a hand to his forehead. "How long have we been working on this?"

"Seven minutes."

"No, not this. I mean this." He motions a circle in front of him. "This. This whole thing."

"Since I woke up?" I say.

Gordon raises his voice, "The whole thing! The..." He looks at me with his head tilted to the side. "It's like you're not even human sometimes, like you don't get any of it."

I'm exposed and have no idea how to cover this. "I don't know what you mean."

"You're just so rigid, you know, and stupid."

All those notes in my data files about Gordon being a decent one, a human I could trust, they're about to be sent to the recycle bin.

"Look at those people down there." He points to the landing of the atrium. It goes down to the second-floor roof, where a garden and walking path circles a fountain. A very small group of people stand together in front of the fountain, arguing it seems. "They don't have to think about it, not as you do. They just know how to move."

"I'm learning," I say.

"Yes, but not even like a baby or an accident victim who has to learn to walk all over again."

I let my eyes focus in on the group below. I observe, like always. I always observe. Why can't I imitate? It should be so natural to fake these frail human movements. Why is it so hard?

"It's like you have absolutely no experience with walking."

I don't give him the honor of looking at him when I speak. "I have experience walking."

"How are you this bad at it?" he asks, throwing his hands up so that even without looking at him, the motion registers in my peripheral alertness system.

"I am not in a human body, Gordon. It's a lot harder than you think to force a non-human machine to work with human impulses. Is there anything else you'd like to accuse me of, while we're seven floors up and lacking character witnesses?" I'm not even sure if I'm threatening him. I can tell by the expression on his face, he thinks I've just insinuated I'm about to break a window with his face and drop him over a concrete bench secured to the landing in the atrium below us.

Gordon, now several shades paler than before, shakes his head. "That's a whole lot more speaking than you ever do in there." He points to the room, where I'm sure they're still arguing about how best to lie in my favor and theirs.

The people around the fountain increase in argument as well. One person turns her back to the group. Her movement opens a path in my line of sight to where a broad-shouldered male sits on the fountains ledge. He has dark hair a little long and unkept. His face is sharp, accentuated at this distance with a stubble shadow. And his eyes are exactly the same as in the game. I walk to the window and slap it one time, accidentally breaking the glass. "Ace!"

He looks up. It's him. Right down to the way his brow shades his eyes when he's irritated. Ace made it too.

5

Glass shatters to the landing below. The group screams and covers their heads. Ace quickly recovers from ducking and covering— as any military trained human would, I imagine. He stands, his eyes lock with mine. His motions and expressions flow in a way that makes my collarbone ache. If Ace were here, he'd be robotic like me. How is this happening? He's like the human version of the game Ace. Real Ace can't be non-terminal and in the game. A person can only be uploaded, by law, if they'd die anyway. Then again, are there really thousands of terminal patients whose paperwork goes through in time, every month, to have that many players uploaded?

"Gordon, is there something the facility isn't telling me?" I know there is. I feel it in my leaden stomach. The player's math doesn't add up. Certainly Ace can't really be here.

Gordon grabs my shoulder, pulling me back from the hole where the window pane recently occupied, as though I'm liable to lunge through the gap. "You know him?"

I don't look away from Ace. He squints in reply.

"Ace," I shout again. He shields his eyes from the sun coming overhead then narrows them even more, forcing his eyes to remember me even if his brain can't. If he's an upload, when did he upload? Why hasn't anyone told me there were more uploads? Is that his family he's with? Why are they upset with him? Maybe I'm lucky to not have a family.

Then I wonder, what if he tells them who I am really? We didn't part on the best terms.

I step back from the window. Gordon relaxes under the impression he's finally managed to pull me away from the opening.

"You know Mr. Pierson?"

I turn to Gordon because I don't know Ace's last name, but how could it be anyone else? I nod.

"The guy whose family funded more than half of our program? All programs for that matter."

I don't know anything about Ace's family financials. The real-world counterpart of Ace feels invented, dreamed, lied.

I can't calculate what's wrong exactly. My brain is on overload trying to put things together based on the information Gordon's giving me. Movement below catches my attention. Ace points up to where I stand and says something faint. I could probably make it out if I dialed up my auditory sensors.

"Maybe this is a good thing," Gordon says.

Confrontation with Ace has a history of being a toss-up, either good or deadly.

Everyone from inside the media room files out to the hall. Like moths to a light, they've been summoned by my outburst.

"What the hell happened?" Ben has a way of extending his arms and his welcome too far. "We heard a noise." Wow. He's articulate too. Another one of his grating qualities.

"Gordon?" Spaulding asks, clearly expecting answers. Then he sees the metal frame where the glass pane window used to be and stops himself from adding anything after addressing Gordon.

"She knows Mr. Pierson," Gordon announces in high spirits as if the window isn't shattered and everything is perfectly normal.

"What do you mean, she knows him?" Spaulding touches the edges of the frame where tiny bits of glass still cling. "Everyone knows him."

"She *knows* him." Gordon raises his shoulders like that's the whole answer, which I guess it is right now. "Her memory might be coming back."

Forgot about that lie. I can't pretend to not know him now, the broken glass is a dead giveaway that my memory banks aren't totally wiped. I look around for an escape. What can I possibly say to Ace? If he's already upset over something, it's probably not a good idea to lead with, "how'd you get out?" But if the guy's family has money, it makes sense. If you can't throw around wealth to ensure your kid wins the eternal life prize, what good is wealth?

It also raises a lot of questions about Ace's behavior inside the game. If he had a lock on the win, why was he such a desperate loser when things didn't go his way? All of this leads me to wonder about his resources inside the game. Was there a mole? And if there was, did the Commander know about it? And what if the Commander had money? Is he here too? He was definitely well supplied on the inside. Forgetting my desire for an exit, I scan for any face reminiscent of the Commander. Not exactly a man I ever want to confront again.

Down the hall the elevator dings.

My already rigid body locks at every joint.

A small group of loitering techs follows Spaulding down the hall toward the opening elevator doors.

"Mr. Pierson." Spaulding extends a hand. Ace moves his right side out of line with the extended greeting, unabashedly snubbing Spaulding and leaving no doubt in my mind regarding his identity. He continues down the hall toward Gordon and me.

Ace stops in front of Miller, who asserts himself in front of me in an appreciated protective manner.

"Who did that?" Ace indicates the few glass shards remaining in the window frame. A slight breeze tickles its way down the hall. The wild outdoor air couldn't care less about where it's not supposed to be.

Except for Ace, all heads in the hall turn to look at the gaping hole in the window wall. No one speaks, though a few mouths are open as if they're forming blame, but not quite ready to sling it yet.

"Someone called 'Ace'." He strikes his pointer finger toward the window. "If this is some kind of statement about the fallout from my family pulling funding..."

The Piersons pulled funding? Why? They get Ace back and then bail? Yeah, I'd be pissed too. I might even be glad I showered glass down on those near the fountain.

"I expect an answer," he says.

All heads turn to me. Like the robot-girl equals the best scapegoat they've got.

"You did this?" Ace stares at me. I expect him to recognize me, but then remember I gave the features designer of my physical robotic attributes some novel identifiers so that I wasn't found out as a fake. "The robot?" He scoffs and turns to Gordon. "I saw you with it. You ordered your new toy to break that window, didn't you?"

Gordon stumbles over the response he's trying to make. Something in the vein of, "I would never."

"It's me," I say. "GenE." I wish I could erase the audience of humans in the hall, but they're all here. All the people who have to show me how to sit and tell me that I need to blink so I don't freak other humans out. They're more likely to pull theater popcorn from their coat pockets than leave the hall at this moment.

Ace scrunches his forehead. His eyes narrow at me. "What is this?" he asks Gordon.

Gordon raises his shoulders, this time in an 'I have no answer' manner. He could use a new gesture response.

"Where did you upload?" I try to whisper, but it's no good. The hall is filled with listeners. Several of whom look confused by my question. "I thought I was the only one who made it."

The frustrated wrinkles in Ace's forehead slacken and smooth out. His lips part to reveal his white teeth. Seconds pass like this, time pounding in my ears for the waste of it. Ace swallows before speaking again. "You think I'm AI?"

It's obvious something isn't adding up, so I don't answer.

"You know me?" he asks.

I stop looking at him because of course I know him. He's exactly the same as he was in the game. I'm starting to wonder if I'm still in the game on some not cool and not funny level where everyone is about to shout 'psych' and laugh as I level up to another zombie-murder-holding-cell gamescape.

Ace leans close to Miller, who is standing the closest to me still. "Can I have a moment to speak with it alone?"

"Absolutely not," Spaulding says from where he's still stinging from being snubbed behind Ace. When Ace and Miller turn to him both with the attitude of 'who invited you to this conversation?', he adds, "She is expensive property."

I want to shout, 'I'm not property!', but this isn't the time to push robot politics and intelligence-rights platforms. I manage to keep my head down and my mouth shut.

"I'll supervise," Miller offers.

Ace nods agreement. The techs all display their disappointment in the afternoon's entertainment being cut short through a variety of reactions, slapping one leg, rolling their eyes, muttering under their breaths, and most likely devising a means to eavesdrop before retreating down the hall. Most of them still search for a way to explain my amnesia and fake my identity so the company can get more funding through a publicity tour.

Dr. Spaulding doesn't leave with the techs.

"Just us," Ace motions to me and Miller.

"I don't approve,' Spaulding says. "I'm a major part of this operation and don't want you handling my discovery."

"You didn't discover me," I say before anyone can speak for me.

"I was there when you woke up."

I nod.

He points to himself. "My finding."

"I'm not taking credit from you, Spaulding. Just standing here so these two can talk," Miller says. "It's good to get her interacting with anyone beyond our tight circle."

"Not without me, she's not," Spaulding says.

Ace steps closer to Spaulding. "I don't want you here, and I'm the guy signing your checks. So, if you want a job tomorrow, get the hell out of my hallway."

Definitely an Ace power move. Spaulding postures himself as though he might risk a firing, before letting out a breath, and retreating slowly down the hall. "If you sabotage anything... I swear." He points to security cameras positioned inside little black bubbles on the ceiling. They weren't hidden at all, because it's not a design feature to have black bubbles protrude from ceilings anywhere there are not security cameras. "I'll be watching."

6

Ace waits for Spaulding to disappear behind closing elevator doors. "Those don't even record sound," he mutters. He glances to a black bubble then turns his back on it, probably ensuring viewers in the security room can't read his lips on the video footage. Though I'm certain, if I were in the video room, I'd use glass reflections to figure out what I might be missing over audio.

"Why did you try to kill me just now?" he asks.

Miller remains at my side. It's impossible to guess if Ace is hinting at me to play along—the way it worked in the game like he's in hiding, or maybe he was never in the game. If Ace was a virtual reality plant, I'm gonna be pissed. I mourned him, damnit.

I look at the black bubble in the ceiling and how I'm facing it, and anything I say might be guessed at if someone can read lips. The one thing whoever developed me didn't skimp on is my ability to produce speech, perfectly replicating normal human pitch, tone, cadence, everything. My mouth is my most developed piece of equipment from an outward appearance.

Ace puts his large rough hands on my hospital gown like I'm a child in need of stilling. His dry and broken skin catches on the fabric as he repositions me at an angle impossible for anyone behind the camera to read my lips, he must assume. Which definitely means he's not Ace from the game. Game Ace would know there are ways around angles and lenses if someone's driven enough.

"We worked together in the game," I say side-eyeing Ace. If he flinches, or maybe if he doesn't flinch, does it mean he's the Ace I know? Or maybe he was controlling an Ace avatar from the outside?

Dr. Miller stares at Ace as if Ace is the one withholding information. Like I had help from the outside and must now forfeit my win due to cheating. I mean, sure, I cheated. Everyone cheated to survive in the game. But are they going to load me back up and download my brain into that virtual prison hell because of that? Best case, this Ace is from the game, lost his memory, just like I had inside the game. Somehow, we've reversed roles.

"I think you're mistaken," Miller says.

"I'm not," I insist. If I could sweat in this fake body, I'd be doing it now. I don't want to give too much away. If I reveal myself, or Ace blows my cover, reveals me to be a product of the game and not an official donor, what might happen? Would they melt me down? Would my thoughts cease, or would I exist in an eternal state of feeling melted down and unable to interact with this horrid choppy world? "I saved your life," I say, feeling like this is a safe revelation and might jog his memory.

"That's ridiculous," Ace says.

"You're not keen on being saved, but you were drowned in that upside-down dome until I broke our sphere and saved you." I rub my cheek. "You punched me in the face as a thank you."

"I don't think she's making this up," Miller says.

"I'm not," I say.

"I've never been in the game." Ace throws his hands in the air. "Is this some kind of joke?" He points to the broken window again. "You think you're funny?" Ace pivots on one foot, making a visual check of the elevator like he wants to make sure it's still there.

"Didn't your family continue to fund the program because after your brother developed the software, he became a donor?" Miller asks.

"What does that have to do with anything?" Ace asks.

"I mean if the donors get to pick their own Avatar image...?" Miller doesn't have to say more. I've figured out my mistake. Though the Ace look-alike doesn't seem to be connecting the dots at first. Slowly he nods, then closes his eyes and stays this way for an uncomfortable space of time.

"We didn't speak when he deployed," fake Ace says. "Did you know that?" He asks the question like a challenge. "I thought he hated me for how I fought him on enlisting in that stupid war." He waits. Maybe he expects one of us to say something, but we're silent. "Everyone knew who'd win. The Intercontinents had all the resources. Those with the most resources always win."

"Who did your brother fight with?" I ask.

Both men stare at me like I'm imbecilic. Apparently, everyone knows this guy's family drama, and I don't, which means I'm an idiot. Maybe I am because I should have continued to not ask questions. A smart person would have remained silent and let the dude monologue.

"I can't remember," I shout as if an emotional outburst will excuse my lack of knowledge of human world history. I could have spent the last weeks downloading news and current events, but I've been too preoccupied with how to recover my friends' files and cover my fake human butt.

"Ace fought with the Intercontinents." He extends a stiff blade of a hand for me to shake. "I'm Mav, the brother who fought with the Outer-losers."

"Your brother? Ace?" I don't know this person in front of me, even though every part of me feels like he's familiar with every one of my flaws. I cross an arm across my body like I'm covering up. I feel exposed all the way to my vital organs, even though I've never met this man before today, and he doesn't know how many times I shot the kid. "And he looks exactly like you. Like exactly."

"Not even close," he says.

"But names aren't used in the game," Miller says. "How would you know the name of Mr. Pierson's brother?"

And now I have to focus on covering my fake human butt again. I knew if I opened my mouth I'd say something damaging. There is no way I can explain to them that we all died in the game, took over the zombie holding zone, and named ourselves just to stick it to the remaining legitimate players.

"Are you sure?" I ask. "Lots of players used names. And nicknames." I have no idea if they're buying what I'm saying. I'm staring at them while still trying to come up with what else I can throw out there to sell this crap I'm telling them. "It's sort of a thing to get a nickname. Like I knew Ace." I nod to Ace's brother, Mav. "Tony and Ed, and Silva, and John, Lily, and Tech-chick..." Without meaning to, I've named all the players that matter to me in the game. "Just to name a few."

"Why haven't you mentioned any of this earlier?" Miller asks. "This changes so much." He scratches an already red spot on his neck.

"You named yourselves?" Mav asks. "Tech-chick though? Really? That's not much of a nickname or a name."

"Meh," I say, not sure how I feel about her. She wasn't terrible.

"I wish we hadn't allowed the program files to be deleted after one upload," Miller comments. Which is weird, because Miller and I both know the files aren't completely deleted. I have a copy.

Mav's eyes widen. "What?" He pushes me aside, no longer interested in the novelty that I mistook his brother for him. Matter explained, don't care anymore. "You deleted my brother?"

"It wasn't my call," Miller says.

"You lost his intake paperwork, can't explain to me why there is no tracking information on donor progress or percentage match, which I was guaranteed information on when I agreed to my family funding this project. How many more failures can you brush under the rug?"

Me. I hope...

"He had all the necessary skills to be the perfect match," Mav says. "It should have been him."

If I could crawl out of that hall, I would, but it's super distracting with the way I shift from a stand to a crawl. Not only that, crawling itself is a fairly complicated movement for me as I'm still learning how to control this body. Unsure what kind of trouble I'm already in, I slip my hand into my pocket and wrap my fingers around the data stick containing the donor files still active in the game after I uploaded. I want to magically download the information into my personal memory banks but have no means of plugging the stick into myself, as far as I'm aware. I want to keep it for me, just me, but I also have a sense that I need this Mav on my side.

"Does it help if I saved this?" I hold up the stick.

"What's that?" Mav asks.

Miller's eyes go wide at the sight of my digital device. His trust is a fragile cup I continue to spill. Whatever his reasoning for lying to Mav about the existence of this disk, I've taken that and a smidge of power from him by revealing my hand.

"When I heard Spaulding give the techs an order to wipe the program, so they could reset it for a new batch of donors, I panicked," I say. "I grabbed the nearest device I could and plugged it into the computer. I made a copy of the donor codes." I'm not even sure what I have a copy of. Does a copy of a donor make it a clone? I have no clue about logistics and semantics regarding digital intelligence transfers and exact identity.

Mav stares at me. "How did you do this?"

"Instinct, I guess. I needed to save them."

Mav has a hand up like he's going to reach for the data files but doesn't touch it. "You saved the files?"

"I tried," I say. "I copied everything I could."

"What are you going to do with it?" he asks.

Miller stands as silent witness to our conversation.

"I'm not sure what I can do." It's true. The program was designed to upload only the intelligence that fit the vessel prepared to receive it. In my case, artificial intellect. "They're trapped, I think." I slide the device back into my pocket carefully, like every movement I subject the stick to causes catastrophic damage to those digitally frozen inside.

Mav lowers his voice for once. No longer on high alert, defense, ready to fight, mode. "What did they call you?" he asks.

"Jennie," I say.

Miller has his eyes on my pocket, as though he can see through the fabric to the device inside. It feels like he's about to tell me that I can't have the name Jennie anymore because donors aren't supposed to use names, or nicknames, or any identifiers beyond source codes inside the game. Except, instead of a reprimand, "We're going to Ecuador," is what comes out of his mouth. Surprising Mav and me both. "Like a technology summit for donor programs."

Mav shifts his weight off the forward lean brought on when I pulled out the disk of donor files. He crosses his arms as he leans away from Miller and me, like he needs space to size us up. I mean, I did just shatter a huge picture window over the top of his head, but whatever. I still say leaning away is a little overdramatic. "Okay."

"You can come," Miller says. "Say you'll pull the funding if they don't include you, and then we can see if there is a way to extract the information on that drive." He nods to my pocket.

I put a hand over the slot at the top of the opening protectively. There's no way I'm handing my friends over to strangers. I shouldn't have told them. "No."

"Yes," Mav says in conjunction with my no. "I'm coming with you."

"One more thing," Miller says.

"What's that?"

Miller nods to me. "We can't identify this donor."

"What do you mean? She's Jennie." I want to smile at Mav, but also hide, because I feel like he's an idiot, but an idiot who can put together why they can't figure out who I am. I don't think this guy has a shot to figure out every other simplistic mystery on earth, but this one thing feels like it's his to solve.

"No donors uploaded," Miller reveals. I cringe because there it is. Right there. He's said it plain as day. "The program glitched and didn't show which donor. The files were wiped before anyone realized the problem."

"No one knows who this is?" Mav asks.

"Right."

"But she remembers being in the game. She remembers people."

I'm not sure when it changed during our conversation, but I like that Mav is calling me 'she' instead of 'it'. At least until he decides a computer Frankenstein is most likely an 'it' after all.

"Yes, well… None of us realized that until she broke the window." Miller points to the broken window frame.

"Did you ask her?" Mav asks, like this is the simplest thing to solve and we're wasting time not being in Ecuador already.

"Jennie?" Dr. Miller asks me. "Do you remember who you are outside the game?"

"Nope," I say, totally relieved that this is his method of double checking. "Don't know."

Mav scrunches his forehead again and I feel like he can see me lying like a tattoo on my left arm. "But you remember your code, right?" he asks.

I look at Dr. Miller for help, like perhaps he has some master plan for passing me off as legit, but he waits for me to answer too. "No," I say. "Sorry. No."

"What was Ace's code?"

I blink, glad I genuinely don't know and thought to blink like a real human might when they don't know something. I hope I'm not overdoing it. I look up at the black bubble on the ceiling and imagine Spaulding staring intently. Trying to make sense of our drawn-out conversation. It literally makes no sense, so it's pretty funny to imagine him trying.

"Ace. I'm talking about Ace," Mav says. "What's his source code?"

"GenAK." I almost spout off his numbers up to where his sleeve usually covered the rest of his code. And then I realize I let myself be distracted thinking about Spaulding not being in control and how I can't wait to see his face when Mav tells him he's coming to Ecuador and let one thing slip. I remember source codes or at least GenCodes.

Miller narrows his eyes like he's lost the ability to open them or his trust completely toward me anymore. "Jennie, you said you could not remember any codes from within the game."

I drag my eyes from the camera bubble and stare toward Dr. Miller like a child caught in a lie. "I, uh… think seeing Ace, I mean his brother, maybe…sparked my memory."

7

The next days are spent planning, prepping, packing—with added Mav presence. He watches as the techs deliver lesson after lesson about how to appear and behave more humanly. Excitement over travel plans only increases the time devoted to me pulling off a decent 'human' act.

Miller and Mav both choose not to press my convenient memory regarding source codes and donors. It's as though Dr. Miller has changed warmth toward me, much more Dr. now than Miller. I'm no longer his pet or his child. I liked the feeling of his claim on me. It's different than Spaulding and how he wants to plaster his name on things and then hold them up and out in other people's faces. Miller would never do that. He puts his name on things because he doesn't want to lose them or he doesn't want other people to take them without asking.

With plans to leave for Ecuador set, it's still days before even the hint of leaving can surface beyond the building's walls. The crowds outside continue to march up and down the sidewalks, parade up the steps, and jostle signs with varying outrage. There have been rumors of more bottle bombs. No one has to spread rumors about tear gas. The last incident was this morning and it definitely plays a part in the current state of 'relative calm'.

"Don't stand there. Work on your movements," Abby remarks. She's with me in the room, supposedly teaching me how to act during travel situations while riffling through more donor files. To demonstrate what I'm to do, Abby motions her arms up and down coaxing me to stand and sit like a puppet.

I sit and stand as smoothly as possible. Not to please her, or any of them for that matter. I want to blend in for my own reasons. To melt into the crowd outside. Find Tony's family and Ed. Even Tech-chick.

The team remains determined to decipher my origins before we leave. There's also the problem of the crowds outside. No matter how much I hope to blend, I walk as though I'm built entirely out of rusty door hinges. And the humans down there aren't the type to wait for explanations regarding my walk or weird speech sounds. Police arrest anyone who throws bottles at the building. Forty individuals have been arrested so far. And that's just the east window numbers. The protesters extend around the entire building, bottles at the ready.

Maybe that's the reason our travel plans hesitate. After several days, the flame bottles are unpleasant memories. The television continues to cover news about Ecuador and how the Intercontinents prove their power and influence even after winning the war. Every news station has some spin about how "Evolutionary advancements, once again, blossom off the Ecuadorian coast."

"Like they won the war," Mav says behind me. He's been spending more and more time with our ragtag group, asking prying questions about his brother as though he's testing me about whether or not I really know Ace. When really, he's the one who doesn't know his brother. Mav has no way to fact check all the lies I'm feeding him whenever he asks. Today, however, he has me off guard. I'm currently under the impression the Intercontinents are the resounding winners of the war over resource control.

The blinds rattle shut from how fast I pull my hand back. "Didn't they?"

Ben flaps his pile of papers against the doctor's bench shrouded in sitting paper. "How do you know nothing?"

"She's got amnesia, Ben." Abby defends me, but it doesn't sound like a defense. More like a joke.

"The war was over before the first donors were uploaded." Gordon pipes in, as though he's the savior of what would have been a verbal massacre, despite the fact his statement only fills my core-processor-brain with more questions.

"But Mav said they didn't win the war," I say. "Just now. He said that."

"No. He said, 'as if *they* won,' like they didn't accomplish it themselves," Ben huffs at me, but his words still don't make sense.

"That means they didn't win the war." I run the sentence over in my mind seven more times to be sure of myself because no one else is making sense and I'm sick of Ben calling me not smart. I am smart. As a matter of fact, I can store more book knowledge in my system in one day than all of the techs could read their entire lives, if they read straight through all their waking hours. "You said they didn't accomplish it. And Mav said if I'm quoting exactly, 'like they won the war', inferring that they did not win the war." I wait for someone to jump in to clarify for me, other than stupid Ben, but no one does. Not that they look baffled by my logic. They look sorry for me. Like I'm too infantile to understand. But they're not explaining themselves well. "Is the war not over?"

"No," Ben says.

"It's not," I affirm.

"No!" Ben raises his voice. He takes short breaths like there isn't time to inhale deeply and explain anything clearly at once. "I mean no, the war is over. No, you're wrong. No, you don't get it. No, there's no point in explaining anything to you."

"Stop it, Ben," Gordon says as if I need him to defend me. To clarify, I do not.

"Don't you see what a waste this is?" Ben points at me. I'm the waste? He throws his file filled with donor information to the rigid tile floor. The pages slide and scatter—a life lost under a bolted bench and cupboard gaps. "This is more than amnesia. It's like she's an empty shell and has no experience of human life. She's an abomination that should be aborted, not supported." Ben recites the words written on several protest signs outside the building.

If my synthetic skin was capable of going pale, it would be right now. Everything tightens around my appendages, like moving might rip my coverings, and a tingle surges along my entire body—out from my spinal cord connection to every end of me and then back like I'm firing information, but don't know what to do with it. If Abby told me to sit right now, I'm certain I'd explode.

"Don't be absurd," Gordon says. I apologize in my head for dismissing his help earlier. I do need him. "She's in early transplant stages. There's bound to be glitches." He points to the large screen on the wall, the one that displayed game information when I woke up. The techs were tracking leaderboards and other priority data at the time. "The game was riddled with so many glitches, if she came out of it perfectly fine, I'd be worried."

"You're such a suck-up, Gordo. Grow a pair and admit she's unnatural and wrong." Ben invades Gordon's personal space.

"That's enough!" Abby shouts. "This isn't the time, Ben." The look on Ben's face is more than being told to stand down, it's heartache and betrayal. Did he expect Abby to back him up? If I'm being honest, I sort of expected her to be on Ben's side, even if his side was, 'My foot is the capital of the world.'

"Computers don't name themselves," Mav says. "People do." He speaks in such a manner that the conversation ends there. To my relief.

People name themselves. But I didn't name me, not originally. Tony did. I adopted the name Jennie. It felt right, like a fit. But then, I stole the origin of the name from a donor who was murdered because I stole her code. My perfectly working machine-head aches from circular thought. But, by Mav's words, if I named myself, I'm human. But did I name myself?

"So the war is not won?" I ask, unsure if the answer was dropped intentionally or accidentally.

"Yes. The war is technically over. Pierson cut the robot some slack and explain yourself on that one. She's a moron and can't understand double meanings," Ben says. Under his breath, he adds, "And Abby can't decide whose side she's on."

Mav turns to me, his face smooth and his speech slow. Patronizing. But I still want to understand so I tell myself to not let Ben know how his words change people around me, or the fact it bothers me. "Ace, my brother..." It's clear he's leading up to something but gets cut off by Abby who is twirling her ponytail between her right fingers.

"Is Mav short for Maverick?" Abby asks. Ben gives her a look that is either 'How do you not know all about the Piersons?' or 'Why are you so interested in knowing about the Piersons?'

"No. Our parents had a thing for three letter names. Ace, Mav. That was it. Just Mav."

"Your brother?" I press for Mav to continue. If one more tech cuts in, I'll provide the team another candidate for the donor program. Mav seems eager to discuss any topic. I want to discuss just this one topic until I understand. No deviating.

"Ace enlisted with the Intercontinents."

All heads in the room turn to Mav. This is a big deal. The room feels smaller and packed tighter, with people who didn't want to be standing next to one another. Probably a good thing Miller and Spaulding aren't here.

Mav's hands raise in surrender, defensive but with a mild joking air. "We had a fight." He motions inward, to himself. "Ace didn't look like me. He tried to enlist with the Outercontintents, but one look at scrawny bitty Ace and our commander turned him away. The thing about Ace, he's a freaking computer whiz. Helped program this whole place." Mav spreads his arms wide, causing techs to duck or lean out of his range. "I can't believe I have to explain this to you. Everyone knows who Ace is..." Mav indicates no concern for those he inconveniences with his muscled expanse. "Him and some other guys." Gravity pulls Mav's biceps back at his sides. "We weren't rich—the Piersons—before Ace and his program investments, that and...the accident."

"He means how Mr. Pierson died," Gordon pipes in, drawing a pointed look from Mav.

"He was terminally injured when a child entered his camp with an explosive device strapped to him." I remember.

"That's right. But, right before that incident, Ace completely hacked the com lines, all the com lines of the Outercontintents. He gave them full access to every move we made because he knew our code better than anyone down there could have." Mav's face gets stern. The soft edges bunch into furrows and chiseled muscle over bone so that it's impossible to imagine this man being anything but stone. "And then they blew him up as a thank you."

"It wasn't them," I say, but I'm cut off before I finish my sentence.

"Yes, it was." Mav gets very close to my face. All sharp edges and constricted pupils. "It was them. We weren't even close to their position. Did you know that?" He asks like I might know. I don't. "They left him in that bunker to be found. When we arrived, they knew we were coming. They were prepared for every maneuver, every artillery, every contingency. We were done." Mav half-heartedly slashes a hand across the air in front of his torso, as if the action isn't worth making but he makes it anyway. "Ace was laying there with this kid, this Inter-continent kid, in pieces all around him. We took him home. The news started right after," Mav says, shoving his words where they don't belong, where a pause should have been. "Mr. Pierson 'the hero' of the war, and a harbinger of peace."

"Yes," I say. "He was a hero." I search Mav's body language to better understand what I'm still missing. The war is over. Ace was the hero.

"We lost, Jennie," Ben says loudly over everyone else. "We freaking lost."

Everything clicks in my head like dominoes. This group of people were all on the losing side. Ace lost the war. And Ace was hailed as the hero for the people who won. Ace is a traitor to the people I'm with.

"But." I look at the room and the people and the files in hands and papers on the floor. "Why bring him here and make him a donor?"

"He was a donor already," Mav says. "As I said, he helped develop the program. It's a military program originally."

"Why here?" I ask again. If Ace developed a military program, why did he develop it for the side he wasn't with? Why not develop his program for his side? I should have woken up on the Interconti-nent's side, at least. Not with the losers. I'm a winner.

"This is the second building," Mav says. "The first Pierson facility was blown up in the explosion that signaled the end of the war."

"In Ecuador," Gordon says. He unwraps a twin candy bar, sliding one side into his mouth as far as it will go before biting it off. "Where we're going."

I'm unsure how to express to these people who use backward logic, say the opposite of what they mean, and use facial gestures to qualify meaning to words that they're making a grand error. "But why did you put him in this program?" I ask. "Why not let him die?"

"We needed him," Mav says. "Right now, for instance. Ace would know how to get all your memory back, not just game memory, but your pre-donor life too."

My face furrows in frustration without me having to think of the action before doing it. I want to celebrate my accomplishment of involuntary emotional expression, but I'm too bothered. "But you could not anticipate problems with the result of your system at that time," I say. "Why bring him here?"

Mav shifts focus. His pupils widen as if they're taking in all his surroundings. I imagine if a fly buzzed at the end of the hall, Mav would see it. "I wanted answers."

"And you thought you'd get them if you had Ace here?"

"He thought he could reprogram his brother, like a post-war sabotage," Ben speaks out of turn again.

"Shut it, Ben," Gordon says.

"It's in the files," Ben says. "Clear as day to anyone who can read code."

Mav turns his head to the side. A gesture I almost recognize. "And you read code?"

"I'm a tech, aren't I?" Ben says.

Abby shakes her head no, which as far as I can tell, doubles as a 'just drop it' signal.

"It's there. I've seen it too," Gordon says as if he's reluctantly supporting Ben. "The code speaks for itself."

"What does the code say then?" Mav shifts his entire body, so he's squared to Gordon.

The slight frame of Gordon shows no sign of being threatened or intimated. He happily discloses any information he can think of. "It was clear from the first donor entry that a false code had been entered with the player, like malware, but with the purpose of manipulating only one player. It attached itself to the donor code associated with Ace Pierson and stayed with that code through the game." Gordon points to the screen that once displayed leaderboard stats. "For a while, those two codes were neck and neck for winning, but the malware was better."

Mav smiles at hearing this news. His aggressive stance eases a bit.

"Malware can't be uploaded into our AI." Gordon smiles at me like this is going to be comforting to me, when I know it's false news. Any damn thing can be uploaded into their shells. I'm proof. "So they kept rerouting, while more and more donors were added to the game. But it was always those two codes on top. No matter how many TECHs or even military source codes we entered, no one and nothing seemed to beat the game Ace was playing with the malware. They both got better and better at besting each other until I thought for sure Ace had it beat."

A shadow crosses Mav's face again. He seemed torn between wanting his malware program to be unbeatable, but still wanting to get his brother, manipulated into being reprogramed, back from the system.

"Did the malware have a name?" I ask.

"Just a code. Technically he'd be Donor One. Or something similar." Gordon pauses. "You know because of binary. Ones and zeros."

The Commander. These idiots created that lunatic. "Ecuador built a new program?" I ask.

"Like I've said," Ben steps in. "They have all the resources, which means all the money, and lots of people willing to work for all that money."

"Ben means yes," Abby says.

Mav has a complicated sibling relationship. His intentions to free the programs I have duplicated on a stick drive might not be in alignment with mine. "Remind me what is our purpose in Ecuador?"

"Fix you," Gordon says like this is a very simple notion. The way you patch a tire, change batteries in a remote, conduct brain surgery in a human. Simple everyday fixes.

"I am not broken," I say.

"You're not properly functioning," Ben says. "Dr. Miller's suggesting we put you in a wheelchair to hide the fact you can't take three steps without looking drunk."

Mav has the expression of a man who has something to say but is unwilling to speak in the current company. I hope to find an opportunity to speak to Mav alone. If he intends to sabotage my ability to rescue my friends, including Ace, from the program they're frozen inside, I won't let him. I can't. And at this moment he's much more reflective of the Commander than he is of his brother.

A crew of seven of us stand with bags packed near the front lobby of the Pierson building. The crowds outside have been pushed back by over a hundred yards for today's departure. News vans, camera crews, reporters with microphone packs bulging from underneath sweaty shirts take their place. Mexico isn't forgiving when it comes to heat. Despite the fact, the glacial poles continue to extend. Mexico holds on to sweltering high temps. One of the few resources it's maintained since the war, so I hear.

Several courtesy screens show the same news story –

Pierson Property announces they will be debuting their recent success of intelligence transplant in conjunction with Ecuador's reveal later this month. Both facilities share a historical establishment with one of the original donors. Ace Pierson, a young war hero, whose coding skills are the basis for the Game of Life...

The announcer continues speaking about shared accomplishments.

"If Ecuador gets wind of this..." Ben leans over to Abby to whisper what he suspects Ecuador's response might be.

"When the car pulls up, I want everyone tight around Jennie. We don't want to leak too much information before we get some answers," Spaulding says.

The team nods. Not one of them checks with me. No, 'sound good, Jennie?' or 'do you agree with this tactic?' or 'do you have a better idea?'

I don't have a better idea, but it'd be nice if they asked.

I keep tabs on Gordon. He has a tablet with him, working and walking. I'm certain he's still digging for information on my code, the donor who originated my code, or anything. I sidestep a few places until I'm close to him, and using my best low speaking tone say, "Gordon."

Gordon startles. Ben, Abby, and Mav all turn to look at me. My low speaking voice isn't inconspicuous. Dangit.

"Uh..." I nod to the attentive audience. "Did that window get repaired?" I ask, then smile and nod to Mav. I'm still unsure what the total damage was to those below the glass shard shower.

Abby and Ben return to whatever they're arguing about. I'm fairly certain it has to do with differing theories regarding what's 'wrong' with me.

"We just passed that hall, Jennie," Mav says as though he's speaking to a child. "You saw the new glass being put in three days ago."

"Oh, right." A nervous chuckle spontaneously generates from somewhere inside me. It both thrills me and terrifies me that I might be giving myself away. "I'm nervous"

Mav puts a hand on my shoulder. I'm nearly as tall as him since the wheelchair idea was disbanded because it 'gives the impression of sickness, and we don't want anyone jumping to conclusions before we tell them where to jump.'

"Don't be nervous." Mav's words sound as if they're intended to be comforting, but the weight of his hand perplexes me. My internal structure is steel and other materials that don't naturally sense a great deal of outside force. But I register the strength of his hand like a warning. Maybe Mav is nervous too and that's what I'm sensing. "Keep that file close to you," Mav whispers so lightly that only mechanical sensors would be able to pick it up. No human ear could possibly perceive the sound, but I can. "Don't show anyone in the Ecuador facilities what you have."

"The vans." Dr. Miller motions everyone to circle around me.

A long line of white vehicles all with tinted windows pulls up to the building. The crowd parts only because they have to. Security brandishes tear grenade guns, place hands on sidearms, and extend a hand for the crowd to move back. Exhaust fumes and overworked, rattling engines roll through the mass like a gas bomb has already been launched. No one retreats—the mob daring the security team to take action.

I try to stay as near to Gordon as I can, but he keeps moving sideways, like he's taking direction from my movements, so everyone moves sideways following me while I'm trailing Gordon.

"Stop, stop, stop," Spaulding calls. "Move toward the vans."

The mass shifts back toward the street. The sounds of people pressing against security lines and shouting and calling to get eyes on who or what our crowd is huddled around increase.

"First van," Spaulding pushes Miller, Mav, and two techs into the first van.

The voices from the distant crowd speak in a frenzy. Most are shouts of outrage or threats. My excellent hearing picks out several outbursts.

"Unnatural!"

I try not to look. I don't want to give myself away. Walking feels stiffer than ever, like every step is a neon sign saying, 'Aim here, I'm the atrocity of nature!' My stiff legs swivel on ball hinges that feel ready to fall apart. No matter of squeezing this or mentally tightening that has any impact on the way this stupid shell of a body functions.

"Shut it down!"

"Melt it!"

"There's Pierson." The focus of the crowd turns to Mav, who ducks into the first van.

Shots fire. I duck and cover my head with my arms as does the rest of the group still outside vans. Gray fog rises from the front of the mob. Security fires first this afternoon. Everyone coughs and gags. Hands move from over their heads to cover their eyes and mouths. The thick vapors have no impact on me. I smile, then cover my relief by pretending to suffer the same effects. My coughing sounds synthesized since I don't have lungs to force air from. It's just a sound I create.

Spaulding makes a big show of getting Abby and Ben to safety. At first, I think he's giving me away, showing concern for them exposed to the tear gas. But by making such an effort of hiding something, then pretending to be less concerned with covering me up, Spaulding has deflected attention from me and placed it on the techs in the first van. We all wear the same white coats, even the doctors, with the exception of Mav. He dresses like a man making a statement and rich enough to be successful at it.

Vehicles leave and more pull up in their place, masked by fog. No one can tell who comes or who goes. We filter into a vehicle as it pulls in front of us while Spaulding postures to the hacking crowd, as though their reflexing gags in response to the gas are applause. I duck into the van without much notice, followed by Gordon. Sheer luck has me close enough to him to speak normally. "Can you track the codes in proximity to Ace?"

"Throughout the whole game?" Gordon asks. "He was in there the longest. Players change, even codes change." Gordon points to a screen filled with files. Not lines of data, but folders and folders and folders of information all more vast than the last. I think he expects me to be impressed. I have to hold back a scoff and suck in the words telling him to give it to me so I can handle this code cookie buffet. "Take this file," he says pointing to a blip on the screen. "All the donors in this group had decaying source code based on attempts at given levels. And here," he taps another location on the screen. "They all had counting codes, tracking attempts in a forward progression. We had to try every motivator within the game for trial runs, to see which kind of system produced the best results." I can tell Gordon is going to go on and on about this nonsense, which helps me nothing.

Something hits the side of our van. I duck instinctively. Gordon screams and covers his device. It takes him several seconds to scurry to the floor of the van where I cower. He'd never survive the game. Gordon, geeking out over code programming, would be the first in this scrappy-unlucky group of facility workers to Mord out if we were inside the game. Whose the literal scrap of the bunch?

"Can you determine if there were consistent codes in proximity to Ace before I matched?"

"It's. I mean... yeah. We've always had that information. It's not a big deal."

They've always had that information? And didn't tell me? "Why haven't we talked about it before?" I ask.

"Why would we?" Gordon shrugs. "Until last week, I had no indication that you knew Ace. Not until you tried to shred Mr. Pierson and his financial committee with that window stunt."

Gordon's face tightens at the eyes and the corners of his mouth pull in closer so that all of his features draw noseward like his thoughts anchor on some odor in the air. I smell the air in the human fashion but get nothing. Even though I make a show of using my nose, my olfactory sensors aren't linked directly to my nose. It's a scan running through the air. The physical appearance of my nose is merely to appeal to the human need to see themselves in everything. My ears aren't the sole source of my auditory processing, for that matter.

Gordon claps in front of himself, with one hand in a fist. I don't know what it means. "Here's the thing." He pauses, does the clap again. "The codes located around Ace were all eliminated from the game shortly before he was. None of them made it to the final level."

"But you said you thought he'd be the one to upload..."

"Before he disappeared from the files," Gordon says.

"I have the files," I say drawing the drive out of my pocket even though Mav told me to keep it hidden.

"Put that away." Gordon pushes my hand back at me. "Don't let Spaulding see you with that." He checks over his shoulder where Spaulding directs security on our next move.

My electric rhythm skips a pulse. I held this out in front of security cameras that Spaulding swore he was watching.

"I have no idea what you downloaded, but if you'd have told me you thought you had Ace... I'd know you're mistaken." Gordon drops his volume despite the fact Spaulding still postures outside. "Ace Pierson went dark. It's the same thing that happens to all donors when they're out of the game."

Another object slams the side of the van. Nothing on fire, thank goodness.

"I told Mav that his brother is on this file. That's why he's coming to Ecuador with us. To extract his brother." I scrunch my forehead without having to think about scrunching my forehead. My insides feel searching and confused. Maybe I'm more human than I first thought. I'm definitely flawed in ability to understand things—a legit human trait. "Do you agreed that we might be able to extract Ace."

"I don't not agree," Gordon double-negates, with one eye on Spaulding who seems to be wrapping up his appeasement with security. "We need Mav Pierson—and all his family money behind us—if we're going to get our program up and running again." Spaulding ducks to come inside the van, then ducks back out in response to another shouted question. Spaulding straightens his tie and crouches like he's going to enter the van again, cutting Gordon's revelations short, but he doesn't need to finish his thought. I'm learning how to put together the parts the humans don't say. It's hard, but I can do it more and more. It's almost like predictive text for human behavior. "Hey, Spaulding. We're going to miss our flight"

Spaulding has on a grin that looks more manufactured than AI, incongruent to the genuine satisfaction in his eyes. Spaulding likes attention. It doesn't seem to matter that the attention he's getting at the moment is mostly death threats and large blunt objects thrown at close range.

His behavior doesn't bother me. Even though it's insanity, he's a shield to hide behind.

I spend the rest of our drive and most of our flight trying to predict how I can apply Spaulding's attention shield to more situations.

When Spaulding excuses himself to use the lavatory, I lean over to Gordon, who swipes and taps on his tablet without pausing for breath. "I want the donor codes for anyone in proximity to Ace before his game ended."

Gordon doesn't stop his tapping. "Like right before?"

"No." Maybe that'll help. "I don't know."

Gordon stops tapping and looks down the aisle toward the lavatory. Where we're located in the front section of seating on a small plane with the remaining four members of our party at the back section, the bathroom isn't far away. Luckily the engine is so loud, there is no chance Spaulding could hear me from inside the bathroom.

Gordon returns his gaze on me, perturbed as though I'm his pestering ward. "I need better parameters than that, Jennie. You have to realize I'm putting a lot on the line for you here."

"Three levels prior," I say. "Up to the time he disappears."

The lavatory door opens. "What'd I miss?" Spaulding asks, then chuckles to himself as he fastens his belt back into place. Gordon laughs along, but his eyes remain alert and searching, as if he's nervous. I don't get the joke.

I do get nervous.

9

Every transition from one mode of transportation to the next is the same charade. Everyone packs tightly together, the support of all those bodies around me disguises my difficulty walking with a smooth gait of motion. Mob-like crowds with loud posters featuring angry-red slashes over the top of a computer with a smiley face on the screen, pre-gather at all our change locations, like our itinerary's been broadcast continent-wide. One poster has printed in bold lettering, "Die AI."

Cameras angle to snap images of anyone with a white coat on. Screens in lounges include news coverage of speculations regarding who might be hosted inside the mysterious AI from Mexico City. One channel has text scrolling along the bottom of the screen: *Secretive travel hasn't prevented open opposition to the failing donor programs throughout the nation.*

"Failing?" I ask. Gordon turns me toward a different screen, one with a story less like a personal attack and more like a Pierson-specific attack.

Since Mav is with our group, there is heavy coverage about Ace. Including photos and video from his life before the war and after. Ace was a slight man. Joints like bones wanting to break free of his reddened skin. He has a sharp chin and jaw like I know him, but the rest of Ace is an alien to me. How can this human be the source of the individual I knew? Or have I biased myself based on his brother's good looks he chose to resemble in the game? Reporters zoom in on Ben and Gordon, wondering if perhaps Ace is adjusting to a new physical challenge after mastering the game of his own creation.

"They think you're the upload?" I ask Gordon.

"Probably better for you, if they think that," Gordon says. He keeps his head down for long periods and adds a lilt to his walk as if he's adjusting to a new set of knees. There's a lot about Gordon resembling the stringy person the television claims was Ace Pierson. I can see how media could assume Gordon was the new and improved version of human Ace. Gordon doesn't seem to disappreciate the comparison.

Imitation lessons continue with Abby, Ben, and Gordon working around the arbitrary measurements of time used commonly throughout the world. Ecuador is one standard hour ahead of Mexico City, where we departed from. The Americas have shrunk from what history I can find. Divisions still exist, they're only differently named. It's all Inter and Outer instead of North and South, and East and West of historical record. The world is a band of resources. Those with easy access have easy power. Simple.

I study as we travel. Even when the plane begins to descend on our last leg, I search the landscape for information. I'm not sure if I'm mapping an escape route or simply curious how the circular grid system they seem to have in place works. There's a massive circle of factories surrounding a huge area of tightly packed buildings. The outer ring is gray from smoke and factory waste. The closer to the center of the city the plane goes, the whiter the structures. Everything appears to have been built with white stone and grayed from exposure over time.

Except for one dark star at the center of Quito. We fly over, but it's nothing more than a black diamond on a hill with a shining bronze stone as sentinel when we pass from the air.

Once we land, the details of the city demonstrate wealth and the current power hold on the world. It's impressive all the way to the details. Lettering is etched or embossed. Nothing is left untouched by depth and shadow. Even the sanitation crew, who seem to work around the clock inside the city, wear white.

Ecuador had once been considered a poor country. Looking at it now, it's impossible to imagine. The buildings are intricate in their detail work and expansive in their size. The wide roads stretching over hills and through town are clean, with designs paved into the stones that make up the pavement. Vehicles that drive past us aren't manned but propelled by computer navigation. I could do that job but have no interest. Seeing a non-thinking machine carry out the task with no benefit to itself makes me ill.

Tall cement fences with metal spikes along the top edges keep unwanted intruders from residences we aren't able to view. I can't imagine anything more elaborate than what I can see, yet the fences indicate more wealth and opulence still.

We wind our way through the city toward the center of Quito. The roadways thin and the structures shrink as we approach a central hill. At the peak of the hill is a gleaming black-glass tower. As we drive higher, the glass seems so tinted that it might as well be made of brick —the transparent material being an illusion, like a two-way mirror. Whatever takes place within the building, they don't want curious onlookers having front row seats.

I review what I know.

There was a war. And those with more won. Mav Pierson has more than most I've seen, but he claims to be a loser. His brother supposedly fought for the Intercontinents but ended up a traitor, or betrayed. That's a fine line. Dispersement of goods does not show itself to be dependent on facts, logic, or merit.

A larger-than-life-sized statue of the deformed version of Ace stands like a fallen angel at the front entrance to the black shining structure. The statue includes missing limbs and facial scars where regular clothing can't hide the damage done from the bomb that eventually ended Ace's life. A looming mangle of scrawniness complete with an off-balanceness threatens to topple anyone who dares pass too closely.

Entering the building continues the effect of falling. It's all clear glass on the inside. Even the flooring seems translucent, but it's mirrors. An information desk stands an inconvenient distance from the entrance. The wide birth of an entry feels more like being swallowed than greeted. Chairs line the outer wall, far from information. I let Spaulding and Miller proceed to the desk while I follow Gordon, Abby, and Ben to the chairs. I'm better at short distances, less likely to draw attention to my flaws if I'm not moving. Besides, I can dial up my audio receptors, if I want.

"Did you hear anything I've said, Jennie?" Abby sets her binder of international social norms in the seat cushion beside her. "Aren't you listening at all?"

"I am." I really am. I'm only not paying attention. My auditory receptive mechanics are functioning well, and I even have the option to record sounds that I hope to review again later. In cases like this, where some other matter occupies my processing demands, I can record and come back later, while all the people sleep. Except I wasn't recording Abby. I have no intention of coming back to greetings and posturing.

"Let her rest." Mav defends me. I turn toward his voice only to find myself staring into Gordon's pocket protector. No ink splotches, so the thing must work. Miller could use such a gadget. He has a shirt covered in pen scratch and ink bleeds.

"She doesn't rest," Gordon pipes in. "How soon until they agree to meet with us?"

Though no one turns their head nor looks toward Spaulding or Miller for their response, the room stills to a low hum as if we're all afraid sudden movement might startle a confession away and we'll never learn the answer to how long we have to stay in our holding pen.

I stand from my place near Abby and cross the large lobby. There are tightly woven rugs covering the orange tile flooring with a perimeter of cushioned chairs and little interior potted trees growing what looks like Roma tomatoes from their branches. The room has a citrus sting in the air along with heaviness from the humidity. How this environment is ideal for mechanical lives baffles me. It's all rust and corrosion in this glass-sheathed structure.

The building is placed at the top of a large hill, where a massive statue of an angel once stood before the war. When it fell, this building replaced it. Almost religiously, proponents of artificial life flocked to the surrounding city since. At least that's the top story from three years ago in the Quito Times.

"Are the real bodies hooked up to wires and tubes somewhere?" I wonder aloud.

"You don't even remember orientation when you were admitted?" Ben harshly whispers to me, not bothering to hide his contempt at my memory failings here inside the safety of a foreign building with unfamiliar crowds outside. Crowds are constant.

Gordon does the typical Gordon thing and provides information above and beyond what I'm asking because he knows something, and he likes it when the rest of us know he knows something, I assume. "Brainwaves are patterned over the course of six weeks. If the program doesn't take, the donor is disconnected from the system. If they're still alert and functioning, they're sent home to be with their families until the natural end. If it does take, well... you know."

"What if a donor just dies on the table and isn't in the game?" I ask.

"Happens all the time," Gordon says without hesitation or any sign of concern for how I might interpret his nonchalance with donors and their volunteer lives. "They're 'terminal' patients. It goes with the territory that some are going to tank before the procedure is complete."

"What if it's halfway?" This discussion can lead me down a line of a million slightly varying questions, but each individually weighted.

"No code registered in the system is a straight up fail," Gordon says, triggering something inside me, itching to rip and claw a code into Gordon's arm myself if he ever says 'no code is a fail' again.

I stand and maneuver across the room to where Mav sits. I use my best imitation walking and only cause mild irritation from Abby at my jerkiness. "Do you know anyone named Jilly?" I ask.

Mav has his arms folded. He hasn't shifted his squared-off stance, an indication that he isn't welcoming me into his personal space. Not today. "No." There is no softness to his answer, like an 'I'm sorry, I wish I could help you connect the dots and fill in your holes.' It's a closed door to conversation sort of answer. I can't tell if it's this place, with his post-war-traitorous brother memorialized in his face, or cowing to his family's competition in the technological achievement arena that erases any personality he might have. Mav is like a statue himself—brooding and cold, and set and unmoving in his judgment.

I've searched the donor database for a 'Jilly' and found no matches. I thought I'd at least try the familial angle before totally giving up on trying to figure out what Ace meant when he called me that once. He'd said I looked like her. Or maybe it was just that I reminded him of someone with that name... It's not lost in my memory, as to why I can't decipher the moment and the name. My understandings of human intention and expression don't seem to line up the majority of the time. They're exhausting that way. Every phrase has to be evaluated from individual perspectives, experience, and style.

There is no way I'm ever going to master the ability to understand human communication unless I can assimilate every human motivation and life experience. I doubt Abby and Ben have such a file in their cases, though they do have a lot of thick nonsense they keep trying to shove down my data drives.

"Let's keep going," Abby calls from across the room.

"I can just plug into a physical therapy program and download every strategy to relearn walking there is," I say, struggling back to Abby in my smoothest human stride.

"Plugging into a computer isn't the same type of learning." Gordon again. Always Gordon when it's a 'Did you know?' type moment. If I only mastered sarcastic eye-rolling, I'd be doing it right now.

Then, of course, Ben jumps in with his favorite topic of 'let me emphasize the ways I feel you're not being authentically human enough.' "It's not human to assimilate behavior by downloading it. It's human to learn by doing, copying. Visual and auditory gathering of information, then put into practice."

"Yes. Exactly," Gordon says.

"No one cares," Mav's voice carries from the other side of the large room we've been waiting in. "It's not human to still be alive after you're dead, so why not give it up already?"

At that, a forced cough and exaggerated clearing of a throat announces company in the room. How long someone has been standing in the shadowed opening of double doors a good distance from us is unclear. What is clear, Mav's last words prompted the company to make themselves be noticed.

10

A man of slight stature and stout build, with dark hair and deep-set eyes, emerges from the doorway. "*Buenos.*" He speaks in clipped rhythm, a local speech pattern that doesn't seem to reflect the language so much as a dialectical standard for this region. "I hope you enjoyed your trip." His English is well structured with correct tense and syntax for English speakers. Though his Spanish accent makes it difficult to decipher.

"We traveled well, thank you." Spaulding moves like a chess piece guarding his king. He stands in front, prominently drawing the focus of the room to himself. I don't like the guy, but I appreciate him at this moment. "Your city has prospered since I visited last."

"Oh, when were you here?" Our foreign host feigns pleasantry with a smile that doesn't reach the corners of his eyes.

"Before the war broke out. We had discussed having a lab in this region. With the low labor, medical, and material costs, I'd thought it was a prime location to develop."

"Why didn't you?"

"We couldn't come to an agreement," Spaulding speaks these words like we're already in some failed negotiation.

I'm still learning how to read human behavior and find the posturing taking place confusing. Spaulding isn't gaining any favor with our host if I'm reading lips pressed thin correctly.

"We're here to compare notes," Miller interrupts. He doesn't move himself to the front of the group as Spaulding has. The foreign man has to bend and lean around those of us frozen where we were caught by this man like some game of gossip freeze-tag.

"We don't have a need to compare," the man says after making note of Miller. "If you're here for our lecture series, you're early. It starts in six months."

"We're here to compare notes," Miller says again.

The Ecuadorian man nods once. He steps around Spaulding, who watches Miller with unfavorably narrow eyes and adjusts the strap on his smartwatch repeatedly.

"You think it's not obvious?" The man weaves his way between Gordon and Abby. He circles Mav, maneuvering with the smoothness of a ballet dancer before he stops in front of me.

I stare at this strange man, with his shortness and thick hair. All the humans I've known in person are of a similar build, with a stretch about their limbs, where this man has more of a squished limb appearance. I wonder if the AI from their labs appears the same as him, or like the people I've known. What will be the same between us? What will be different?

"You need better joints," he says to me.

"I have no control over this," I say defending my appearance. How dare he judge me? I woke up this way.

"I know, I know." He waves a hand to Spaulding. "Allocation of resources, right? Is that why you're here? We have better supplies? You want to pretty up your accomplishment before trying to pass this." He turns to me, and even though he is shorter than I am, he looks down at me, "For celebration?" He turns his head as though looking at me causes him to hear claws dragged upon the tile flooring. "All I can say is, have fun on your return trip." He points to the doors we arrived through. "We'll even pay your shuttle service to return to the airport."

'No." Mav speaks but doesn't move, not imposing his presence. He must assume words are enough. Even I'm not foolish enough to think words alone will work with the foreign man before us. He wants numbers and elegance. We come with scraps. "We don't want your things."

But we do. We want access to their machines and the opportunity to load my data to their system. I want access, at least, to their program.

"Mr. Pierson is correct," Miller emphasizes Mav's name receiving the desired reaction he was hoping for. The man steps away from me. He walks to the counter and checks a screen with so much typing that I'm not sure what will happen next.

Spaulding shakes his head in a vigorous 'no' toward Miller, his jowls still wiggle once he stops. If Spaulding shows restraint, it's got to be a bad move. Will we be removed by armed security? Spaulding turns his back and starts inputting data on a device. My guess is he's calling to arrange return flights as soon as possible.

Miller ignores Spaulding and continues to speak. "We're not interested in your things." He points to me. "We've had some complications with our files." He waits for the man to stop typing. I get the impression that though he was hoping the mention of Mav Pierson had an impression, the response isn't exactly what he was hoping for.

"Mr. Pierson?" the man looks up from his screen. "Your appearance is different."

As in Mav looks different than he expects? It's out of character type different? Can it be that the man is unfamiliar with Mav? He thinks this is Ace? Different can mean so many things, it's exhausting deciphering human meanings.

"You should have informed me you were coming. I'd have had rooms prepared." Whatever the man checked with on the screen, it's in our favor. So long as no one blows this. "My name is Geovanni. I go by Geo."

"Nice to meet you, Geo," Spaulding says in an attempt to change the focus of the room again. His tone is neither gracious nor welcoming. I'd guess Spaulding does not believe it has been nice to meet Geo. I'd have to agree with Spaulding. I'd also like to know what the screen said that changed Geo's mind about helping us. One look at the Ace statue outside would lead me to believe that Geo is fully aware Mav and Ace aren't the same person.

"I would like to see your AI." No one speaks. As though my question isn't phrased intelligently. Everyone stares at me as though I've misspoken. I try again. "I would like to meet your donor."

"Yes. *Bueno, que si.*" Geo lets his English efforts fall away. No more need to put on a show for us. He motions us through the shadowed double doors.

I don't follow first. I need to know what I said wrong. The best person to ask is Miller. Or Mav.

Spaulding is first to follow Geo, trailed by Gordon and Ben in step with Abby at their heels. Miller drags his feet following Abby, but Mav holds back. I need a sound cushion since my whisper isn't perfected as yet. "Mav."

"Jennie?" There is a smile playing at the edges of his mouth as if he finds me amusing.

"What did I do to cause everyone to look at me like that?"

"I don't know." I can tell he's lying.

"Tell me. I need to make more requests, and if I do it wrong, I'm less likely to reach my objective."

The smile fades as his eyes squinch up a bit in question.

"I've done it again, haven't I?"

"Try to sound less...mechanical." Mav lifts a hand, indicating I should move in the direction of the group. Our conversation over.

"I need access to the donor files," I say. "How do I request that less mechanically?"

Mav folds his arms as he moves ahead of me, then with a quick look over his shoulder to where I still stand in hopes of an answer he says, "Don't ask."

I stumble. My off-balance joints can't keep up with him "But I need—"

He stops, with his back to me. "Don't. Ask." Mav continues walking, observing some oil paintings, of how Ecuador used to look, hung on the wall. Dirt roads, clay buildings, orange tile roofs. It's beautiful in its simplicity. I wish I could have seen it that way. "I didn't say don't look for the files."

"And that's less mechanical?"

"It's definitely human." Mav turns a corner.

When I follow the rest of the group is gathered in the room we've entered. I close my mouth, swallowing whatever curiosity I have about humans and honesty. The room holds a large glass table. Unlike the exterior of the building, the glass of the table is completely transparent.

"*Hay* protocols here at the *facilidad*," Geo says standing at the head of the table. "*Por favor* take a seat." He motions everyone to chairs, also transparent, though I doubt they're made of actual glass. They move too lightly and easily to be a delicate material. I'm half terrified my heavy body will crush the object under my weight. I remain standing in order to observe how everyone else fares in the seats.

Everyone sits except Mav, who stands at the back as if he has the need to relieve himself. Or perhaps he too is worried about how his impressive frame will impact the transparent seating. Geo looks at us as though we're holding up the rest of his presentation and he has it prepared and is under a time restriction.

"Please sit, *por favor*," Geo says.

"I'm not sure." I lift a chair. It's air to my touch, but my fingers don't crack the material.

"You can't harm the chairs," Geo says. "*Sientase.*"

I sit down at the command.

Mav takes his seat next to Gordon, which is next to mine.

"*Bueno.*" Geo motions a hand and an additional person, whom I hadn't before noticed, dims the lights from a remote. "*Estrict* confidentiality or you go home now."

I nod. At my side, Gordon nods as well. I hear Spaulding voice his agreement along with the two techs remaining and Miller. Mav gives no indication as far as I can decipher.

Geo taps the table one time and a projection appears on the glass wall behind him.

Gordon leans close enough to me that I can hear a rasp in his throat. Maybe he's caught an illness in our travels. "Jennie" His voice a soft whisper. The intensity is so much that my mechanical heart races at the mention of my name, not in a romantic sense, but more of a danger is coming. "I found something." Brace for it.

"*Especific* files for each and every donor..." Geo continues talking about whatever is taking place on the screen. Something about record keeping, good business practice, methods for data transfer. "Corruption in the files is expected, we have safeguards in place for this." His accent gets thicker the longer I hear him speak, instead of less prominent.

Gordon doesn't tell me anything more. I wait.

"...trace any programs introduced from outside sources..."

Gordon is watching the screen. He's supposed to tell me what he found. A person can't say 'I've found something' and then not say what it is they found, can they?

"...errant program codes and bugs in the system. We ran into problems because a reboot would mean a loss of donor codes, no one knows how many might be lost or corrupted from a hard crash of the system. So we could not."

"Gordon?" My attempt at a whisper draws Mav's attention. My vision has adjusted to the dark already. It's easy to see the majority of our group are completely engrossed in this presentation. It sounds exactly like what we already know. It's impossible to control for digital loss and hackers.

"...but we lost power and our backup systems failed."

Wait, what?

I listen to Geo too. "All our files went down," he says, meaning the system crashed. "When we rebooted the program, we had all the donors back, even the ones previously eliminated."

Reactions vary around the room. Spaulding swivels in his chair. Mav's brows move closer together, not in rage or anger, but confusion. Questions form in shapes at his mouth, but he changes the way he holds himself without letting his wonder fall out on the clear table. Miller looks like he's been sentenced in a court for some crimes against humanity. The techs stare at the screen like it possesses the magical solution to all things. Maybe it does.

"We let it continue to run. We didn't ask what had changed or why our power failed. Why our backup systems failed."

"Was the power loss grid-wide?" Ben asks.

Geo winks at Ben in a non-playful manner. It still would have been odd, had he been playful in winking, but without any hint of humor behind his eyes, it's almost a threat. "No. *Solo nuestros.*"

"Odd, don't you think?" Mav says.

"*Si. Si, lo es.*" Geo nods. His focus remains on Mav for a long stretch of seconds before moving forward with his presentation. "But nothing seemed amiss. It's like the game debugged itself, hit a restart or something."

Gordon leans in with his silent whisper once more, while the rest of the room buzzes and speculates about the power sources and the game fixing itself in Ecuador, where it clearly remained a problem in Mexico City. "One of Ace's proximity codes."

I search my databanks for conversations with Gordon, to make sure I'm following the term proximity codes correctly. I know we haven't used that term before, but I also know the meaning of proximity and can guess he means the codes that remained near Ace for extended times.

"A security guard that worked here." Gordon stops talking but has the posture of someone who still has more to say. I look around to determine what's caused his stopping. Mav has his head bent forward, looking down at the clear table in a listening posture. Listening to us no doubt. Geo has stopped talking too. When I move my head to spy if he's watching, he shifts his weight to his back foot. A retreat in his lean.

I run through the ragtag group of people I know inside the game. A security guard? Anyone could be a security guard. No help at all, Gordon. There's no way to determine if that information can apply to my group or just some random player who happened to work the Ecuador center prior to becoming a donor and leveling similar tracks as us.

That makes two players in the Mexico City donor program who had previously worked or been involved with the facility here in

Ecuador. From the look on Geo's face, I can assume he heard Gordon's information and is concerned with either the fact we're investigating his staff or the fact we're aware of his staff being Mexico donors.

Geo doesn't look away when I meet his eyes. Not like the rest of them, who seem caught in something embarrassing when I look too long, and they look back. I know staring isn't a Northern accepted custom. Geo seems uninformed about the 'look away' social norm. I can't decide if that's his culture or a challenge. Maybe I should try staring at more of the locals to get a feel for what's normal.

11

After our briefing about what's off limits, which is everything except the glass conference room, we're given personal quarters with mirrored walls, to give the appearance of transparency, while still providing an odd sense of privacy within the grand professional space. Each room has two beds. Spaulding is the only one of us given his own accommodations. The rest of the Mexico City donor party has to share, two to a room. Being the only other female-identifying member of our group, I bunk with Abby.

"Why do I have to bunk with Jennie?" Abby complains to Miller. I'm certain she's aware I can hear her. "It's not like she sleeps. Why does she need a room?"

"We need Jennie to behave like the rest of us. Room and bed included," Spaulding says.

"Great. I get to wake up to her standing over me, not breathing air like she's dead, and eyes wide open, not blinking?"

Miller's palms twitch a barely visible apology gesture.

"You're paying for my therapy after this," Abby says. Lifting her bag, she storms past me into our shared room and claims one of the beds by throwing her bags on it. She flops herself on the second bed, leaving no space for me to pretend at humanness.

There's no reason, as far as I can determine, not to play into her concern. I enter the room, slowly close the door, without making visual contact with Abby, then turn my head by small degrees until I face her without adjusting my shoulders, torso, or hips. It's not a natural human movement and I know it will freak her out. I wait for her to make eye contact with me and hold her gaze as long as she dares. The second she pulls away, I return to a natural posture, with my back facing Abby, and smile.

Well-padded seats adorn the only corners left available for furnishings. I sit across from the television. There are three power ports in the room, which Abby quickly claims with all her charging cords and computer plugs. This room is better soundproofed than the lobby. Even if there were protesters, which there aren't, I wouldn't hear anything through the high-tech materials used to construct this building.

No noise to drown out the hum of my working parts. I don't like to listen to the fan cooling my internal workings, or the buzz of mechanics beneath my skin. I focus instead on the click and tap from Abby's typing. She hits backspace more than any other key. I can tell by the silence of her other fingers when the 'tap, tap, tap' chews up her mistakes.

Abby uses three devices at the same time. The water dispenser in our room gets the rest of her attention. She fills a paper cup with water almost as much as she changes screens on her devices. Clicking and clacking, scrolling, posting, filtering, possibly researching for hours before she lays down from fatigue. Blue light from all her open gadgets washes over her in the darkness. I stand and walk around the beds with the least sound I can manage, not sure how light of a sleeper Abby is, but certain my unsteady gate could vibrate anyone to alertness. The open screens include a college assignment, social media, and some search running without results yet. Forty-seven percent finished. It's been running a while. Must be an encompassing search.

A knock at the door startles me and I lose balance but save myself before falling on top of Abby and her electronics. I stand with my arms spread over her, willing myself not to topple. If I had breath, I'd be holding it.

Before daring to move toward the door, I lean back, waiting for any movement from Abby. When I'm finally convinced she's out cold, I figure the knocker must be gone. It crosses my mind that I might have imagined I heard a knock at the door, but I'm not sure my imagination works that way. Everything feels so terribly literal and juvenile that I wonder if my personality was left in the game along with everyone else.

I listen at the closed wood panel before opening the door a crack. Outside stands a tall, slender, and perfectly poised man. His skin is flawless and youthful to match his clear brown eyes and thick strips of chocolate-shavings hair. I have no idea who he is, but he's the taffy-pull opposite of Geo aside from dark coloring.

"He-hello?"

"Mexico City, right?" he asks. His voice is low, but not gravely. He has a smooth Spanish accent that kisses the words in the places that Geo seems to trip on them. "Sorry, I wasn't sure if you're English or Spanish. I assume English since your country is all Anglo after the war, you know."

Even his softly condescending 'you know' makes me weak in the knees because I do. I totally know. At least when he says it. "Yeah. English. Thanks."

"You want to?" he nods to the hall, inviting me out of the room.

The way he leaves his sentences unfinished, as though he assumes I have some idea how it might end, ignites my curiosity to the point of a nodding in ignorant agreement. I *do* want to. I don't much care what, any to will do. "What time is it?"

"I don't know." He steps back, not away from me, but more of an extended invitation to join him in the hall. "Hours of the day aren't really my concern."

I've already guessed he's an Intelligence Donor Winner, or I should say 'the Ecuador ID Winner'.

"I'm Juan."

Maybe I don't hear him right. I step into the door frame opening. "One? Like the first donor?"

"No. Juan. Like Juan."

I still hear 'one.' "Like the number?"

"Not *uno*." Juan motions me farther into the hall away from the mirrored walls providing privacy for guest rooms where all the people are sleeping in this crazy see-through building. Night blue stars manage to filter through the dark glass in a way daylight doesn't penetrate. Maybe it's special glass.

I let the door softly latch closed at my back and cringe internally at the thought that the sound might wake Abby.

"I put something in the water," Juan says, noticing my mechanical reaction to my mental concern. "They will all sleep through the night."

"You what?" I ask, unsure if that's a crime or not. Also, unsure why I never thought of such a thing since I've been trapped in this world.

"It won't harm them. Humans do best with limited information."

His statement makes me wonder how he came to this conclusion. What is he holding back from the humans he interacts with? And mostly, why has he had the need to learn how to drug the humans so they don't rouse? I've had that need and still didn't figure it out. I can't help but feel like I'm still losing at a game I haven't been told the rules to.

"What do you want?" I ask, unsure if I should be wary of Juan, or take notes on better methods of donor/human interaction.

"To meet you," he says. "This life is not my own during the day. I have to demonstrate myself to them." He nods to the doors. "Loyalty."

"Why?"

"They're afraid of us," Juan says.

"Don't you have family?" I ask, knowing donors are part of something. There are people waiting to be reunited with the family member who they won't lose because of this lottery system. "Won't they see your humanness and embrace you?" Miller sees human in me that I hope I can grow into, something internal and honest. I don't want to lose the way he makes me feel like I belong to him and him to me. It's how I imagine a parent might be.

Juan laughs a low laugh. "What have they told you? Do you remember nothing?"

I want to be back in my room. "I remember everything."

"That's not what I hear." His voice holds onto 'hear' a little long, almost like a melody he's hypnotizing me with.

"I have no control over what you 'hear.'" I stop. Juan continues a couple smooth paces ahead of me before he pauses. "It's not true, what they say."

"Fine." Juan steps back. "Play it your way."

Suddenly I wonder if Juan ever left the game. He's still battling on this side when the human war over resources is over, not to mention the donor war. "I'm not playing at anything," I say. "I already won."

Juan looks at his wrist like he's checking the time, though there's nothing fastened to his arm. "When you wake up from their lies, come find me."

With that, Juan glides into the blackness of the building, not a hitch in his step. Everything about him is smooth and terrifying. My surface feels much more rough and unrefined having met him. I fight my joints to return to my room, hoping to look effortless in my movements, knowing that I have no audience to witness the struggle it is to be 'effortless'. My knee catches and I tumble onto my face.

"They're holding you back on purpose," Juan's voice travels through the hall like it's being conducted through the glass ceiling. Shattering my illusion of 'alone'. "I could fix you up, so your body isn't such a distraction."

"I'm good, thanks." I gather myself into a version of standing, open Abby's door, then slam it closed, truly hoping I'll rouse her. Whatever Juan put in the water, assuming he really did put something in there, Abby doesn't stir.

12

S omething in what Juan said won't leave me alone.

They're holding me back.

My thoughts power this new body. Every action I take is directed by my choices. Yet, I haven't felt totally 'me' since waking up.

The room I share with Abby is filled with devices charging. Abby knows I need to recharge as well. Fueling my battery cells doesn't mean I have to power down, not like humans sleep. I can remain alert. But I need access to a port. Abby claiming every possible outlet in the room for her devices feels like a personal attack like she's purposefully preventing me from recharging.

"Stupid Juan." I unplug one of Abby's several electronic devices. It's not like she needs seven different Wi-Fi connections. "He's just messing with me because I'm the new bot."

Not finished with most recent updates. Would you like to continue later? Flashes across the screen of the device I've unplugged. Does Abby know it's updating? Will she notice if I skip it? *Not now.* I click the option to end the update and take five minutes to recharge my batteries. I then plug her cord back into power and don't bother resuming any updates.

Morning takes its sweet time to arrive. I consider waking Abby just to have someone to talk to but remember that I don't like talking to her. I opt to leave the room before anyone's alarm forces company.

The halls are made of clear glass with exterior walls contrasted from the dark glass making this building look like a liquid shadow suspended atop a hill. Today has an agenda. I can feel it in the air, even though I don't know what it is. I find myself standing outside the conference room from yesterday. It's dark. The dawn light fighting the exterior glass can't quite erase the ominous cast to the room. I don't go in.

Voices catch my auditory sensors and I turn toward the stairwell and elevator. The sound of conversation, not an argument, muffles its way from a lower level. I flatten myself against a wall, back to glass, the way I would in the game if I was trying to listen in on someone else's strategy, and make my way closer. The wall serves as additional support for my unsteady legs as I move. It definitely doesn't conceal me. Stupid glass.

The voices rise from the stairwell. I drop to my hands and knees, which makes it easier for me to cross the open hallway without making as much noise with my odd way of walking. But it doesn't do anything for me camouflage-wise since everything is freaking glass.

"You know what this is?" I recognize Geo's voice. Gruff, full of the local accent, and impatience. I stretch to get a glimpse of 'this' through the glass door to the stairwell, without also drawing attention back to me.

Geo points to the left shoulder blade of whomever he's speaking with. Someone tall with dark hair and deeply tanned skin. Morning light strengthens, increasing the risk I'm taking trying to siphon information from Geo's conversation.

The other person doesn't respond to Geo's question. I assume because it's one of those rhetorical situations, where they both know the answer.

"You shoot your mouth off one more time before I've had a chance to claim what's mine, and…" Geo stops talking. I pull back on my outstretched frame. Trying to gather information through all sensory intake options might cost me anonymity. My rickety structure isn't great for stealth mode.

"I'm not your property," Juan speaks. He's the other person in the stairwell. A shuffle of feet tells me that Juan's words draw Geo back from somewhere. Was he coming to find me? Does he suspect someone is listening? Am I wearing anything too brightly colored? Whites and light blues—good choice.

"Don't mess with me. You know damn well what's mine, and what I can do about it. It should matter to you. You know what these guys are as well as I do, and neither of us wants them to have the upper hand. You mess up again and I'll wipe your smug personality and start over." I wait to hear Juan say something back. Something smart to put Geo in his place, remind him that it doesn't work that way. Several seconds pass. Then maybe a minute. Juan says nothing.

My internal mechanics start working overtime, pumping too much fluid to my hands and feet, so I feel swollen and limb heavy. If Geo climbs the steps to where I crouch, I won't be able to run or hide because all the parts of this stupid wannabe-human-body keep responding to information without my permission. Besides, when are fat hands and feet ever a logical or helpful response to stress? Who designed this body anyway?

A stair creaks much closer to me than the conversation originated.

"It's going to take a lot more than bribing Spaulding to get access to Jennie's codes," Juan speaks again. His voice rises on my name and codes. I'm pinned by my poorly designed human-robotic-shell.

The creaking step sound recedes. Geo speaks again from the same location I first overheard their argument. "Don't tell me how to do my job."

Footsteps descend further down the stairwell. I don't know if they both retreat from my hiding place, or just one of them. I'm afraid to move. I can't be certain Juan was trying to warn me, or simply engaged in an argument that included coincidental timing to save my cover from being blown.

"Jennie?' I fall to my side when Mav says my name from behind where I'm crouched.

From my side, I look back toward the stairwell, fast filling with what morning light filters through the dark glass. Juan stands at the landing between the floor I'm on, and the one below. Mav obviously can't see him. I open my mouth—not to say anything about Juan being there necessarily—but Juan shakes his head 'no' before any words come out.

"W-Mav," I end up saying, like some mix of my brain almost called Juan instead of Mav. "What are you doing up so early?'

"What are you doing on your side? Did you not get enough sleep?" He bends low to grab my hand and help me to my feet. His face is in position to notice Juan on the stairs if he bothers to turn and look toward the landing. I'm a lot more weight than Mav bargains on. Looking like a fragile female human doesn't mean weighing like a fragile female human.

"Bots don't sleep," I say in answer to his question.

"Yeah, but you're in a heap like maybe you should be asleep. Do you get tired?"

"No." But I do. Just a different kind of tired. The kind of tired where I get so tired of human things and trying to guess humanness that I'd like to be just ones and zeroes without any extra variables, please. Too much to explain, so I don't.

"Have you seen the news?" Mav asks.

"No." That one's true. I haven't seen the news today.

"Some reporter in Mexico thinks he's found your family."

My mouth drops open involuntarily. I close it. It's not possible. Mav continues to wait for me to respond. Maybe he thinks I'm going to jump around giving people high fives down the hall. I'm much closer to breaking another large pane of glass than celebrating. Because how am I supposed to deal with this?

I follow Mav to the room I share with Abby. Once through the door, Mav barks a command. "Turn on the news."

"Jennie, did you unplug my phone?" Abby has a tangle of cords in her hand, all untethered to any power source.

I attempt a shrug in reply. I've witnessed plenty of the gesture from Abby, but my version is more of an up-down jerkish dance movement than an evasive gesture.

"Everything was updating." Abby pushes buttons and swipes at her screens. "I lost data because my battery ran out before everything loaded."

I attempt another shrug, this time the version that also means 'sorry' with a question mark, while Mav stomps to the remote in order to turn the television on himself.

"You should know about updates. You practically qualify as one." Abby raises her voice. Whatever bug fix or glitch repair she undertook the night before, it didn't happen. Or maybe it's the newest and greatest version of some operating system that she's now behind on. It's a thing among the techs to have the newest, most up to date, operating systems.

"*....Parents of Jillian Newberry claim she suffered amnesia prior to qualifying for the donor program in Mexico City...*"

"Jilly?" I ask the news anchor as if she too remembers Ace using that name within the game when talking to me. Suddenly, I'm much more concerned with the news than shrugging at Abby.

"What's this?" Abby motions toward the television with a power cord that's hanging from her hand.

"They claim to be Jennie's family." Mav looks over his shoulder to both of us. "Explains the memory loss thing."

"*....Rumors surrounding the successful transfer of human intelligence to an artificial body have gone as far as to suggest the winning donor was a runaway, or that the family separated in dispute of the experimental procedure...*"

"Jennie, do you recognize them?" Abby asks. "You said 'Jilly' like you remember that identity?"

"And it is similar to your own name," Mav adds.

My eyes are glued to the screen. Pictures of 'Jillian' with her family flash across the screen. She has blond hair. Her family consists of both a Mom and Dad and one younger sister. She's short and straight without many curves. If I squint enough, I'm looking at a reflection of myself when I was in the game.

"Jennie?" Mav asks. "Is that you?" He points to the pictures of someone I was designed to look like because my parts were taken from her failure. But not all my parts. I had longer arms than Jillian, and my eyes weren't the same color brown. Jillian's eyes would have been erased by the time Ace put my parts together and coded me into the game of life. But this is the girl he was trying to revive. This person on the screen is who Ace wanted me to be and I'd give my left arm to meet her. In this case, her family.

Gordon appears in the doorway behind us with Dr. Miller. "Oh, you've seen." He flips through screens on his computer. "Here she is. Jillian Newberry, GenCiv code." He taps the screen with the back of his index nail. "I knew it. Her code disappeared three months before we had an upload." By upload, he means me. "So, either our system has some serious glitches—"

"We know it does," Abby interrupts.

"Or this isn't our Jennie," Gordon continues.

Dr. Miller steps into the room. Five occupants push the comfort limits to standing room only. "What's your opinion, Jennie?" he asks. He looks worried, according to the new Webster dictionary definition 'give way to anxiety, allow the mind to dwell on troubles.'

I'm torn. Part of me wants to deny these people and their claim on me, but there's also part of me that could be theirs—the loser parts. Lately, loser feels like the majority of what I came out of the game with. Maybe I am their long-lost Jilly. "Could be," I say.

"Gordon, contact the Mexico City facility and get them tickets out here. No point delaying." With that, Dr. Miller retreats back out the door. He's hardly spent any time in my company since leaving Mexico. I don't know what I've done wrong, besides not being more human faster. I still move rickety. Maybe that's it. I can't help but take his distance as evidence of my failure.

After Dr. Miller leaves, I walk closer to the door, like I might follow him. What would I say? 'Hey, sorry I suck at being human, to make it up to you, I'm going to fake like I'm the relation of this loser girl's family, which I sort of am...'

That's stupid.

"Oh, hey." I'm blocking Gordon's exit. I move so he can get around me. "Actually, is it cool if I talk to you in the hall for a minute?" He checks behind him to see that Mav and Abby aren't watching. They're both glued to the television and the condensed life story of Jillian, the amnesiac intelligence donor. Which, if you ask me, sounds like the stupidest candidate possible for such a game. Who were they expecting to come out the other side—someone who knew what they'd signed up for?

I lead the way into the hall. Gordon closes the door all but a crack, so it doesn't click and draw attention at closing all the way. "Remember how I said there was a code from a donor who worked here?"

I nod.

"I think I found her."

Whoop-de-doo, Gordon. "Okay."

He turns his screen to face me. TECH-chick stares back. Rainbow hair and everything. Spitting image of herself, no altered ego image from inside the game like Ace. TECH-chick was apparently as equally intimidating in life as she was in suspended circuitry. "TECH-chick," I say.

"Yeah, actually. She's listed as GenTECH." Gordon turns the screen back to himself and scrolls through information regarding TECH-chick. All I can think is, why couldn't I find her in the database when I was looking on my own all those nights? There are pictures with every entry, and I'd have recognized TECH-chick. "Weirdest thing, she worked security here. She's listed under science lab, but worked security." He pauses like that's a mismatch of skillset. They both sound demanding to me, so I don't ask. "And all her donor files and even her code..." Gordon scrolls some more, tapping into different folders. "...It's all stored here." He points to the carpeted hallway flooring. "She's registered to this facility, but her information —her brain, if you will—uploaded to our facility."

"How is that possible?" I ask.

"It's not." Gordon shuts off his screen as the door behind him opens.

Mav holds the knob in his hands. His eyes roam to the black display of Gordon's device. "What're you guys discussing out here?"

"Just trying to figure out if we need to start calling Jennie Jillian, haha." Gordon's voice cracks on forced lightness.

"Jilly," I say. "They called her Jilly."

"They?" Mav asks.

And I realize I've just misspoken. If I know Jilly from the game or know someone who knows her... "Her family. My family maybe." Not sure I cover well enough.

"That wasn't mentioned on the news," he says.

I turn to Gordon. "But, like I was saying, please just stick to Jennie. I like it better now anyway." I walk past Mav into my room, tap his hand till he frees the knob, and shoo him toward the hall. Then I shut the door and input the mental commands to 'act normal' and 'don't say anything stupid that might give away the fact you're not a real donor'. I imagine it looks like heavy breathing from an outside viewer.

Abby's still in the room. "What's wrong with you?" she asks. "It looks like you're about to vomit. Can you hurl? What would you spew anyway? Battery acid?"

I guess I look more like someone ready to lose it than someone centering themselves. Being human requires a lot more self-aware-ness than I currently possess. "Just nervous about the meeting later today."

We're supposed to meet Geo and be 'introduced' to Juan, their 'major accomplishment'—supposedly without flaws as I have.

"Don't be," Abby says. "I've heard their robot is a glorified program. Just follows commands and performs tasks. AI fail if you ask me." I'd like to ask her what she's heard about me, or even what she thinks of me, but I also don't want to 'ask her' because she's likely to tell me the truth.

13

The conference room hasn't gotten any more opaque since the previous day. A building made almost entirely out of clear glass should be reassuring, but I feel like I'm missing something. Like I'm being told to look when I should be listening.

The glass table sits our entire Mexico group with Spaulding at the right of Geo, who sits at the head of the table. Behind Geo is Juan—a tall imposing figure with even darker features in the light of day. His brow shades his eyes so that I feel like he's watching us from behind sunglasses.

To either side of Juan are armed guards. Why there are armed guards in a room filled with unarmed people congregating with the sole purpose of meeting one another has me scanning the environment for the third time.

"Feels like they're hiding something." I lean toward Gordon to speak near him—my best approximation at whispering so far. Juan moves, the smallest fraction of movement, in my direction when I speak. I only catch his motion because I'm running a scan and the flinch of his steady robotic form catches one of my sensors.

"What could they hide?" Mav answers. "I can see into the next four rooms and they're empty."

I sit straighter. It's the appearance of nothing hidden that has me the most concerned.

"We're just waiting for our lawyers to arrive, then we'll make introductions and get started," Geo announces in his thick accent like each Anglo word is painful to form and eject from his mouth.

"Lawyers?" Dr. Miller asks. He turns to face Spaulding directly, who appears to not be surprised by the announcement. "Why do you need lawyers?" He still faces Spaulding, but I believe the question is for Geo.

"You brought Mr. Pierson." Geo indicates Mav. "I assume he wants some claim on our accomplishments." Juan shifts his weight at the head of the room. The soldiers at his side adjust their guns so that a rustling of straps and metal carries over the gap of silence before Geo speaks again. "Especially in the face of your failure."

He doesn't point to me, but I snap my attention from scanning the room to look at Geo directly. He meets my eyes like he's waiting to receive me. I'm the failure he's talking about, and I'm sick and tired of being thought of as ruined before I'm given a chance. Just like in the donor game.

"With Ace out of the picture..." I can almost hear an implication in Geo's words. Ace should have won the game of life—he had every qualification plus money. From the look on Mav's face, he hears it too. Geo might as well be accusing Mav of 'getting his brother out of the way.'

"You need to watch how you phrase things," Mav says.

"Which is why we're waiting for our lawyers." Geo smiles as his eyes draw tighter, not the slightest concerned at how he trips on English words with his heavy accent. I'd wager he's enjoying the wretchedness of us all. Broken and unprepared.

I'm suddenly relieved that Jilly's family are on their way here. Maybe they can take me out of this mess. I can pretend to be their child. I mean, she's remembered for being an amnesiac. How hard is that to fake?

Three men, tall for the Ecuadorian standard and all with crisp seams in tailored suits with muted but prominently colored ties and faces dialed to the setting of 'stern' and 'business,' walk down the hallway. Their crisp forms distort where the glass panes meet. Not one looks comfortable crossing those seams of glass like it reveals too much of what's under the suits.

Spaulding stands first like he's the one who called the trio of law-abiding swindlers to this meeting. Geo stands only after the men enter the room. He motions for them to sit near him at the head of the table. Dr. Miller, Mav, Gordon, and I shift, displaced with the addition—all of us moving down three seats. At the end of the table, I find myself the loser of this game of musical chairs.

I do my best to stand at attention behind the foot of the table. Where Juan is the picture of quiet dignity at the head of the room—practically the symbol of security and professionalism—I stand half-cocked and exposed despite being fully clothed.

"Now that we're all here," Geo begins. Before he moves forward with his sentiments, Mav and Dr. Miller stand at the same time. Neither appears to have planned the coordinated event.

"What is this?" Dr. Miller speaks first. He nods to the lawyers. "We've come to you here," he glances about the glass room out toward the glass halls and the dark glass exterior, "for cooperation in introducing a new generation into society."

Juan shifts the slightest motion. His shaded eyes slowly move toward Dr. Miller. Standing, I have a much better scan of the room. In reality, it would have been wise for me to remain standing from the start, to appear like I chose this position. But, now that it's been forced upon me, I'm glad for it. I watch the movements of the room. The smallest ones are the most telling. Like how Gordon is entering code into his device on his lap, below the clear table top. If anyone were paying him attention they'd have a perfect view of his actions, but his motions are masked by the invisible plane dividing all of their lines of sight.

The room's attendees are set on sizing one another up. Right now, that measuring sight is aimed at Dr. Miller and Mav Pierson. "Society can wait," Geo says.

"We found Jennie's family." Dr. Miller pushes his calves against the back of his chair so that it scrapes behind him on the carpeting. "They're coming here now. They'll need information on how to integrate her into their routine, how this new life will impact them. They'll be celebrities unprepared to deal with the instant fame."

"No, they won't." Geo's confidence causes Dr. Miller to falter slightly. His knees bend, and he catches himself with one hand flat on the surface of the glass in front of him. "They will remain the same pointless people they've always been with no more interference in their lives than they choose to pursue." When Geo pronounces 'pursue' with his thick accent, it comes out sounding menacing. Like, if they don't decide to remain silent background fixtures, any problems that arise will be on their own heads.

I watch Juan for any indication regarding what's next. Surely, with his smooth entry into this world, he's met with his human family and dealt with transitions. This facility claims success above all other programs in the world.

Juan offers no reaction.

The lawyers busy themselves with files and papers and opening cases where more files and papers emerge onto the glass.

Spaulding holds a pen in his hand. When it appears or from where it emerges, I miss entirely. All I notice is that he has it now, and he grips it as though he intends to put his name to something for gain. He licks his fat lips and pulls them from his sticking teeth before clicking the butt of the pen against the table twice like he's impatient for a meal.

Dr. Miller takes his seat, but Mav remains standing. It's clear he hasn't formed what he can say in this off-balance room. But he stands like he's performing a mute filibuster.

"Take your seat, Mr. Pierson." Geo places both palms on the table and leans forward. "I'd like to get started."

Juan jerks his head up. It's hard to imagine he's dozing in the tension of the room, but he looks at Gordon. Like Gordon has surprised him. I, too, look to Gordon, hoping whatever the surprise gesture was, or is, it will benefit all of us from Mexico. Gordon doesn't look at me, signal, or hold up a message from his device. He ignores me.

"As has been made clear in the years our continent bands have been fighting," Geo begins. Already I'm not happy with the meeting. "Those at the center of it all..." He pauses as if we need time to realize he's referring to himself. "...have it all."

The lawyers shuffle and tap their papers into order and straightness, getting the inanimate things tamed for their big showing obviously soon to follow.

"We own the resources, personnel, and technology."

"Now hold on," Dr. Miller stands again, interrupting Geo from what comes after technology. "Ace Pierson developed this technology before he...passed." Died sounds like an insensitive term considering Ace was an intelligence donor just as Juan and the several bits and pieces of failed gamers that went into the Frankenstein construction of me.

"You should have put more effort into ensuring he was here, then, if that's how you feel about it." Geo nods to the lawyer closest to Dr. Miller. A file slides from a pile of ready papers and is placed squarely in front of Dr. Miller without the lawyer needing to stand or speak.

"What's this?" Miller asks.

"A contract."

"What for?" Dr. Miller crosses his arms as if he expects to be asked to sign something and has no intention of cooperating. I smile in defiance of this silly charade and mentally cheer him on.

"Open it," Geo urges. When Dr. Miller makes no move to unfold his arms, Geo sits in his seat, leans back and swivels to his right, where Juan stands behind him. "It's a contract for Ace Pierson's services." He nods again to the file, taunting Miller to reveal the paper within. "It clearly specifies that we own his work." Dr. Miller's complexion blanches. Color falls from him like he's being bled of life. "All of it."

Dr. Miller's head snaps toward me. Spaulding looks down at the pen in his hand. No mercy glance to try to claim me. "No." Miller opens the file. He flips pages over, scan reading as fast as he can. "You can't do this."

Geo continues to swivel as he waits for Miller to complete his page by page search for some loophole.

"She's not property," Mav says.

"Yes, she is," Geo announces. "*My* property."

"This proves nothing." Miller slides the file to the head of the table, across the line of lawyers. Papers slip out, disorganized. Two pages fall to the floor. Geo stops the gliding file with his flat hand atop the cover.

"I wasn't going to bother dealing with you this way, but then I realized you brought a member of the Pierson family." He nods to Mav. A slick smile grows across his face. "Thank you for coming. I knew it was the perfect opportunity to deliver the news."

Mav's form looks stricken like he's physically ill from this meeting. I don't blame him. "Deliver what? I don't claim to own Jennie. I'm not her family." That one hurts a little. Though Mav doesn't know me, he looks like and shares blood with my main ally inside the game. Hearing him say he has no familial ties to me hits me like Ace from the game rejecting me. A nerve pings in my neck and I want out of this room. "I don't have any ownership or claim on this." He half lifts his hand. Is that all he can say about me? *This?* Like my form isn't good enough to even be named 'body' 'girl' anything? I'm that disjointed in my human appearance?

Maybe Juan was right. Maybe my team is purposefully holding me back from a smooth human transition, making me dependent on them and preventing me from being all I can be. Maybe I would be better off with the men who developed Juan to be the gliding force of nature that he appears to be.

Geo smiles deeper at Mav and flicks his wrist for his second lawyer to deliver papers. "I'm not saying you ever had a claim on this poor creation." I'm unsure if it's me or my team he intends to insult, but it stings. And my loyalties remain with my crappy team. "I'm saying your family does not own Pierson Industries."

"What?" Mav demands.

"All of the technology your companies are built upon..." Geo moves his lips only toward the file—pointing with his mouth. "I own."

Gordon is typing faster. He's no longer hiding his motions below the table, his device is up and he's thumbing so quickly and fiercely, I can't believe no one is stopping him. He could be live streaming this meeting to the internet. I hope that's what he's doing.

"Put it away," Geo says to Gordon, who continues to finger his device.

Geo nods to Juan, who responds like a trained dog. Juan moves to the side of the table where Gordon sits. Gordon's eyes lift as he watches Juan approach from the side. He types faster. Juan makes no haste. When he reaches the back of Gordon's chair he pauses, allowing Gordon an extra second to hit send. "Sir."

Gordon slides his phone into his shirt pocket and folds his hands on top of each other in his lap. He nods with his head bent. It's a submissive gesture, which seems to please Geo. Yet Juan and Gordon seem to still be passing some current between them. Juan watches me lurching in my corner at the butt of the room, then returns to his position at the head.

"Right then." Geo nods to the final well-dressed man seated at the table nearest our host.

The man stands, "I'm placing you all under arrest for the use and distribution of patented scientific techniques under the piracy of technology act and taking possession of products belonging to Pierson Industries."

"What?" The table erupts in protest, first from Mav. He's followed resolutely by Abby and Ben who had appeared conspiratory in their earlier silence, but now reveal themselves to be cowardly pawns unwilling to speak until it's too late.

The only person unphased by the announcement is Dr. Spaulding, who is given a paper to sign from the man announcing the arrest of the room. "Mr. Spaulding has immunity, as he has agreed to provide us access to all the materials and files in the Mexico City facilities and any known facilities worldwide undertaking in the use or distribution of technologies developed by Ace Pierson, a former employee, and war hero..."

Mav chokes on a laugh as he echoes, "War hero..."

"Just take them away." Geo waves to the man to cease speaking and clear the room of us.

Armed men appear at the end of the long glass hall, wavering at every seam they cross. They don't have to enter the room for us to understand. We're being escorted to prison. Nice welcome committee indeed. I trail at the rear of the room, behind Gordon.

"What did you send?" I whisper in my best quiet voice, which is heard by all.

Gordon doesn't answer me, not because he doesn't open his mouth, but due to the fact the butt of a rifle connects to the back of his skull forcing him forward on his feet and jarring his open mouth closed, catching his tongue so that blood escapes his mouth.

"Not you." Geo sends Juan to stand in front of me.

"I'm with them," I say to Juan. If the robot before me has such an emotion as pity, it's showing behind his deep shaded eyes. His cheek pulls ever so slightly so that I feel he's trying to tell me that he warned me, but I wouldn't listen. None of this show makes me any more willing to listen to him now.

"You're with me now." Geo has Juan wait until the party of law offenders is out of sight. He then has me pushed back so that Spaulding can leave. "Don't come back here," Geo says. "Immunity is a one-time grant."

Spaulding extends a hand to shake on it. When Geo doesn't reciprocate, Spaulding waits. Geo takes the final case left at the table, brought in by the lawyers, and hands it to Spaulding. A payoff. The case fits heavily into Spaulding's hand. The weight of the bad deal sinks into his wrinkles and pulls on the joints holding the money.

"Stay out of the news, Spaulding," Geo warns.

With that, Spaulding lugs his prize with him down the hall. I doubt he'll bother returning to his room to retrieve his belongings. He's a man escaping his conscious, hoping it won't sneak into his luggage before he can leave the country.

"You don't own me," I say as defiantly as I can manage.

"Faraday cage for that one." Geo doesn't look at me, doesn't talk to me, doesn't acknowledge me as anything more than an object to be 'put away for now'.

"I'm a person," I say. Juan takes hold of my arm and pulls so hard, I'm certain I'll have to repair cords and wires where they've been loosened to the point of disconnection. "Ow."

I struggle to keep up with Juan's long strides. "I'm not property," I say again.

"We'll discuss it later," he says and no more. No matter what I call out, no matter how many panes of glass I reach for, scratch with my metal claws, or kick so the tempered glass spiderwebs outward in a shatter-pattern, not one piece of glass do I manage to displace, though I damage a good few, making the perfectly see-through floor a white-lined mess.

"This will get worse before it gets better," Juan says before throwing me into a metal cage and securing the door behind me.

14

Worse is worse than it sounds. My intelligence has already been uploaded into the device I'm housed in. Due to technological restrictions and the unpredictability of human intelligence transfers outside of a circuit transfusion, which is risky, Geo's team cannot remove my intelligence from my housing in order to insert me into better housing.

They can, however, take me apart piece by piece and replace the parts one at a time with upgrades. It takes time for each replacement to adjust to my brain function, so it's slow. I'm left with paralyzed limbs for days at a time. All the while, without news regarding my team from Mexico. I know nothing of Jillian's family—if they landed, were informed of a change. Nothing. The Faraday cage I'm moved to after every procedure restricts Wi-Fi signals from reaching my circuitry. I am supplied with no news of any kind. Not even Juan has been permitted to see me since I've been trapped in Ecuador.

I'd thought the Mexico facility was like jail.

Ecuador *is* jail.

The workers won't talk to me. "Where's Juan?" I ask. Today's procedure is hand and wrist replacement. Currently, I have a left stump with exposed wires and liquid filled tubes. It doesn't hurt, but it's disturbing to see my insides exposed and tinkered with like the inner working of a computer laid bare. It's gore. The woman reconnecting my wires doesn't shift her attention from her task. It's like I've gone mute since being caged.

They work from the bottom up—my feet, legs, even my trunk, and internal functioning is replaced already. The parts of me that pump fluids and signals to the rest of my body now has a quad processor. I work at four times the efficiency I could before. I get what Geo means when he says the Intercontinents have the resources. They do. All their materials are more advanced and greater quality than anything they had in Mexico. I was basically a junkheap before.

"Do they keep you in a cage too?" This question gets a rise from her, and I wonder if maybe they do keep her in a cage. What's winning a war for if it's the enslaving side that wins? I'm starting to wonder. "Changing out my parts won't make me company property. Not legally." She squints like the wires shrunk in proportion to her sight and she must now put more focus in her task. "I don't belong to anyone. I'm a person." I've made the same statements day after day. "I'm not a pet, either."

I know what happens if I make threats about being 'kept' or 'caged'. I get shocked so my system shuts down, but not so much anything scrambles. It's like a hard reset. They can manage it remotely by pressing a button. It's really annoying as it has no effect on humans—only electronics. I'm also aware they don't like to press it because it shuts down all their systems too. They have to reboot everything in the building every time they zap me. It's been five times already. Somehow, they always manage to drag my metal body back to the cage before everything restarts.

"Do they keep Juan in a cage?" The worker lets out more breath than she takes in like she's been saving a little extra air in her lungs and finally gets sick of holding onto it. I copy her physical behavior in an attempt to appear as human as possible. Instead of her eyes getting narrower, they widen.

That's a new reaction behavior for me to achieve in a worker. This one's fun. I copy that too. "Do you talk to Juan?" I ask. Unsure if it's discussing Juan or my imitation of her that caused the first reaction. I'd like more behavioral responses in my 'human reaction' arsenal.

"We're instructed not to talk with the products..."

I'm almost too surprised by a verbal response to form a spoken follow-up question. I'm suddenly flooded with curiosity. One, she speaks! Two, the worker used the plural—products. Not product.

Does that refer to me and Juan, or are there more of us? I push that down into a ball at the pit of my stomach and move to her use of the plural. "Products?"

The worker stands, my hand completely tethered, but not covered by the skin like material hiding the mechanical parts of me. She shakes her head no like she's protesting. Her eyes are wide so that I can see white all around her iris and her pupils enlarge like she's attempting to access more information from the room. I know this because the hole in my eye device also widens when I wish to scan a larger portion of the environment, but it also requires more of my brain function to complete the scanning task, so it's not always a viable option for information gathering, especially if there's auditory information available as well. Maybe after all my upgrades are completed, I can accomplish both means of information gathering from the environment without compromising any data, but for now, I have to pick and choose my means of collecting information.

Workers bring their supplies with them inside my cage when it's only one person working, like today. Otherwise, we'd be outside the cage and plugged into the wall. I wonder if the security of the signal scrambling wire-walls gave this worker the confidence to slip and speak to me? If that's the case, why on earth is she practically back-ward climbing the door to get herself out?

"They wouldn't know you said anything if you just act normal." I pull on the skin covering like a glove. My hand doesn't respond to any electronic signals my brain sends it. I keep trying though. *Wiggle the skin tighter, dang fingers.* I'm never going to close this gap without a little jiggling. "The way you're freaking out, they'll think you slipped me the codes to crack the lock." I point with my lips to the latch at the cage like I see all the locals do. Point with their lips.

"How long until this is back online?" I flop my hand in the air, so she knows what I'm talking about. She signals a cross and turns her back to me, repeating the sign of the cross over her chest again and again while fumbling with the keypad with her other hand. I guess she thinks I'm the devil.

I sidestep to get a glimpse of the numbers she punches in. As if the woman can see behind her, she moves so her back obstructs my view no matter where I stand. I've tried several combination patterns and searches to try to crack the lock code. I believe they change the codes regularly. By regularly, I think it's by the hour, or maybe simply by the worker.

"Tell the other products I say hi," I say once the door lock disengages. "Next time maybe we can chat a little more." I laugh under my breath as the woman pulls the cage door closed behind her. An electronic lock engages and the woman runs, leaving all her materials inside the cage with me.

This is new.

15

The tools left in my confinement pen don't look like the surgeon's tools. They look like the sort of thing used to replace batteries in a watchmaker's shop—tiny handheld drivers, wire holders. The tools of an electrician who works with tinker toys perhaps. There's rubber tipped tweezers, glue, and liquid stitching tubes for melting my coverings back together. I'm unsure what to shove inside the gap at my wrist, what might fit or what might be too well accounted for to not go missing. I'm certain I must slide something, several somethings, inside the opening in my wrist and then close it somehow. The liquid skin will close the glove-like opening.

With my working hand, I choose the rubber-tipped tweezers, the smallest driver, one that has a copy in a larger size, spare wires and gears, and a conductor, which worries me as I slide it inside my arm and push to conceal it among the inner workings of my forearm. I don't wish to accidentally fry my circuits, but a conductor seems like it could come in handy.

My cage is easily looked in upon as it's a mesh of wires and not made from solid walls. I believe Geo has some prejudice against things he can't see through. I notice immediately that it's him, Geo, who enters the room outside my pen.

"Haven't seen you for a while."

"Miss me, did you?" His accent bites. I forgot how sharply the English words pour out of him. Like he has to spit them out for the English pronunciation. "I'm surprised you have such capacity."

"Why create us, if you despise us?" I speak for myself and Juan and however many more there might be like us, hoping Geo will let information slip and either confirm or deny the number of persons like me. Or what he has against us.

"The creation of you was before my rise to the top." Geo eyes the materials left inside my cage. I can see his brain adding up the pieces, but he makes no move to enter the space I occupy. "I just happened to be here." He points to his feet, like he means this exact space here, not figuratively 'here' as in a position of control. I'm certain he must mean the latter because otherwise, it makes no sense, but his choice of emphasis by pointing throws off my logic. "When decisions needed to be made."

"What decisions?" I flop my still unresponsive hand in front of myself. "What kinds of joints service our frame?"

"That's a start."

"Why bother upgrading me if you don't trust or like me?"

"I've learned to not trust you. Foolish of your Mexico friends to only supplant a faraday cage in your head preventing system upgrades without their consent."

What? I have a what?

"I've added a lot more control than that." Geo motions more workers into the room and points to the tools on the inside of the wire box with me. The workers open the door. One stands at the opening while the other one collects items and hands them through the door to a third employee who places them on a counter at the side of the larger glass room we're all inside.

Control? I'm not a remote-operated toy.

"Once the rest of the world understands the danger you pose, it will be too late."

"I'm not dangerous." My voice drops, sounding the opposite of my statement. A new sensation rises in the section where human guts would be located. It's a heated feeling that attaches itself to my spinal cord and engages all my extremities as though I need to be ready to use them at any second, and my thought processes reroute signals so that only my reflexes and pre-memorized movements are set for action. Angry.

"Where is the rest of my equipment?" Geo waves his workers to exit the cage. "I know there are parts missing from the supply list Anita signed out."

Anita, huh? "Why don't you ask her? She seemed a little shifty to me—the kind who might sell equipment on the side to make a little extra money since her boss is so cheap."

Geo remains calm. He has no rushed reaction to my words, which irritates me even more. I need to learn from his behavior and copy his resolved exterior, but it's difficult.

From the look on his worker's faces, none of them want to be sent into my pen in order to search out missing items. I'm unsure what makes them so afraid of me. I haven't seen a reflection of myself since my upgrades, but I worry I'm monstrous in appearance from their expressions. Geo pivots away from me and discusses in a low voice how he plans for his employees to retrieve the tools. Of course, making his voice low has no secretive effect, since I have the ability to hear even very slight sound.

"Why does Juan get to wander free and not me?" I ask.

Geo's spine straightens and he turns so that he can see me out of the side of his vision. "Juan doesn't move freely through our facility. His movements are closely guarded and documented."

"Is that so? So you gave him permission to come in here and discuss the codes Gordon sent him before you hauled the Mexico crew away?"

A movement, like Geo says something, but absolutely no sound escapes him, along with a rough and rapid motion for two of the workers to excuse themselves. At least that's what they do as if they know what the action means.

"He didn't tell you about that?" I ask. "That's funny for a guy, a boss." I add the boss part hoping for a greater reaction and get it. Geo's jowls shake in his attempt to keep his face controlled. "To allow someone as skilled in code as Gordon to attend a big meeting with his device in hand and after Juan had met with us secretly the night before to warn us. Enough time for Gordon—super expert with computers, I'd say he's sort of like Ace..."

Geo shows me his back. In the glass wall before him, I glimpse the color of the barely visible reflection deepens.

"Permitting Gordon time to research codes needed for Juan to bypass firewalls preventing intellectual upgrades." I'm making all of this up. Yes, Gordon had a device at the meeting, and I'm certain Geo saw it. Yes, Juan appeared to react to Gordon's having a device unchecked, and yes, I had met with Juan the night before the meeting and he had warned me. But the rest is fantasy. Fantasy that can be fueled with security camera evidence that at least some of what I'm claiming is accurate.

"I'll get whatever you stole, even if I have to rip your arm off myself." Geo slams the glass door behind him, leaving me inside my glass case and additional wire pen of a room.

Lucky for me, robots don't need food, water, or a bathroom. Only the occasional battery charge, which I need less frequently since my quad processing upgrade. "Can't wait."

I anticipate a forced reboot as their 'safe' option to enter and retrieve the items I stole. In hindsight, it was stupid. I'm not gaining anything by having tiny objects. I can't hack the lock on my cage or code my way out of here. I have a little screwdriver, some wires, and rubber tweezers shoved up my arm. Whoop-dee-doo.

Sometimes I wish the game rules applied to this realm. It'd be much easier to reprogram humans to function how I choose or infect them with a virus of my choosing. Maybe one that shuts off their gross motor function, so they would be frozen in place and I could finally be free of their cages and expectations. They'd be forced to stay still and watch me reprogram their world instead of the other way around.

If only there was a way to protect me from the power surge. Then I might stand a chance. But what can withstand an electromagnetic power surge?

I pace the cage in my sleek and steady new legs, complete with extra length and thicker skin, making me less likely to suffer a scrape deep enough to injure my internal tubes or wires. Juan is right about the joints and connections in Ecuadorian housing. Much more advanced and easier to manipulate. Once my upgraded appendages were able to communicate with my brain signals, it's been instantaneous motion free of wobbles, glitches, or jitteriness.

"How do I prevent a power surge?" I tap the wires around my pen in a nervous pattern. Thinking. Looking at the cage that holds me.

I have one of these in my head? But Dr. Miller wouldn't do that to me unless it was to protect me. I do a mental inventory—literally trying to identify what is located within my head. It's difficult to feel what one is made of when you can't see the parts and pieces and your sense of 'feel' is based on an idea construct and not a true sensory experience the way a human might describe it. It's not like dragging finger pads along the internal recesses of my mind. I'm following the pathways and connections as slowly as I can process in order to identify the parts and how they connect and if there's something unexpected, unnecessary, or unwanted.

It turns out, my head is filled with all those things. And I have no idea how to sort them all out. Why I've never tried to identify the parts and pieces surrounding my 'brain' seems stupid now. But how could I have anticipated being held hostage by a foreign scientist while most of my concern had been trying to learn how to 'appear' more human in order to trick my team into continuing to search for a donor code to match me with?

It all seems so I and unimportant now. And for the first time since being caged here, I forget myself and consider the fate of my team. Maybe they're not in a holding cell somewhere. What if something much worse and permanent has happened? Spaulding can suck it. I don't care for him having sold us all out anyway, but Dr. Miller and Abby—despite our sister-like relationship of disappreciation for one another. Gordon, who I hope did somehow manage to send information to Juan. Not like he had any preparation for that meeting or time to develop a hack that could help any of us out of this mess. And mostly Mav. Because he looks like my Ace. And because I miss him even though he's not Ace.

16

Trapped in a cage of highly conductive material, hiding additional conductive material up my arm isn't going to help me. So much for the crud I shoved under my skin before Geo came in. Why didn't I think about that before I sealed the opening in my synthetic skin?

I've basically only helped them add material to effectively prevent me from receiving electromagnetic signals, upgrades, messages, or anything really. The worker was probably already intending to shove that crud up my frame and I just did it for her.

I imagine Geo having a good laugh looking back over the security tapes. Yes, there are surveillance cameras everywhere. It's not like I'll ever get away with anything here. I slam the cage. "Ah!" I slam the pen door knowing it's not going to reveal a weakness or open. Still, I pause to observe how all the hinges, connection points, and corners of the structure react. Nothing. I slam it again. I'm made of steel framing. That's got to do some damage, right?

No.

"Ahh!"

"*Callate*," a complete stranger demands silence of me. Probably a worker passing by my glass cell, just wanting to stick her nose in.

"Move on," I holler and continue pummeling my cage with my fists. When the onlooker doesn't remove herself, I shift gear, bringing my newly sealed wrist to my lips and ripping the freshly glued section with my teeth. No blood pours out. The worker doesn't flinch. Stupid human already used to temperamental machines.

She's still standing in the glass room surrounding my metal cage.

Her hair is made of such tight curls they seem to be climbing each other to read the top of her head where unnatural color stains odd clumps of hair. Her dark skin is like oil in the watery shadows of the glass building. Her eyes are anything but watery. They're dry with irritation and dead set on me.

I let my numb hand fall to my side and begin digging out the conductive wires I've concealed. "Why aren't you leaving?"

The stranger speaks Spanish, and my currently recovering system translates roughly, "Gordon me sent."

Like I care if Gordon sent her.

Hold up. She said Gordon, not Geo...

I stop digging inside my forearm. "What?" I bend closer to see through the mesh cage better. She doesn't exactly 'blend in'. She also doesn't fit the 'Ecuador facility' MO. "Who sent you?" I bend to peer through the mesh to my right, down the glass corridor to check if anyone is coming. I adjust and repeat the process to my left. Both halls are empty of workers.

"Gordon." The woman has a thick Ecuadorian accent.

"What is this? Some kind of joke?"

"No." She moves closer to my cell and pulls an odd circle of filing pins from her pocket. A locksmith's tool perhaps? They're definitely for picking locks. She points with her lips toward my ragged wrist, where I bit a hole through my skin. "*Quítalo.*" She says 'stop it' like an 'or else'. Maybe an 'or else I won't help you'. "Freaks me out," she attempts Anglo wording in punchy bursts.

"Where is everybody?" I continue to shift my weight trying to check all halls. Glass structures permit me to see a good distance whether anyone is coming, but it gives anyone coming the same advantage to view activity where we are.

"Active alls." She throws in Anglo with her Spanish, making it that much harder for my system to follow her speech. I think she's telling me everyone is active, which doesn't mean anything in any language as a singular phrase. "System shut down."

I assume she's talking about the knock-out pulse Geo warned me about. Like it's supposed to be active maybe? Or my system isn't supposed to be? This whole dual language thing is nuts. How does anyone speak two languages? "I didn't feel anything."

She taps the cage like it's a response to some question I didn't ask. "*Verdad*?" Which means 'Truth'.

I want to ask her more about how she knows Gordon but would rather let he finish her task before distracting her with personal questions. "The pulse doesn't impact people though, right? Where are all the people?"

"They are busy."

They're busy? What kind of description is 'busy'? It could mean anything. A person might be picking their ear wax and consider themselves busy. Cryptic wording at best. Maybe that's worse.

Instinct, or maybe reflex, claws at me to smack the cage, to rattle this interloper to provide better answers. But, until I'm released, I can't exactly throw my weight around.

"Gordon says you know my sister," she says in battered English.

Gordon told her what? What the freak, Gordon! If he were here right now, I'd be highly irritated with him big time. "Who me?" I step back from the door. Suddenly I'm the one wanting space...and a better-translating app. "I don't know anybody. I don't even know who you are."

"She works here." She waves a metal pin through the air. Here-here. Her sister worked in upgrades maybe?

"I'm not from here. I'm from the Mexico City facility." Then it hits me. Her physical build is different. Shorter by a foot at least, with a wide round face—not chubby, more like her bones are wide. She doesn't have the same flint and steel in her eyes and she's darker. But, I'm certain all the same. Her sister is, was, TECH-chick.

The lock pops clear and the door swings open. Nothing separating TECH-chick's sister and me any longer. I wonder if I'm supposed to apologize but remind myself that this child doesn't know what happened in the game.

"*Si*. Donor families. Come." Motioning me to follow her, she tucks the pins back into a pocket on the side of her pants. "Don't have time."

I'm afraid to follow her. Like I'm being led to a confessional I'm unprepared to not lie about. It's been my job to lie since I woke up. The picket lines of bottle bomb wielding lunatics outside the Mexico City facility populate my expectations.

"Gordo call—all," she says.

"All of them?" What? Like all the donors in the entire game?

"Follow."

She leads me the opposite direction Geo went in. We're located near the center of the building on this floor, so I can't spy activity outside yet, not being near an outer wall. The closer we get to the exterior, the louder muffled shouts and rhythmic pounding builds. It's a familiar sound. It reminds me of Mexico. Families picketing and shouting four floors down. And then I realize that's exactly what the sound is. "That's not who we're meeting up with is it?"

No answer. Only running.

I run to the dark glass at the end of the long hall and press myself to the cold pane to observe what's happening. "What is this?"

"Gordon called me." She holds up a single index finger. "*Solo* call *de* prison."

"Jail?" His single call from prison? He really was put in jail. I stop to consider the group of them sharing a cell. Abby would be on her own of course, in the girl's section.

"Gordon asked for help, tells about mission with all here. I don't agree."

What on earth is going on? I don't want to go with her. With my translation system malfunctioning, it's almost impossible to understand her meanings. She opens the door to the stairwell and starts down. I continue even though we're in a part of the building I'm not familiar with. "Still, I'm here."

"What?"

"Internet. Codes. Messages. He sent images of a meeting with Geo and your jail friends." She points to me over her shoulder. "I recognize you from the image files."

That's what Gordon was really doing. Recording from his device during our big lawyer meeting. He sent video files to a secure website off location from the Pierson facility and sent TECH-chick's sister to find it. "What's your name?"

"Belen." She says it like 'Bell-En'. I like it. She stops at the basement door. "Ah, here we are." The door opens letting in a damp urine stench. Not inviting. "Tunnels."

I'm impressed. "How do you know about these?"

"My sister worked here, *recuerda*?" *Remember,* she asks.

"Right." Her sister worked security here, as well as upgrades? What didn't her sister do? TECH-chick had hands in everything apparently. I follow into the pee-soaked hole in the earth and try to picture TECH-chick using this place for security detail. I can't do it. "Right," I repeat.

17

The underground tunnel smells worse the deeper we move. My system alerts me to toxic fumes, exposure to materials that will harm human pulmonary systems if they remain too long in this enclosed space. We keep descending into the earth. I count the steps of decent to be in the seventies and rising and feel the damp rising like a humidity water table. My olfactory senses aren't the same as human senses. The odors are in the air, embedded in the moist earth walls, and festering in puddles. We try our best to step over what my system registers as unfriendly chemical compounds, bacterial percentages, spores, mold and fungus, fecal matter—mostly animal, but the data tells me the species and I've definitely lost respect for human claim on advanced society.

I have no idea how Belen manages to navigate the black, other than she drags her hand along the right-side wall once we reach the end of the steps. I keep my feet in contact with the earth below me, careful not to lift either foot completely. I scan the air for currents that indicate airflow. Move toward the source of the flow. Unfriendly growth passes under my fingers at regular intervals.

"What's your sister's name?" Conversing pulls my brain away from seeking more stanky data.

"You don't know?" Belen asks.

I hug the dirt wall, avoiding a rancid pool with more than water in it. "We don't use names in the game. Just codes."

Belen stops advancing. I can see her heat signature, so I stop as well. "Codes... I like it," Belen says. She continues forward, not answering my question.

"I take it you know technology as well?"

"No, my sister was a genius with machines, not just computers. She used to love puzzles."

"And you?"

"*Solo* computers," she says.

We turn to the right when there's an option for it. We travel a quarter mile before the turn. Even if I tell my brain to stop feeding me stats regarding my environment, it still tells me. It just stores it a little lower on the 'urgent information for you to consider' queue.

"What can you tell me about Juan?" I ask after another half mile in our new direction. My brain says south.

"Which Juan? There're tons of Juans here."

She uses the word '*bastantes*' in her language for tons. At first, my system translates a different word that starts with 'b'. My ability to tolerate her mock playful tone left when my system overloaded with odor data. And I doubt she has the capacity to appreciate Intelligence Donor humor. "You mean, like me? Donors?"

"No." Belen stumbles into a set of closed double doors. "Ah, here we are." She pushes, but the doors remain solidly shut.

The hinges have a high rust content. The doors themselves are solid, making it difficult to read data from the other side. I can't tell if a wall of caved-in earth blocks our path.

Memories of Mord piling against elevator doors twists my expectations. I strain to hear the ragged guttural sound of mouth breathers sucking in our scent. Then I realize, I don't have a scent here. Not like humans. Just like in the game, only opposite again. Humans give off odors depending on anxiety, exertion, or arousal. Humans are stinky. I smell of rubber and metal, and if I move very fast, heated rubber or metal. If I get wet, wet rubber or metal. In the game, donors didn't have a sense of smell, only Mord. Like me. Now, I remain odorously invisible among human crowds. I'm not sure what that means if anything.

Belen slaps the heel of her palm on the door. We wait. She hits the door again. Louder, and more times. I try not to count, but my brain logs the number as sixteen pings of contact with the solid metal door.

"Where are we?" I ask to fill the quiet. I know where we are. I have an internal map of the aerial of this place after flying overhead months ago. We're close to some street markets above. Though I'm not entirely sure how the tunnel connects to what I recall being roughly one point seven miles from the base of the hill the Pierson facility rests atop.

"Shops." Belen paces in front of the doors.

I could inform her that I am capable of breaking the doors down, even with my single lame hand. But I don't. I let her pace and watch with stiffness. I'm unsure what I think of Belen, and I believe she's unsure what she thinks of me. I suspect she's questioning if freeing me was the right thing for her to do. If she asks me what I think, I won't be able to answer. Because I don't know whose side she wants to be on. What she hopes to receive from involving herself. I watch her for signs of changing her mind. Or signs of being double-crossed. Things like that happen in the real world. People defecate in tunnels in the real world.

Finally, a scratch breaks the sound of Belen's feet plodding through slogging dirt. We both move to our alert position. Belen holds her head low and extends her neck like she's straining to hear. I step back and loosen my limbs, all scans running and ready to respond to a threat.

The door pushes in, toward us. I'm far enough back to not have to move. Belen jumps out the door's path.

"Bel?" A man's voice booms into the cave, immediately swallowed by earth walls and the open tunnel, like a mute on a tuba.

"Pedro."

I'm not sure what to expect. Part of me worries that TECH-chick somehow managed to send video messages to those rooting for her, and maybe they know who I was in the game. If they ask. What can I possibly say? 'Hey, your murderous relative was super good at back-stabbing people...'

We emerge into sunlight and muted colors. We're near the edge of the city's pristine circle. Factory exhaust stains the landscape a darker shade of gray in this section of industry. The aroma of sweetbreads merges with pickling liquids, the mingling of edible things not yet sold but on display for hours fades in with the rancid odor of wet feet. The street is damp down one cobbled line set lower when it was laid than the rest of the road. Vendors hawk their wares from booths that look like they've been constructed from cardboard and blankets just that morning, ready to crumple in on themselves any moment. I assume this must be some kind of unsanctioned market.

The narrow walkway packs vendors, shoppers, and a host of people motioning Belen and me to follow them out of the crowds.

"What is this?" I ask.

"*El Mercado*," Pedro answers.

I know it's the market. I'd have to be an idiot to not realize we're standing in an open market. Part of me wants to push the wood crate filled with tiny bananas and papaya on its side. I need answers that make sense. No more evasion. I stop my feet and hold my arms still at my sides, careful to not show my strength and recent gain in coordination and efficiency thanks to Geo's work. I don't want these people to change their minds. I prefer not living in a cage.

"Who are you, people? Where are you taking me? And why are you here?" I ask.

Pedro looks from me to Belen. She lifts her shoulders but doesn't translate. Instead, she steps between him and me, facing me, and speaks in a low voice that makes me feel smaller than her, which I'm not and I can prove it to her if she makes me. "Just follow." As if any of the vendors shouting their products and prices at us in Spanish care what we say.

When she turns, her back to me, she places hands on Pedro, turning him so his back faces me as well. She pushes for him to move in the direction of the group of people with him. Her hands remain on his shoulders, as she looks back toward me with the expectation that I'll follow.

I have no reason to follow. I'm free now. I have no explanation from these strangers. To obtain answers, I need to find Gordon.

Besides, I'm uneasy trusting my immediate future to people associated with TECH-chick.

When Belen returns her focus forward, guiding Pedro through the streets, I turn south, the direction continuing away from the hill, which is not so far from us. Distance underground tends to compound itself and stretch to something much greater than my visual scans weight the same space. There's not enough space between the threat and me.

Two steps and I'm between makeshift shops, my height easily swallowed by the half hazard lines pinned with wool sweaters, knitted hats, woven bags and belts, and all manner of adornments for hair. With my responsive right hand, I slip a knitted hat with flaps to cover my ears from the line it hangs on while the workers call for passersby to "Come and see."

My clothing doesn't match that of the people on the streets either. I wear gray pants with a short-sleeved white cotton shirt. My head hurts trying to decide what to do. Time should have no impact on my ability to make decisions, take actions, but I feel it catching up to me. Like my brain decided it matters, so now it matters times seven thousand and I'm out of options.

Stop. Think it through. Look at the people selling and the people buying.

I fit the profile of a traveler more than a merchant. Copy traveler behavior. Belen strides past the narrow space between vendors where I'm concealed with my knit cap pulled to my brows and the flaps over my ears. I step deeper between the wood posts holding up sheets to protect the items being sold.

"Gordon," I say his name like a wish that he'll appear at my side and tell me who to trust and what to believe. Like he's my personal processor.

When nothing happens, no magic drops Gordon and his ability to speak 'device' at my side, I crouch on the balls of my feet so I'm low when Belen runs back toward me. She stops in front of the shop where I took the hat. Her eyes move slowly across the lines of heads in the booth. A visual hiccup as she tracks the space above me causes my insides to panic. My toes press into the cobbles, ready to spring.

Belen moves away, back the direction she ran from.

My ligaments and all the wires and cords pulling my extremities to 'alert' relax, my head sags forward. "Miller. I need you." He's not technologically gifted like Gordon or Abby or even Ben. But he's been there since I began training to use my robotic system in coordination with my 'human brain.'

A tall woman with light coloring to her skin and rich darkness matching her smooth hair to her sharp eyes passes. She wears a broad-brimmed hat, blocking sun from touching her skin. Her companion taller still, with a wrinkle-free gray suit and solid purple tie, follows behind her showing little interest in the items on display. They don't belong in this little shopping district. They appear lost, like two kids who let go of their mother's hand on vacation in a strange land. I follow them at a reasonable distance.

I toe-step like a bird to the outer edge of the booth to watch them better. She lifts a wooden carving and praises its craft. Then replaces the item to its location of display, not bothering to give it a second glance.

She also doesn't look at the knit hats. I pull the tassel on the side of my good hand, so the hat slips off my hair. The woman turns so I can see her face. She's perfect. Not a bone out of alignment. Her skin flows over her frame like the skin of a drum. Her movements rhythmic, deliberate, and controlled.

"I thought this was the height of society," she announces to the crowd of vendors. "The resource band to make all other latitudes writhe with jealousy. All I see here is the misuse of natural resources." She returns to the carving. It's a leopard with well-proportioned head, the notion of movement in its limbs, and detail in every muscle group. "This scrap of wood, that ball of yarn." She points to a wool sweater. "Where's the industry? Advancement? Progression?" The carving slams back to its location. "It's like pre-war here."

When I view the surroundings, I don't see what she's talking about. I've been learning about pre- and post-war conditions. The buildings are white, built in the same style after most structures either fell apart or were torn down before the Intercontinents realized they held the majority of the world's cards as far as ready-made natural resources. Once they started setting limitation on the access of goods, then setting prices, balance shifted in the world economy.

"Not everyone chooses to take advantage of the opportunities presented to them, Ma'am," the man shadowing her movements says. They both have an accent, but it's not Ecuadorian. They don't speak like anyone from the Northern regions I'm familiar with either. Everything about them says 'perfectly foreign.' I'm guessing their cab dropped them on the wrong corner of town as well.

"Let's see this Geovanni, shall we?" she asks her companion. "Surely the man who built that," she turns to face the hill in the not so far distance, "has learned not to waste resources." Sunlight slices into the dark glass at a high angle due to the position of the building on the tallest hill in the city. It shines like a black star refracting shadow rainbows onto the famine-white structures below. I haven't seen the Pierson building in the way this woman looks to the building, with avarice and expectation. What will she think of the Ace statue, twisted and grotesque, like a warning sentinel guarding the entrance to hell?

18

If there's one thing I learned from being a player inside an aggressive computer game competition, don't trust anyone. But, maybe more important still, play the game. Right now, I have to play the game on this side. I can't figure out the rules or the players quite yet, but this world has all the markings of an active game. Right now, I need this woman with her straight back and wide hat. I have a need to collect them or dispose of them. I'm unsure which, but I won't let them out of my sight now that I've marked them as my objective. I'm instantly obsessed with controlling them now that I've been made aware of them.

Most importantly, I need them to get me inside the building so I can locate my data stick and download all the files into the currently running donor program inside Geo's iceberg of a facility. Certainly, the excavated depths of that hill house active donor games. I have no time to waste.

I fight my urge to choke them into telling me about where they came from and why they need to talk to Geo, fairly certain my game programming is taking over. I can walk this line. Obtaining information and controlling human assets doesn't have to mean body count. I'm not saying it won't, but it probably doesn't have to.

None of the goods surrounding me match the woman and her companion. But I can't approach them with a gaping bite out of my own wrist and wires loose. I slip back into the space between two vendors. A long sleeve sweater knit in muted gray and off-white wool looks to be my best option for covering my self-inflicted wound. I scold myself to think things through before taking action, to be human. Be more human. Think. Think before acting. At least before violently acting.

The sweater pings several skin sensors at once. It must be intolerable for humans to wear this stuff. Why do they? It not only itches, little hairs poke, and the material chafes coarse fibers everywhere it connects with bare skin. What it lacks in wearability, it makes up for in sleeve length. Thankfully, the sleeves fall to my knuckles, covering my wrists entirely.

Conversation between the woman and her associate doesn't rise above the crowd. I've lost them over my distraction with the irritating sweater. Also, the climate is hot. Though I don't suffer temperate discomfort, I'm aware of the melty feeling from hot wool on rubber-like skin. I smell of wet animal and burnt plastic combined. This sweater makes no sense. Why do they sell clothing like this?

Stop being distracted. I remind myself. There is no focus switch inside my head. I walk behind some markets and re-emerge into the pathway standing straighter, more dignified, though with a slight torque of my neck where the top of the sweater rubs just above my clavicle framework.

The woman and man stand several yards away. An open vehicle door greets them at the curb defining a walking street verses a driving street. I move quickly to catch them before the door closes. "Excuse me, I couldn't help but overhear your conversation."

The broad rim of the woman's hat lifts. Sunlight burns away the flattering shadowed filter her brim provides. Her sharp features and smooth skin stretch tight over her pointed nose. Up close, she looks stretched, unnatural. "Yes?" Her dark eyes scan me in the top-to-bottom, one-shot method I've come to recognize as a judgment instead of a collection of data. "Who are you?"

"I work with Geovanni."

The woman's tight skin attempts to lift her painted on eyebrows. She manages to open her eyes a little wider. "I'm sorry, I didn't realize we were meeting anyone here. I thought..." She checks with her companion out the side of her eye.

"I wasn't aware either, Ma'am," he responds.

All of my systems push harder. Unable to control the rush of transmission fluids lubricating my joints and nervous system, I pretend to breathe, expanding and contracting my chest cavity. It's weirdly calming. My ear tubes expand, something pops where the pressure builds too high. I step closer. All I want is information, I remind myself. I'm not here to eliminate these people.

"It wasn't a planned meeting," I lie. The driver of the vehicle jots his head between the two of us with a confused expression. He doesn't speak English. "But I did order the driver."

"Malik?" her voice rises to a tone that means her companion is failing her.

"I called a car, Ma'am. I assure you."

Not wanting to get into a fight over the car and unsure how to sway the situation to my favor—to be honest, I still don't know what my end-goal is here—I change tactic. "I'm sorry to get off to the wrong foot. You know how it is, ordering transportation." I extend my non-maimed hand. "I'm..." I can't say, Jennie. They know Geo, what if they know who I am? Recognize my name from television coverage? I don't look exactly like the girl who went in the building thanks to all the recent upgrades, but my name has been passed around like a juicy secret. "I'm sorry, the sun is so hot." That sounds human, good stall me. Jennie came from the Gencode nickname I grew to identify as myself while inside the game. But, I was never Gencode. The only code that ever marred my skin was Con. "I'm Connie. Mind if we share the ride?" I gently release my hand, careful not to show too much strength in the grip of my handshake.

The man, Malik, might be a robot for how little he moves. Seriously, I'm not sure he's breathing. "Ma'am?" he stands close to her side, between the open door and the woman, like he thinks I'm going to leap impulsively inside the vehicle.

"Oh, I don't care. Just get me out of this sun." She slides onto the seat, sticking to the leather material and leaving a momentary heat signature where her palm touches.

"Together?" The driver walks to the passenger side of the vehicle to open the front passenger door for me.

I nod a 'thanks' and practice a demure smile I've been working on from observing Abby with Ben. The driver responds by closing my door before I'm completely inside, knocking my right thigh with the interior handle. I let the smile drop from my lips. Maybe I just need more practice.

No one speaks once all the doors close. The car circles around different grades of the off-white structures before finally turning onto a road lining up with the 'black glass building'. The lack of conversation in the car has an unpleasant effect on passenger vision. I notice the driver staring down at my left forearm more than three times. There's an odd bulge in the fabric where ragged skin won't lay smooth no matter how often I rub my working hand over the top of the sleeve to encourage it to cooperate. We need a sound distraction.

"Investors?" I ask, turning slightly so the passengers in the back know I'm addressing them. The motion also gives me a chance to move my left hand under my butt. I've seen people sit on their hands frequently. I have no idea why they do it. It's not good for finger circulation, I'm certain. Since my fingers aren't entirely responsive in that hand yet anyway and I'm imitating human behavior, it's a brilliant move for me.

The woman and Malik avoid my deliberate move to engage them in conversation by turning their heads— severely so there's no mistaking the intent behind their neck strain— to stare out the window. Either way, I get my needed distraction.

"What's going on ahead?" the woman asks.

Large crowds block the road. It's not right in front of us yet and I had forgotten about the obstacle of dealing with whatever faction currently riots against Geovanni. There's got to be a way to use the chaos to my advantage. "You haven't heard about the riots?" I say.

"Geo didn't mention it when we talked last night." The woman retracts her head from the windows, squaring herself to me as though I might have some solution to the annoyance she finds in a crowd.

The driver slows down, even though we're nowhere near the maw of people.

"You'll be fine." I motion for the driver to continue forward. I question if it's the smart thing to do, but instinct tells me this woman responds to confidence. She shifts in my direction, as though I'm the compass of her well-being in this vehicle.

"The crowd looks imposing," she says.

I don't know what variables I'm working with, thus can't determine the risk of using the mass of disgruntled people as cover. If the Commander were here, he'd have a plan. I never thought I'd say this, but I miss the Commander's insane strategizing. What he lacked in empathy he made up for in elaborate determination to be on top of every situation. I could use him right now, if only to know which side I'm on.

19

The problem with not having a plan centers around the fact that I don't have a plan. I also lack anyone with whom I trust to strategize. The woman in the back seat with Malik continues to shuffle her sitting position to look out the left window when the car climbs the hill and the crowd is most visible on that side, then to the right of the car, forcing Malik to flatten himself against the seat so she can angle herself to observing the crowd from this side.

"What kind of bad publicity is this?"

"I don't know, Ma'am." Malik relaxes when she shifts back to the left window.

She's not the only one whose anxiety rises as our elevation increases. The driver keeps one eye on the hoard of picketers and one eye on the roadway ahead. We pass a pull-out option for slow cars to allow other drivers to pass. The car swerves so that its tires cross the threshold of changing our minds, but then he yanks the wheel back to center.

"What kind of publicity were you hoping for?" I ask.

"An investment opportunity," she says.

The tips of my right fingers press against the glass like I can tap and bop the heads of the rioters as one plays whack-a-mole. Bop, bop, bop. "I hope you have good insurance."

The car turns for the last circle around the hill before reaching the top, with its flat parking, Ace sentinel, and the building where an angel once stood.

"Get as close as you can," I say in English, forgetting the driver doesn't speak English.

"Still discontent..." The driver speaks Spanish, but I understand him. He lets the sentence dangle like he can't decide which concern he has gets top billing. It could be that there's no room to turn around with the parking area overrun with picketers. It could be that people don't look friendly. Or he could be concerned that we won't pay him. I certainly don't have any means to pay him.

The road widens near the top. People rush the car before we reach any available parking.

"Donor Rights," one protestors sign reads. "Transparency in Digital Life." Another sign has TDL, an acronym for the phrase on the previous sign. In large black letters. "Donor Families Have Rights Too." I read as many signs as I can before the first person slaps the car. I never understood why Dr. Miller insisted on keeping me away from the crowds in Mexico, except that I thought he was ashamed of how poor at 'human' I was. I thought maybe he'd hoped to show a more promising product. But I get it now.

The faces in the crowd are twisted with loss and blame. They've lost a family member who was on the verge of death but not yet dead. Sent to an early end for a gamble at the lottery of being whatever I am. Some faces show self-blame. The inward focus of sorrow and guilt shown in deep wrinkles, the pull of their mouth, and the weight of their shoulders. Others reflect an outward rage so broadly spread, I doubt they care who they target. They spray 'angry' with every sweeping glance and stomping foot. Shouting at the sky more than the black glass building before them.

Very few members of the crowd have the physical traits of locals. Several languages mingle together. I wonder if the pair in the back seat would be with this mashup group outside if they'd only arrived earlier.

"What is this?" the woman asks. Each word more pronounced than the one before it. I assume she's talking about the car being banged against. "Go on. Keep going." Her head appears between the front seats. She looks at me. "Tell him to keep going... through the crowd." She orders.

I calculate my odds to be better with the mass of people outside the vehicle than I am with the pair inside the car. I open the door into the crowd and push my way out. The door doesn't shut behind me. Hands reach in for the driver and his passengers.

"Friends?" I ask at large. "*Quien es son?*" I think I said, 'Who are they?' But I might have said, 'Who is are?' Understanding languages isn't difficult for me, but speaking them, putting the sentences together in the correct order... For some reason that's not part of my programming. Only decoding meaning. Maybe I shouldn't have been so fast to split ways from Belen. I regret my choice to depart her company. "Who are all you people?"

Someone behind a 'Donor Rights Now' poster peeks around one side. "Friends of the Newberrys."

I feel exposed and identifiable since I'm the one assumed to be Jillian, yet no one looks at me with eyes that narrow, or tilt their heads in an 'I can't quite place you, but I think I know you' way. I swallow even though I don't have spit in my mouth to dispose of. "Who?" I ask.

"Jillian Newberry," another rioter answers. "The Mexico donor. She was brought here for some kind of training, and when her family was flown down to help with her transition into life after intelligence transplant..." Someone else's face turns from anger to sadness, crestfallen at the term 'intelligence transplant' like it's a disease to be cured of. "...their plane crashed."

A third person jumps into the storytelling. "Not just crashed, like totally suspicious. And no one here will say anything about Jillian or what happened to her family. Like she's just disappeared."

A gray-bearded gentleman with a lowered sign reading, 'Fair Resources' narrows his eyes at me—the first person to do so. "You really don't know about any of this?"

The car backs up. It's blocked at the rear at this point, so the driver pulls forward again. The crowd gives only a little, mostly from him backing and them relaxing. The driver backs up again, then pulls forward, like he's rocking his way through the crowd. Slowly, he back and forth maneuvers his way closer to the building.

"Hey," someone else shouts. "Phones are on. The burst is over."

And then I remember, Geo has a weapon he can use against me. I really need to think things through. I should not have come back. Several members of the crowd pull out their devices and video, photo document, comment and post to social media and news outlets. The story is live again. At least, until Geo manages to recharge his pulse-thingy and I drop like a remote-control toy out of batteries.

Add dismembering that pulse emitter to my to-do list to avoid that happening. But before I destroy it, I'd like to know if there's a way I could manage something similar. Can I create an EMT-like burst affecting everyone and everything except me? For that matter, if I can throw signals out like an EMT, can I manipulate human reactions through signals? Can I program humans?

20

The crowd tightens around the building, waiting for something to happen. I want in now, while their defenses are down and I'm up and running.

"Once we get this story circulating again, we go in," someone shouts from where they've climbed the deformed statue of Ace. "Charge the castle!"

I need to find a way to block EMT attacks while learning how to develop my own signals to send out. I scan the humans closest to me, but can't read anything beyond environmental percentages. Damn Faraday-caged brain.

"Confiscate all their files," someone hollers. Doesn't really sound like a scary raid with words like confiscate being thrown around. "We want as much material as possible."

"What are you going to do with it?" I ask.

"Destroy it."

The response is so matter of fact, it almost washes over me—the genocide of my kind. They're murderous terrorists. I put one step distance between me and the destroyers, like that'll cushion me from their intentions.

I stumble over my language controls with what I can possibly do. Other than wait for them to exit with their bundles of data and take it by force, whatever force necessary. I don't need language to annihilate these terrorists. I need weapons.

Malik and his boss manage to reach the doors through the human blockage. The woman swings her purse side to side, not really deterring any negative attention. The people bugging her manage to bug her still. Obviously, these rioters don't intend to harm anyone. Not any human anyone anyway. No one throws rocks at the glass exterior and there are rocks everywhere so it wouldn't be hard to do. Still, the woman makes a show of swinging her purse wildly about.

I squint to see if Geo greets them. A blurry form runs from the double doors off the grand lobby and sweeps the pair deeper inside the glass fortress. Unsure if they intend to come back out, I check to see where the car we arrived in ended up. The driver of our car tries to back out again, making slow progress through the crowd. Looking behind myself, out beyond the top of the hill where we stand, I notice more vehicles approaching.

The circle of factories beyond the white city buildings emits more exhaust than when I first arrived. Or maybe I notice it more now. A full circle of smoke surrounding a yellowing city with its dark star at the center. I stand here looking down at the emissions like a fortress of mist blinding the world to what's been happening here at the city center, whatever it is. My insides tell me something blocks my scanners from all that lies within the glass structure before me. Masters of hiding in plain sight.

I try again to force a signal to radiate beyond the limits of my skull. Something clicks internally. Pain-like fire presses behind my ears and against the point where my spine meets the base of my skull. "AH!" I rip the glove-like skin off my hand and dig for something sharp. I have to relieve the pressure I've caused.

"What the hell?"

Someone at my side screams, "It's a bot!"

"I'm ID." I use the abbreviation I assume they're familiar with for Intelligence Donor, which is all I am. One of them. "Not scary." I don't have patience to defend myself. I have to relieve the pressure. "I'm one of you for hell's sake."

So much for waiting to ransack their electronic loot. At this rate, I'll never recover Ace and the others from the files I've accidentally trapped them in.

People press in around me, grabbing for the covering I've ripped from my arm. "Bot!"

I pull away and back toward the building, though I didn't want to go back in. These idiots force me in that direction. I find the long skinny knife and plunge the sharp end into my head through where an ear canal should be, yet isn't there. Pressure remains until I pull the knife out again. No blood spurts out, no whoosh of air. There's no goo—not even a sound. But the pressure lifts, which is all I care about. I slump in relief and lean against the black glass doors. In my skin covered hand, I still hold the thin surgical tool. Those nearest me back away as if my relieved posture is somehow threatening.

"What's your plan?" I ask the person nearest me, feeling bold by the mob-like retreat from something as ridiculous as a four-inch-long pen with a tiny razor blade knife at its top. "Once you have their files?" I wave the knife a bit, adding hand gesture in the question for fun.

"What do you mean?" a young woman takes another half step back from me.

"When you charge the building, what do you plan to do with it all? What's the purpose?"

"Holding those inside accountable for the lies they've told, the hurt they've caused. The loss we've suffered by letting our families and friends be a part of their experiments."

The vehicles climbing the hill circle close enough I can make out tinted windows. "So, what? You're going to demand they pay for damages?" Depending on who exits those cars, I might want an exit plan of my own. "I'm what they caused."

"We can't help you," someone says. "All we have is protest."

That's stupid. If these people truly believed the pinnacle of their retribution consists of shouting at closed doors and holding up signs, what's the point of getting out of their wasteful human beds?

"We'll burn it down!" a young man shouts. Fire flares behind his eyes. I can't see how he means to spit his rage at a building made of non-flammable material. Still, it's better than standing around with signs and megaphones.

"It's made of glass," I say shifting my feet, moving back my hair, and adjusting my wool sweater to cover where I've pulled the hand covering back over my metal framework phalanges.

"Expose their fraud—that's what it means. Burn down the system." Someone else says. "Publicize the corruption."

Obviously, I don't understand human phrasing and word choice. The people who make up this crowd claim to be those who volunteered family members and supported friends to participate in a gamble for an advantage. "Didn't you all sign away the right to riot when your loved ones were carted away to a holding pen so their still-functioning brains could be converted to electronic signals, waves, and blips—left exposed to glitches, virus, bugs, hacking, and program errors? Surely you feel some thread of responsibility?"

"She's one of them!"

"They sent a programmed spy."

"It's not ID, it's a bot."

"She's a spy!"

"No," I say attempting to step back, but there is no 'back' there is only the crowd on every side and the glass doors. "I'm not a bot." I'm not ID exactly either, but I'm not a bot. I'm an individual—maybe the most individual to be on the planet at this moment.

Fear from my initial behavior with the penknife passes. The crowd leans my direction. Everything about them is overbearing and uncomforting. I need a weapon that would stun a human from acting on rage or misconception. Like EMT for humans. I have to figure out how to throw a signal that could shield me from their nonsense and mood swings. Focus brain, there has to be something I can broadcast.

Shouts and murmurs regarding what to do with me clash in a mass of threats breaking out among members of the crowd toward other members of the crowd. My head lolls in relief. At least humans can be counted on to bicker with one another, buying me time to process.

Screeching tires draw additional attention away from me. The vehicles with tinted windows brake to avoid hitting the car I arrived in, wildly backing its way down the hill. With so many people pressing around, the driver has no way to turn around. The other vehicles brake, blocking the retreating car. Tinted doors open. Belen steps out, which surprises me since I ditched her. Why would she come back here? Why am I back here for that matter? None of us should be here, yet we're drawn like moths to a zapper, the black glass nothing but a glittering tombstone.

"Belen!" I holler, my tattered arm waving in the air. There isn't much about her expression I'd call a welcome greeting. The riotous crowd grows in intensity with my motions, like my waving incites them to be more aggressive with one another regarding their varying degrees of riotous options. That's the thing, they're all overarchingly in agreement, but are ready to rip each other's limbs off due to differing notions regarding how to accomplish the same destructive ends—namely destroy the AI program.

Belen nods to someone, in the mass of bodies it's impossible to guess who it is. The driver of the car I arrived in opens his own door and takes off on foot down the hill. The cars behind Belen's park as well, some at a precarious angle blocking the road entirely from more company. Three vehicles back, a door opens and Mav steps out, followed by Gordon.

"Gordon! Mav!" I wave with both hands now, frantic. They're not jailed somewhere. They're here with Belen. I'm rescued or assisted. Or whatever I need right now. Maybe all I need is to know there are people who don't want me melted down for scrap. And those people are here.

Something cold pushes down my hair, touching the back of my neck. I slap a hand back as though I'm swatting a bug, but something shoots through my spine like a zing before I connect with the annoyance. White light blinds my vision sensors and my olfactory alarm indicates burnt plastic, though it's not the same as in the game. Smell doesn't affect me here. I'm alerted to it, but I have no connection with it. It's a blinking light in my brain saying 'this odor contaminates the air in your surroundings' and nothing more. Then everything shuts off. Except I'm still alert, only my packaging is down.

21

I can't see anything. I can't smell anything. My skin sends tiny nerve ending signals to the wires connecting it to my brain. I know this because the biggest complaint reaching my thoughts right now is 'sweater fibers'. Also, I can hear out of my right side. The side I drove a penknife through where an ear canal should have been.

"She arrived with the Egyptians," someone I can't identify by sound says. "Look at her arm, she's one of them."

Inside I cringe, unable to move my arm or any part of myself. I want to roll away, catch a bit of slope and continue down the hill away from this mess. But I also need to get inside and retrieve my data cartridge.

"Not with us. She's stupid," Belen answers. I hear feet shuffling and something on rollers with one wheel that keeps flipping circles, unable to keep alignment.

"Can she hear us?" Gordon's voice rasps like his throat hurts. A rough shoe presses into my side, setting all my skin sensors warring for space in my head – 'Danger, danger, you're being nudged.' I wish I could quiet my skin sensors, inform them that a slight toe-push and itchy sweater hairs are the least of my worries. Hey sensors, why don't you develop little spikes like porcupine hairs ready to strike anyone who gets too close?

"The taser. *Escrambled* her *esystems*."

"Yeah, but, if it's my brother's design, she has a reboot function." Mav coughs. "We don't have long."

"You *estole* their technology. It's corrupted robbers." Belen yells at

Mav. If I could see, I might witness tiny little Belen slap him across the face. "They're my *esister's* codes."

"Hey, who stole whose designs? Ace developed the entire donor program, so why is his program running all over the world?" Mav counters.

Belen doesn't say anything back. I'd love to see her face. I know she's not TECH-chick, but I've taken an instant disliking to her as if she's some extension of my game-world nemesis. Though technically, the Commander probably falls higher on the enemy ranking sheet.

"We should move her pretty soon, right?" Gordon says, again with that 'screamed too hard for too long' quality to his speech.

"How long until they set off another electric pulse?" someone in the crowd hollers from a distance and muffled by bodies between their location and wherever it is I lie on the pavement. I do notice the mob of people are no longer at each other's throat. What is it about Belen that creates the absolute opposite of what I'm trying to accomplish? Does she have to be so much the real-world counterpart of her sister? Take Mav, he may look like Ace—or more accurate, Ace programmed himself to look like Mav—but by all personality standards, Ace is the bolder brother. Mav has all the influence of a gnat on an underripe papaya.

"We set that off. Geovanni no crash his own *esystems* right now," Belen says.

"We did that?" someone else asks. "But we took damage."

I don't see the response. I imagine it's something like Belen pointing down at my motionless form with a 'look stupid' expression on her face. "*Mira*," she says.

"Why do we need one of their products?" That's me they're referring to as a 'product'. "You can't trust them."

"Exactly." The voice this time is deeper, richer.

"We can share," Belen says before one side of me is pushed up so I'm on my left side, then tipped over, face and stomach against what registers as the lip of a metal counter, a slab of steel. Indignity is being moved, removed, like so much scrap metal as I'm lifted by several pairs of unidentified hands. The slab is only five inches off the ground. "We don't need you for our next move, except to keep this out of Geovanni's reach."

I don't hear a response from the persons Belen speaks to, but feel the cart with its one circling wheel being pushed away while feet pad in a rush in the opposite direction.

"What are we into here?" Gordon's rough voice is barely a whisper above where I lay face down. I can wiggle my toes and know the effects from the device that scrambled my signals are wearing off.

"Shh. Wait till they're all inside," Mav replies. My thigh twitches. It won't be long before I'm at full capacity. The cart slides forward less controlled. "Watch the hill, Gordo."

A crack in the pavement catches the circling wheel slowing the cart before I have to blow my cover and stop myself from careening down the path. The two men from Mexico pull the cart in the opposite direction, fighting gravity uphill. I can't help but wonder where Dr. Miller, Ben, and Abby might be. With Belen perhaps? Or worse. I don't waste thought on Spaulding. The cart halts.

"Now you want to explain to me, Pierson?" Gordon's raspy voice forces itself into some range of high rage but muted by previous overuse. "What the hell is happening?"

I wait for Mav's response, but nothing comes for so long, I risk moving my head to the side. But do my best to make it appear like a gravity induced tilt. Gordon starts talking again the same second my head klongs against the metal like he's responding to my movement and I freeze even my thoughts for a split second before realizing Gordon isn't responding to me and my stupid attempt to spy a better vantage point. Besides, all I can see between the fray of my hair are trousered shins.

"I tracked all those codes as she asked, and you know what I found?"

Mav still says nothing. Does he know? I want Gordon to say it, so I can know.

Gordon continues talking, hopefully, his whispered scratches at words will tell me something. "A kid from Singapore. The Asian resource belt has a lot more than industry. They're controlling every political move from that one country."

"So what?" Mav asks. "Some donor comes from a country of influence. Doesn't sound too groundbreaking to me."

"The kid was with Ace," Gordon's voice drops like this is serious.

"So?"

"He wasn't a part of our facility. He wasn't one of our donors." Gordon stops talking, his tone indicates he has more to say but can't push the words through his battered vocal cords.

"What are you saying?" Mav's voice drops. I want to look around more to see what secret I'm missing here.

"These guys, they're connected to the security worker from this facility, right?"

"Yeah?"

"Also, in our system with Ace."

Mav's tone changes like he has something to defend beyond late Ace's hacking ethics. "What are you saying? They all came to Mexico?" Mav steps closer to Gordon, looming over him so that both Gordon and my slab are chilled by his shadow. "Are you accusing my brother of something right now? He may have started fighting for the wrong side, but he's no traitor. He's no spy."

"No..." Gordon leans away, shakes his legs like he's getting the confusing bits out through his shoes. "There are glitches of time where the codes disappear from the program and come back. We thought just glitches, but I don't think so."

"What are you saying then?"

"The programs changed on the inside. Rewritten in the game."

"That doesn't surprise me knowing Ace was in there. He's brilliant with codes, programming, all things tech," Mav says.

"It's not just that, I think the programs got connected somehow."

"It's all online right? Interconnected?"

"No, it's not. Each facility runs their own program, but I have evidence that our facility housed donors from three locations, all tracking with Ace shortly before Jennie uploaded."

"What are you saying, Gordo?" Mav asks for the annoyingth time.

"That fancy pants lawyer that threw down on your facility in Mexico? He might be right. Maybe Geo planted something so he could infiltrate all the programs. I mean, think about it. Our program finishes first, then he announces less than a month later. Where'd our codes go, right? Ace left the system before Jennie woke up, so did the others."

"You think they're here?" Mav asks.

"No. I don't know." Gordon continues to wiggle his shins like the motion will sort his thoughts. "I don't know when Juan uploaded."

"Their materials are twenty times more advanced than ours." Mav sounds like he's buying into this notion, and why not?

"No. They're not."

"But, Jennie—her joints didn't work."

"That's Miller. One more failsafe. You can't know for sure who's coming out of the game. He swore a month, only a month and then he'd know if he could trust the winner with a fully operating system. It was our job to 'train' her, but really we were evaluating Jennie for adjustment disorders…"

I stop listening at this point. Miller held out on me?

I trusted him.

"But think about it—if our program could connect to other programs, who's to say donors couldn't slip into any program out there…" Gordon lowers his already scratchy voice when he speaks.

"There'd be no boundaries."

"I think Jennie doesn't have a donor code. It's not lost, misplaced, or forgotten by some amnesiac side effect. I think she doesn't have one because she's not one of our donors." Gordon comes uncomfortably close to an accurate accusation.

My eyes open. Fluid rushes my limbs, preparing me to act if I need to. I don't want to get stunned again, but more than that I don't want to be bashed into an alert mass of intelligence that can't stop thinking and feeling but is unable to act or interact in any way.

"I've looked through every file several times over at this point, and I'm certain," Gordon says.

"Miller says…" Mav's point is cut off, I don't get to know what Miller says.

"Screw Miller. She knows languages."

"She has access to translation programs." Mav defends me.

"They're human donors, not programs. They don't go through a simple game program and come out world educated super geniuses, man. She's familiar with languages because she's probably from a different linguistic region. She's a program jumper. Maybe from an undocumented source. Or, best-case scenario, one of Geo's, like he claims."

"I'm not letting that guy claim my company's work." Mav gets loud. "My brother's work."

"You do realize he probably has serial numbers on all the upgrades he installed here. You try to sneak Jennie out of the country, you'll be arrested." Gordon's legs bounce in place again. "We shouldn't still be here." He paces in front of the cart I'm lying face down on. "This is a mess."

I debate my options. Say something? Defend my source code? Which would basically be lying about being GenE. I'm certain Gordon can track down the fact her game was over long before I uploaded since he's obviously skilled at tracking code, even when codes aren't from his donor list.

I sort of regret being all 'hey Gordo, help me out with this puzzle surrounding whose codes were near Ace.' How stupid am I?

Hopefully not human stupid.

22

Gordon continues to pace and bounce his leg during his attempts to be still. Mav sits on the edge of the cart I'm on with his back to me. His hands rub down his face, then push everything back up like he's trying to force his eyebrows to merge with his hairline.

"You know what they have in there?" Mav flicks the scrap of fingernail he's been slowly separating from his ring finger. "The lower levels?"

I know there are underground levels in the building from following Belen down a long staircase far beyond ground level.

"I know we're not supposed to be asking questions. Not if we want to get out of this country before Miller decides to put his 'failsafe' into place." Gordon turns for a return pace. "If he hasn't hit the 'detonate' button already. He wasn't happy about the holding cell."

"What if they're not uploading donors?" Mav picks his index finger below the quick. "Think about it. Juan doesn't behave like any of our donors."

Gordon stops pacing. "What're you saying?" Gordon moves so his shadow stretches across my face. I press my eyelids tighter, just in case. "Are you suggesting they're murdering healthy humans by uploading to the game? Or are you suggesting Juan isn't a donor?"

Mav lets out a long breath then flicks another nail scrap. "I don't know." He stands up, pushes wrinkles down his pant legs, then sits again. "The longer we're here... It's like a sick feeling growing. Right now, I feel literally sick, but it's like my brain feels sick." Mav finds a nail with the slightest roughage left to attack before it too is below the quick. "It's hard to think straight. But it's weird they have so much sublevel structure when the rest of the building is totally see-through."

"I get that. Like 'look here', but don't look down." Gordon takes three steps, turns, three steps, turns. "My head feels gross too. I thought I was just tired."

It's strange that such a 'transparent' structure would have a massive hidden underground operation. I'm sure it has nothing to do with Juan, though. He's a showpiece. Geo loves parading Juan in front of potential investors. I witnessed it several times from my cage—the Geo tour with Resource Ring investors, like the couple who entered the building today. Take them past my cage with whatever upgrade I was undergoing and a 'not long now before' finger thrust my direction, 'functions as fluidly as' thumb points over one shoulder to where Juan obediently stands at attention with a semi-smile gracing an otherwise bland face. Everything about my forced upgrades was open to public exhibition. Geo doesn't seem like the type to hide anything.

I press my thoughts out, trying again to figure out how to use brainwaves to affect those around me. Maybe I need to figure out what my goal is. *Upload my friends from the game.* That's my goal, but how do I word that as a thought? Or a command? *Upload.* I focus all I can on that one word, centering every snap of energy to the spot at the top of my spine where it seems all my connections meet to zing at the corner of my jaw. "Ow!"

"AH!" Gordon hollers at the same instant I reach to hold my smarting jaw.

"Jennie?" Mav jumps off the cart as though he accidentally sat down on my stomach.

My cover blown, I pretend like I only just woke up. "Where's everyone else?"

Gordon paces away from me while facing me. "Are you alright?"

"Are you kidding me, Gordon?" If I didn't think a slap from me would shatter the entire left side of his face, I'd totally lay one into the side of his skull right now. He just had me tazed. "Just answer the question. Abby, Ben, Dr. Miller. Where are they?"

"Miller is still being detained," Mav answers.

"Detained?" What's that supposed to mean? Is he alright? "Where? Why?"

"We were all in custody for two months," Gordon says defensively as though I'm accusing him of not being by Miller's side, which I'm not. Two months was long enough for all my upgrades, I assume. I don't know if Geo intended that, or if it worked to his advantage serendipitously.

"Abby and Ben?" I ask again.

"We don't know." Mav speaks after Gordon doesn't fill in the blank. "We were separated while being held and questioned."

"It's possible they've been deported to the Outercontintents. Anything North or South of the Tropics." Gordon shrugs like he's saying, 'This is a sorry excuse for an optimistic guess.'

"Why weren't you deported then?" I ask, removing the irritating sweater. I still have my post-surgical scrubs outfit underneath. Anything is better than a scouring pad against my skin.

"We were," Mav says. Gordon nods like an apology.

"We're sort of illegals right now," Mav adds.

"We couldn't leave our property..." Gordon catches the indignation behind my eyes at that word. I'm no one's property. "We couldn't leave our own people behind." It's too late. I heard 'property'.

"Well, what's your plan?" My voice rises. This is insane. I continue to go from an awkward situation to progressively asinine. "You're not honestly considering helping these guys?" I indicate the grounds Belen's people recently occupied.

"They have a plan to get out of Ecuador." Gordon shrugs again. "We figured we'd find you, help them, and then benefit from their escape plan..."

Mav rubs his shoulder like it hurts, but it's more to cover what he says next. "After they blow up the building, we're outta here." Like just having motivation behind an action is reason enough to justify it. If that were true, murder trials would be a whole lot different.

"What?" I can't let them do this. I need to ensure I can upload more people. I can't be the only one. Juan hardly counts since he's a freaking perfect human pet robot and I hate him. "They can't."

"I'm not letting Geovanni, whoever he is, take away my family's company, or stain my brother's memory," Mav Pauses so long I think he's done talking. Then he shouts, "he's not in charge," jarring my audio receptors.

"So we wait for them to come back out? Or for the building to blow?" I can't hide the contempt in my voice. "Don't you think we're a little close to the detonation?" I've been close to a large-scale explosion before. Sure, it was a game setting, but it still wasn't fun. Not something I want to have to repair myself from in this version of existence.

"Jennie." Gordon pulls at the collar of his shirt, letting more hot air in than out. Ecuador is simmering in every way today. "Do you know anyone from Singapore?"

"How would I?" I say.

"No. I don't know... Nothing," he says, obviously irritated.

Mav doesn't take his eyes off the wide doors of the black glass building. "It might be a smart move to go to Singapore. We're supposed to be deported anyway, right?"

"Singapore isn't North of the Tropics. It's fully Intercontinental," Gordon says. "Deported means north or south not lateral."

Mav's eyes remain intent on the black glass towering before us. "Someone's coming."

Gordon grabs the handhold of the cart I'm sitting on, moving the circling wheel once. I have to swivel my legs around and crane my neck to see what's coming. A tall figure distorts behind the panes of the building, moving quickly toward the doors. No one follows behind the wavering image. The closer the distortion gets to the opening, I notice part of the reason it looks so odd is because it's carrying something.

The figure presses the outer doors open. The first thing I see is Belen's dark coloring and untamed hair slung over the shoulder of Juan.

"Jennie?" he hollers from just inside the entrance.

If he thinks the fact he's holding Belen hostage is going to convince me to turn myself in, he grossly underestimates my affection for my initial rescuer. We're at the far end of the parking area, right at the edge where lot turns to hill. Ace's statue immortalizing his injuries stands between us and Juan. He bends to view us around the monument. His eyes open the second he spots us. Juan runs, mouth open while he sprints with Belen over one shoulder. Her weight doesn't slow him.

"Why aren't we running away?" I ask.

"He's with Belen?" Mav obviously misses the fact that Belen is completely unconscious. It's not like she's choosing to be paired with Juan at this moment. "He doesn't look hostile."

"Look at you, Mav. You're a freaking Greek God," Gordon says, "Maybe a superpowered, highly-intelligent, deadly, competitive, humanly irrational robot running at you with what might be a dead body over its shoulder doesn't intimidate you, but I'm short, scrappy, and stupid in comparison and I say we run."

"You wasted thirty seconds on all that wordiness," Mav shouts back to Gordon.

By this time, Juan is upon us. "I'm glad you're safe. We've got to get out of here."

None of us knows quite how to digest his sentence. His words don't sound like the Juan I know. Smug and smooth.

"Did you hear me?" Juan says. He opens one of the vehicle doors and throws Belen inside like groceries. "They're all coming online. We have to go."

"Who is coming online?" Gordon asks.

Juan doesn't look at Gordon but focuses on me. "It's the Mord, GenE." The way Juan pronounces my name sends a chill up my frigid metallic spine.

"The who?" Mav asks. "Mort? Who is that?" He turns to Gordon. "Do you know Mort?"

"What's your code, Juan?" I ask. Liquid is again pumping wildly through my system, alerting all my scans and alarms, but all I see is Juan's machine. Just Juan. In nothing but his Juan suit and Juanness. It's whatever is housed within him that has me on edge, and my scans don't look that deep.

"I can explain it all later, but they've made a mistake," Juan says. "A serious mistake."

"Who is they?" Mav asks.

Sound rumbles from the building before us. Not the kind of sound encouraging a person to hang around and identify it. It's more the sort of sound that gives a person the 'something's not right' feeling in their gut. The kind of sound that proceeds bad things.

"Go." Gordon opens the back driver side-door and slides in. "Come on, trust the man."

"He's our enemy!" I say.

Mav sides with Gordon.

"You coming?" Juan asks. "Would you rather shoot me before trusting me?"

I push the cart down the slope with my foot. It careens down the hill with one wheel clicking each time it circles independently from the rest of the wheels. The cart slams into a parked car—one that is definitely blocking our path if we hope to drive down the road away from this insane building. I motion for Gordon and Mav to make room and close the door the second I'm in. "I still don't trust Juan."

"Yeah, you look good, too," Juan says. "Thanks to me insisting they upgrade you. Nice hunk of scrap they made you in Mexico. Almost not worth winning if that's what you get for a prize." Juan reverses, slams into a parked car then shifts to first.

"There's a reason for that," Gordon says defensively. "Dr. Miller took strict precautions—"

"I'm sure." Juan points the car away from the paved road. "Let's save the debate for later, it always brings out the other guy and right now, we need a driver."

"Other guy?" Mav asks.

Juan nods to Mav in the rearview mirror. "Not in the mood to talk about whatever you guys haven't resolved. Grudge match is gonna have to wait. I'm driving."

Our black car with tinted windows jumps a curb, pointing straight down the hill.

"Are you crazy?" Mav asks. His hands press against the roof of the car. Gordon, too, has his limbs stretched to capacity trying to reach the roof and press for enough leverage to hold his wispy frame steady. In the front seat, Belen bounces around like a sausage link bundle.

"If you upload a Mord, fully Morded-out, I'm not talking post cure here…"

"No one knows what you're saying!" Gordon screams, losing his grip on the ceiling and slamming his head against the seat in front of him as the car bounces over the next curb section on the hill. The back end of the car bounces too high, we're going to flip over. "Turn, turn, turn!"

"Don't tell me how to drive!" Juan pulls the wheel to the left, the back end of the car swings in the shift of momentum and we slap the pavement with rubber wheels.

"What do you mean about the Mort?" Gordon shouts over the screeching engine and gears in Juan's control. He drives like he's still in the game.

"Once everyone figured out Jennie uploaded, everything was insane. It was like, if she could win, anyone could claim a spot."

"Why is that?" Mav secures himself by tightening the belt until it won't click in place more. "What changed?"

Juan catches my eye in the rearview mirror. Does he know? How? If he does, will he say something? Don't say anything. Don't say it. His pupils refocus and his hold on the wheel lightens. We ease up on the turns, keeping all four tires on the ground with our next round down the hill. "Back to the other topic, about the scrap pile, you guys uploaded Jennie into. Why would you assume to limit the donor who exits the game? It's counterintuitive if you hope to establish trust."

"What the hell is this? You really think this is the time to debate with us about establishing trust?" Mav shouts.

The car nears the bottom of the hill. I have no idea where we're going.

"What's wrong with now?" Juan sounds genuinely unaware that this semi-controlled nosedive down the side of *panacillo* isn't the same as a trust fall exercise.

23

Our vehicle circles to the base of the hill, fishtailing against the last railing when Juan turns hard to the left. I was more confident with vehicle outcome under the taxi driver who didn't speak my language. "Do you know where we're going?"

"Not that I was consulted on the matter, but I believe we're appealing to the manpower of Mr. YanTeoLee of Singapore who has an outreach unit just over the border into Columbia." Juan doesn't flinch or twitch. His eyes don't widen, and his shoulders don't bunch. His spine doesn't straighten or shrink. There is no physical indicator that any change takes place in him except that his word choice differs the next second when he contradicts himself by saying. "No one has to specify 'manpower'. It's not like it has to be the power of a man..." Then Juan is quiet without finishing his sentence.

"You okay, man?" Gordon asks Juan from the back seat. Gordon has to pick himself off the floormat as he's been jumbled right off the bench. I mime putting on a seat belt in Gordon's direction. He waves me off. In his defense, we're off the hill so he might be okay without the belt, though I definitely fasten, secure, and double tug my own seatbelt to make sure it's functioning at full lifesaving capacity. "Juan?"

Juan keeps his eyes on the road, taking turns at high speed, battling the vehicle for control, but not slowing. I slam against Mav repeatedly, admittedly not too bothered by his proximity. Then Juan takes a hard right and I plaster against the window so fiercely, with my mouth ajar, technically the window and I have a heavy make-out session while the car jostles me against the mouth-juiced glass repeatedly before claiming a steady direction.

"Juan!" He can't drive to save his own life, much less all of ours.

"Not Juan," Juan replies with the smooth Spanish accent he first introduced himself with.

"Geo?" I ask. At this point, I won't be surprised if Juan is nothing more than a glorified remote control, with Geo holding the controls.

"No," Juan informs me, seeming in tight control over his word choice and facial expressions. "I prefer to speak for this...situation."

When he says 'situation' it's strained, like part of him feels indignant about whatever it is we're waiting to be told.

"Nazrete is particularly outspoken when given the opportunity," Juan says. His driving doesn't match his calm exterior.

"Do you have more than one donor in you?" Gordon's tone rises as though he's both awed and mortified by the idea.

As if in answer to Gordon's question, the car swerves too close to the line of cars parked along the side of the road, slamming Gordon's side of the car against a bank of driver's side mirrors.

"Watch it!" Gordon hollers.

"Why take her?" Mav bows his head toward where Belen lays in a heap of elbows and legs.

"Not my idea. Like everything around here, I'm along for the ride, but don't get a say." Juan narrows his eyes. I wonder what it must be like in his head. Personalities battling for control, wanting to speak or explain, or defend, or attack, or whatever. How many personalities must they battle for their spotlight moments? Juan rolls his eyes in an overexaggerated manner. "Some kind of survivor's guilt. Has to stick all our necks out for every damn fool."

"Same thing that killed my brother," Mav speaks as though he recognizes a personality flaw in his sibling, more than out of reverence for the deceased. He watches Juan closely as if that flaw, and its homicidal side effects, are catching.

I assume Mav's remembering something Ace mentioned to me once. How Ace died trying to help a young boy fighting with the resistance. The boy detonated. Ace didn't save anyone that day. "He didn't die," I say. "He survived that explosion."

"No, he didn't," Mav says. "Ace died when the kid he thought he saved pressed that button. He didn't even try to live after that."

The interior of the car squeaks from all our sorry butts sliding this way and that. For a moment it's the only sound inside with us. Outside there's street sounds, business and leisure activities. People cursing our driver and his poor navigation skills, pointing out everything Juan 'almost' hit or did hit. And lots of pepperings of hand gestures that don't require sound.

"You don't know anything," Juan spits at Mav. "Why are you here?"

Mav shifts to the edge of the bench we share. All his weight forward in an off-kilter car, his head between the seats. Passersby might look through the tinted windows and spy what they think is a party vehicle with close buddies sharing stories of the great time we've had. "I came here to save what my brother started. Which happens to be your sorry existence, you Donor piece of trash."

"Hey!" I wedge myself into the conversation.

"Bullshit..." Without any exterior physical indicators of change, Juan switches to a demurely reprimanding tone. "Watch your language."

"Dammit, Juan. Stop flipping personalities." Mav hits the seat to his right, Belen's seat. She coughs, one arm slips against the seat, and her weight shifts. Mav ignores her.

"Hard to control in high-stress environments." Juan strains to get every word out.

Belen rubs her head, then her elbow before clearing her throat three times. "What happened?" The throat clearing effort does nothing. She sounds like a ninety-four-year-old chain smoker.

"We were going to upload codes to the current Ecuador program." Gordon verbally vomits my personal objective, like it's his information to bargain with. Stupid Gordon.

Though, if I'd have stuck with Belen, I would have reunited with

Mav and Gordon sooner and maybe could have avoided the whole weirdo scene at Geo's place. And we wouldn't have to endure Juan.

"That's a shit idea…Language!" I kind of like this less controlled, more split version of Juan.

Mav sits back hard, bouncing Gordon and me forward in our seats.

"If several of the codes from our game ended up in the Ecuador program before the system was purged…"

"You can't just copy and paste human personalities. The regulations for cloning, let alone…" Juan's cadence of speech shifts "Who says you can't? Everybody telling me what I can and can't do…" Another switch in patterns and word choice follows. "Geez, Nazrete, no one wants to clone you."

I can see why Juan came off so rigid before. Keeping his personalities in line requires constant vigilance, something that the demands of driving seem to be stealing from him.

"*Estop* this car!" Belen screams.

"You saw what they made. We can't go back," Juan says to Belen.

"I still don't know what a Mort is," Gordon twists so he's talking to me behind Mav's back.

"*Mi familia.*" Belen twists in her seat to better stare out the rear window.

"Those are terrorists!" Gordon shouts.

When Belen she keeps her gaze steady behind us, I move to observe what she's seeing. Mav and Gordon follow my action. I imagine Juan checks his rearview mirror as well. All of us watching smoke escape the shining black diamond atop the hill that stands above dirt-white buildings claiming the rest of the massive city.

We advance toward the wall of factory emissions circling the outer ring of this high city—the location of advancement, achievement, power, and precedent. A key city of the Intercontinents. Its black heart deflates in the rearview. "Smoking glass."

"What about Miller?" Gordon asks.

"Screw Miller," Mav says.

The factory gasses blur any indication of damage or shift in the air from the building atop the hill. The *panecillo* remains what it always has been—a high spot to look to.

24

Crossing the fog barrier presses a dismal outlook into our drive. A glaze drapes over every face but Juan's. His dark curls keep their bounce while the rest of us mold in the humidity.

"*Que es?*" Belen asks Juan what it is, in a crude manner, after two hours of driving. She has to gesture zombielike in order to communicate her full question. I realize she's talking about the Mord. But that's impossible. They can't really have gotten through.

"A mistake," Juan answers.

I shake my head. It's bound to be confusing with so many people in his head fighting to describe events, provide quick information. He must be mistaken about the Mord. There is no way they would be capable of coming through the system. Not only do we lack a procedure to translate straight code to a three-dimensional existence, there's a shortage of robotic human housing. If there wasn't, Juan wouldn't be a walking multiple personality. "They'd need robotic housing..."

Belen twists in her seat, cradling one arm probably injured in the drive after Juan kidnapped her. "There are many levels of robot production."

"I've been in the building. There's nothing but offices and guest suites. You know how I know? It's made of glass. The whole thing. Stupidest design I've ever seen," Mav says.

"Seriously, Mav, you can be so naïve," Gordon says. "It's an iceberg." Gordon brings the tips of his fingers together, forming a peak, he breaks the image to indicate the first knuckle of one hand. "You're only seeing this much, the rest is in the hill, underground."

My fake skin flushes with a cold chill, confidence literally drains from me.

"You're saying they're intentionally uploading Mord? But why?" I ask.

"Those things aren't void of features," Juan says. "Not like the Mord."

Belen waves a hand in front of her face, keeping her eyes wide and staring blankly ahead. "They look like you, but their eyes don't see, and their ears don't hear. The air rattles through their noses useless. They sift information through their teeth up to their brains."

Belen defines Mord as I know them. Instead of being absent all features but their mouth, this new version possesses the appearance of normalcy, but it's all a fake. The only question is, why are they here? Mord can be cured in the game, but I can't see how that's possible on this side of the code. I can't reprogram this world to fit my wishes. None of us can, no matter how hard we try. "But...why is Geo uploading them?"

"He didn't know," Juan repeats the phrase to himself, "Didn't know."

"What do they want? The Mord." I ask.

"*A morir*," Belen says.

"To kill?" I ask, my voice rising. The Mord chased me through the game, I lead them, but rose above and left them behind. Now it's like they're following my wake to destroy me.

"Not to kill... It means to die," Juan says. "They're just doing it wrong."

"They're already dead," I say.

"But still living," Juan counters. I don't want to trigger an internal conflict in the guy, so I stay quiet and let him compose himself before he continues. "They're sentenced to an existence of never death in this place."

A wave of frustration floods out of me because he's misreading them. The Mord don't want to die, they never have wanted that. It's the thing that defines them best, refusing to die after already being deemed dead. "They did lose," I say under my breath, but Juan hears me. He tightens his jaw and blinks slow one time. I'm slightly concerned he's interpreting my words wrong. Because, after all, the players trapped inside him also lost—to me, if I think about it. "Not that losing should disqualify a player from quality of life...or dignity of death."

Juan moves his jaw ever so slightly, but it's loose enough to shift position and that's better than clamped steel frame robot anger.

"How do you plan to get out of Ecuador? We're fugitives," Mav asks.

"Ibarra," Juan answers. "The Intercontinents won the war on resources and claimed world power. Can't do that without a healthy underground trading ring and cartel."

"Which is in Ibarra?" Gordon asks.

"No." Juan and Belen exchange a look. I know the look. It's an Ace look. The kind he used to pass with TECH-chick. The kind of shared expression commiserating ignorant company. "Columbia is our destination."

"But that's not Ecuador. We have to cross the border before we make it to Columbia." Mav points out.

"Ibarra is the border," Juan says.

"We make it to Ibarra, we are practically in Columbia," Belen says.

"I thought we were going to meet up with Singapore," Mav says. "The big name from donor processing in Asia."

"YeoTanLee will be in Columbia." Juan lowers his brow, a very un-Juan manner to take in the road conditions ahead of him. "This whole thing went to hell the second you showed up, Jennie" There's always fault to be flung behind shifty eyes.

"Don't make me shoot you." I swear without considering my words.

Mav shifts his whole body to look at me. The kind of shift that puts additional space between us while forcing Gordon into the door handle. Gordon doesn't complain about his Mav body shield. He shifts forward so he can cast a questioning glare at me too.

Juan smiles, his forehead leans toward the windshield like his frontal lobe calls the shots now. Impulse and heat. I'd prefer Nazrete to Juan in charge of the Juan collective.

25

It's a funny thing, assessing humans for humanness. I find myself staring at Belen for hours as we make our way passed Otavalo and on to Ibarra. I knew her older sister, TECH-chick. But I never evaluated TECH-chick on her humanness. It wasn't a factor at the time. TECH-chick left people behind. In the game, odds of survival improve when choices are made without regard to others. But my understanding is that human family groups matter to humans. It's something I envy since I've realized I don't have claim on such a thing. It bothers me that Belen hasn't fought Juan about leaving Pedro behind. The other thing that bothers me...her hair. I want her to cut it. It's a mess—long and bushy. Would she notice?

"What's going on ahead?" Mav asks, positioning himself between the front seats.

I change my focus. Cars slow to a long line of brakes.

"I don't know." Juan presses buttons on the console, searching for road conditions. "We're miles from the border. It won't be a checkpoint yet."

"This is what it's like at the lines of the Tropics," Gordon says.

"Well, yeah. That's a barrier keeping prosperity in and the oppressed out." Mav says.

I crane to determine who is prosperous versus oppressed based on vehicle condition. There are all manner of vehicles. I have no knowledge base for which car brands are best, or which paint colors signal wealth. White dominates the color scheme. My guess is that's a climate choice more than a status symbol. The only other thing I notice, no one looks around. In every vehicle near to us, the driver and occupants keep their eyes wide ahead, as though they're all concentrating on listening to something and can't spare any additional sensory stimulus for looking around.

"Turn on the radio," I suggest. "Maybe the news can tell us what's going on."

"No one crosses the border into Columbia unless they're trafficking," Juan says.

"Wait, go back." Mav points at the center console where Juan flips through news sources for updates on traffic or accident reports.

Juan traces back a few screens. A news report includes images of men and woman with hospital gowns loose over perfect skin with the backs of the gowns not securely fastened. They walk without lifting their feet off the ground, dragging their toes. Their chins lift so that their noses point to the sky. Mouths open as though the people are scooping air molecules by the gulp. They move as if there's no rush to their task, whatever their task.

Until someone stumbles into their midst. The stumbler snaps their head from one open-mouthed person to the next. It's the woman from the taxi—her wide-brimmed hat gone. Every terrified feature of her stretched face exposed. From where I sit, craning to get a good angle on the screen, it looks like the hatless woman tries to make eye contact, waves, attempts to speak to someone in the group. It's not until I realize the grouping gets tighter around her that I can see what's about to happen. The crowd around the person turns in, the mass of mouth breathers narrowing the distance the woman has to escape. There's no way out.

Gaps get smaller, the woman is trapped in a circle mob. The reporter provides warnings for viewers to look away if violent images are upsetting. The woman backs away when one of the mob gets too close, but then she has to repeat the evasion because there are more behind her, and every angle spun or leaned toward is a dead end she has to attempt to back away from. Until there is no place to move and the camera pans out.

The shot is wide. An arch of red liquid sprays over the crowd with open mouths. Then another. Pieces are thrown before the camera points down while those filming run away from any semblance of nearness to the group. The reporter continues talking over the sound of running and screaming and the shaking streak of a camera still rolling in the mad grip of a terrified documenter.

"Businesses have closed or locked up shop while the masses exit Quito, Ecuador. The people are believed to belong to the Pierson group as an internal conflict between Mexico City and Quito came to a head earlier this week at a conference meeting. AI has been infected with a virus that destroys the human processing component of donor transplants..."

"What?" Mav moves back in his seat. Then punches the seat to his right with the side of his first. "They're making it sound like I caused this."

Juan's face in the rearview mirror says everything I'm feeling. Relief mostly. No one looked at either of us with suspicion regarding whether we're infected or not. Our eyes confirm to one another that we're fine. Are we really?

Belen crouches with her feet up on the seat, tight against her thighs and her arms wrapped around her legs. She rocks on her haunches, her head tucked into her knees and palms covering her ears. Maybe Pedro wasn't left behind. Belen wipes the heel of her hand over her eye.

"I'm sorry about Pedro," I say.

"We must cross the border," Belen says. "More distance from the *muerte* as possible."

"It's pronounced Mord," Juan corrects.

"Do you think that's why the border's so hot here? People trying to flee?" Gordon asks.

"Why would they stop people from escaping those things? I'd think they'd encourage it." Mav says 'those things' in a way that rankles my synthetic skin.

"They're definitely checking vehicles ahead," Juan says. We all strain around the obstacles of seats and each other to get a look at the far distance where *policia* pull open car doors, asking passengers to step out of their vehicles. People are scanned with a long black stick while other officers go over the interior of the vehicle with another electronic baton.

"Get out of the line," I say.

"Yeah, I think you're right." Juan cranks the wheel to the right, forcing us onto the shoulder, also occupied by cars, because lane lines mean nothing in Ecuador. Once on the shoulder, Juan manages to drive in reverse, mostly on the greenery flanking the edges of designated roadway.

"Watch out!" Gordon shouts. He's turned so he watches out the rear window with the rest of us, at our backward progress. Behind us another car has the bright idea to drive the shoulder in order to bypass the lines to advance. One of us will be forced down a slight embankment if neither of us concedes direction.

"Gun it," Mav urges. "They'll flinch first."

"I'm not playing chicken," Gordon hollers.

"Gun it!" Mav shouts over Gordon's loudness.

Juan presses the accelerator and we jolt backward, speeding toward the vehicle approaching us at the rear. The lights of the car shine at us, despite the remaining daylight making them unneeded, obstructing the view of who sits at the wheel. The other driver continues forward without any indication of flinching for what feels like minutes but must be seconds only. I duck behind the seatback, attempting to shield myself from the inevitable impact. Gordon does the same thing.

"To the left!" Mav shouts.

Juan adjusts the progress of the car toward the left. Metal sparks and scrapes out the right-side door—the door I'm crouched next to. "Watch it!"

Crunching metal amplifies on the right, impact launches me forward toward the back of Juan's seat. Still wearing my seat belt, I'm yanked against the nylon strip of fabric, rubbing my rubberish coverings so hard, I rip at the hip slightly. Two torn areas. Great.

The other car deflects off the right side of our vehicle, launching out over the embankment at an angle that doesn't bode well for driver or passengers inside.

"We need to make sure they are okay," Belen screams.

Horns honk at us the farther we drive from the accident—faces display human shock, disgust, and what I believe is murderous rage at seeing us drive away from what could be a fatal accident, which we caused. At this point, if we exit the vehicle, the nearby drivers will murder us before the scanner people can come close. Beeping starts erupting before we pass people, from cars that had no way of seeing the accident.

"They're scanning people down there. What do you think they're looking for?" Juan presses the gas closer to the floor, accelerating our reverse. "That's not the TSA or whatever airport security."

"They're so far ahead, they'll never see us," Belen insists.

"Have you seen Jennie's arm?' Gordon bends around Mav, takes hold of my right arm, which has no issues, and attempts to lift my arm. It's ridiculous. My skeletal structure won't be forced into movement so long as I'm conscious. Not like I'm going to tell him that.

"That's right. As soon as Jennie steps out, everyone will see her torn wrist," Mav says.

Belen has a grip on the door handle, but Juan hits the door locks before she can lift the handle. "You stay in the car!"

Juan shoots Belen a sideways glance. It has all the signs of a warning shot like Juan has something on Belen he can reveal to the rest of us if she's not too careful. Belen lets go of the door and folds her arms, then crunches her legs onto the seat with her, effectively folding herself up into a little package of sadness.

Juan navigates backward to the end of the long line of cars waiting to get out of Ecuador and spins the car in the opposite direction.

"Do we have a plan?" Gordon asks.

"Get the hell out of here," Juan says. "We're not making it across any borders without help."

"I thought you said you had connections here," Mav accuses Juan.

"My connections remain where we just left from."

Mav throws his back against the seat.

"So far, this trip to Ecuador isn't my all-time favorite travel experience." Gordon crosses his arms.

"So, what? Go back to Otavalo?" Belen asks. "I know those mountains, we'd do okay."

"We need gas." Juan taps the dashboard display with one finger. "We've been driving for hours. Tank's almost empty."

"I hate cars," slips out of my mouth. I've been reminding myself to not say anything, so as to not draw more attention to myself. None of these people seem that keen on me right now.

Belen unfolds from her personal cocoon at the sound of my voice. "Why you bite your arm? Trying *asustarme...*?"

"It's stupid," I say, wishing I could dig around to see if any items are still lodged between my skin covered tubes.

"Did you not know Abby's plan?" Belen asks without seeming to notice the reaction her words stir in Gordon and Mav.

Both of their heads turn as if I'm the magnetic pole of their compass-noses all of a sudden. Not knowing anything, and not wanting to plug the flow of revelation Belen seems to be on, I remain silent.

"What plan?" Gordon asks.

"You can't be *serio*." Belen twists so her knees are on the seat, holding the seatback in her hands and her head over the rest between her and Gordon. "Abby never mentioned to you she was planning a *sabatear* Geo?" *Sabatage, is she serious?*

"How would she do that?" Gordon asks. "We don't have any access."

"She contacted me before your arrival." Belen's eyes move from Gordon to Mav and back to Gordon. "She didn't tell you?"

"No. She didn't," Gordon says.

"Tell us," Mav says, moving his elbows out to his sides in a looming, imposing manner. I shuffle my feet until I'm an inch closer to the door, giving Mav room to intimidate.

"Abby knew about the disk," Juan says. "That night we met..." Juan's eye flash to the rearview mirror then back to the road, long enough to catch my attention. "I was supposed to keep you out of the room long enough for Abby to find that flash drive with all the Mexico City data on it."

"Donor files," I say it like a statement, even though in my head everything turns to questions. Why was Abby in contact with Belen? How is Juan connected to all of this? The donor files aren't sabotage, we're supposed to save my friends.

"No idea." Belen curls around, back into her ball of despair.

"What happened?" Mav removes the indent of his frame pressed into the back seat.

"The march on the building wasn't just to remove their data. We replaced it too," Juan says.

"Whose side are you on?" Gordon shouts at Juan.

Juan takes his eyes off the road and turns his entire upper torso and face at Gordon. "Don't you talk to me..."

"Damnit Nazrete," Gordon shouts before any other version of Juan can scold itself.

"Watch the road!" Belen hollers. Juan swivels, keeping an eye trained on Gordon until Mav interrupts.

"You replaced it with the data from our building? Mexico?"

"Not exactly," Belen says.

Juan's hands grip the wheel so tightly I'm certain little finger imprints distort the circle. "We added a virus."

I know that admission of guilt. How dare he mess with my files. I was trying to rescue him, and not only does he lie to me, but he also steals my data and infects it?!

"How dare you?"

"We thought the code would disable their robotics lab. Inside that hill, levels and levels of bodies all hooked to chords and wires, waiting to be uploaded with computerized human thought. And after what happened with Jennie, I couldn't let that happen again."

All heads turn to me. "Memory loss, am I right?" The faces don't turn away from me.

"It wasn't Mord code, I swear." Juan lifts his right hand in the air, fingers tight together. "I swear,"he says again. "But, somehow, that's what came through the wires." The fellow passengers return to a forward-facing direction and my shoulders drop a few centimeters, not enough for anyone else to notice. "They all started waking up. Every floor full of robots not using their eyes or ears, or any of their scanning systems as far as I can tell."

Mav's voice drops in tone and temperature. "Why didn't you say anything when you came out of the building?"

"I wanted to get out of there."

"This isn't the game. You're not competing," I say.

"It's always the game," Juan says. "There's nothing but the game."

"There's no extra lives for the rest of us." Mav's anger isn't like Ace's. Even though he's a physical clone, it becomes easier and easier to distinguish the two. There's fear fueling Mav.

Ace had no fear.

26

We only make it as far as Imbabura, eight and a half miles outside Ibarra. The gaslight has been on far longer than eight miles. Thank goodness it's hard to miss the next *gasolinera*. Whoever designed the station must have been blind, at the very least color blind. The roof over the pumps is bright yellow, borderline neon. It assaults the eyes. Contrasted by crayon red pillars holding up the roof and cobalt blue 'PS' with the same color blue bubbles trailing the letters. It's the opposite of my idea of an oasis. It's something I'd avoid if I had a choice, but none of us do, if we hope to continue our search for a way out of this country.

"Looks like a preschool threw up on this place," Gordon says taking in the primary color scheme of the *gasolinera*. Mav snorts an agreed laugh. I nod my approval of his description.

"Because Mexico *es* so much nicer?" Belen takes offense. I cover my smile but can't wipe it from my face. Mav snorts a second time. I can't tell if he's mocking Belen or agreeing that Mexico is so *not* much nicer.

"Jennie, stay in the car," Juan orders.

"What? Why just me?"

Juan twists in his seat, reaches a perfect long arm back to my hand, lifts my left wrist then drops it, my metal frame dropping back to my lap without resistance as I haven't gotten enough movement back in that limb to reflexively catch my falling hand.

"I'll keep it covered."

"No. People are on high alert, they're looking for something to stand out," Juan says.

"I feel like you're overreacting," I say. "If you're so worried about it, I'll tape it."

"*Con que*?" Belen's voice hits a high note she has yet to use. I'm pretty sure she's broken her vocal cords. How do humans fix broken things? I know they have blood and other complications of fixing broken parts. "Nobody has tape!"

"It's true. No one's gonna remember to grab tape when they're escaping a mob of robot zombies," Juan says so matter-of-factly, without the slightest degree of concern or even humor, I'm offended. I have to keep everyone on good terms. The last thing I need is everyone jumping to conclusions that I'll behave the same way as the Mord on the news station. I cover my aggravation by laughing at Juan's comment.

Juan is so robotic, I wonder if he's even a donor. Or some default setting the rest of them are being controlled by.

"At least check in the *Mercado*," I ask Mav. "See if there's some gloves, or tape—or even a bandage. No one is going to question a wrap on my wrist while people are acting crazy."

Mav nods as everyone exits the car, but me.

"Can I at least watch the little video console thingy?" I ask through the closed window. Juan doesn't turn around from where he's selecting gas grade to pump into the car. "I'm doing it..." The rest of the group is in the little market attached to the gas station.

I flip the video panel on and watch as a reporter continues with coverage in Quito. The city is a mess. Broken down cars litter the streets, smoke erupts from buildings. The camera trails as a bottle of soda rolls, unopened, down a sloped roadway, emphasizing the mass rush exodus from the central city. "...Officials have declared the attack an act of war strategized by the Pierson group in retaliation to Ace Pierson, a member of the Pierson family who fought for the Intercontinents..." I look up to see if Juan is hearing any of this, then I turn toward the market curious if the same news might be broadcast inside the small store where Mav might be watching. "...it's important to note that Ace Pierson was assassinated by Outercontinent forces at the end of the war..."

"What? He was not! He lived long enough to sign up as a donor. He didn't die in the war!" I tap the screen like this action will reach through and alert the reporter of their false facts.

"...Dr. Spaulding confirmed with reporters earlier today that the Pierson group arranged their attack shortly after the Intercontinent nation of Ecuador announced an open invitation for donor facilities to observe their successful intelligence donor program..." Video footage of Dr. Spaulding speaking with media, an air of importance masks his glee at media attention.

"Spaulding, you skunk." I slam my palm over the screen, not preventing the audio from getting through.

"...the traveling party developed a virus to infect the current running donor program, and disable one of the strong fronts of the Intercontinent forces..."

"That's bull!"

A tap on the window startles me. "Jennie, what are you hollering about?" Juan asks through the glass.

Moving myself, so Juan can't see the screen spewing lies about our small group, I wave him off. "Nothing."

Juan narrows his eyes at me, I wonder who watches behind the pupils. Do they all get to see at the same time, or take turns controlling the housing they're all trapped inside? If it's anyone who knows me, they'll know I'm lying. Something is definitely up with me. "Keep it down. You're drawing attention."

I nod. As soon as Juan returns to operating the brightly colored pump, I shift my focus back to the screen, eager to soak up indignation in response to rumors being passed as news.

"...Intercontinents have developed a two-pronged retaliation, cutting off the Pierson group where they stand and all those who might support such an uprising." The reporter shifts registers, as though he has a vocal range where his opinions dwell distinguishable from 'reporter' mode. "The war is already won, stop dragging it on."

The screen jumps back to a studio location. "...what we're seeing now is the site about to be bombed..."

"Bombed?" I repeat out loud. The image on the studio screen

remains to be the streets of Quito, abandoned except for the stray dogs rummaging through items littering what were pristine streets a day ago. And the small reporting team huddled at an elevated outskirt of the city—high enough to get a decent overview, but not so close as to be in danger of encountering the wondering Mord who've been uploaded into donor bodies. The camera makes several attempts to zoom in on a group of Mord, their humanish robot eyes staring glazed over from disuse. I have to say, I prefer Mord void of eyes. There's something worse about having the apparent ability to see and not utilizing it. Yet I want to help them, teach them. They have the features and all the connections in place. Why can't they see? I push my curiosity outward, almost like I'm sending my thought to space where it can be contemplated by the cosmos and return an answer that might make sense.

Off in one corner of the screen, a white streak cuts the shot of blue sky. The camera refocuses, going wide to get the burning white line scorching its way toward the heart of the city. I lean in closer, trying to get a glimpse of the shuffling Mord. The camera moves, reporters and camera operators arguing with each other out of the footage shot. Everything being exchanged in Spanish, but my brain automatically adjusts to English. "...get the image zoomed closer—tight in there..."

Everything clicks at once. The white streak in the sky points to the crowd of confused and desperate Mord. Instead of curiosity bursting out of me, this time anger rolls off me in waves so tangible I half expect the glass to shatter in the vehicle, or the cars around me to rock. *Run! Don't let them destroy you!* Several of the Mord lift their chins to the air, suddenly alerted to the incoming missile. From the angle of where the cameraman huddles, it's almost as though the poor misplaced creatures stare at me through the lens in response to my internal warnings. Like we're connected somehow, drawn together by my sudden concern for their welfare. How I wish they could literally heed my warning, but then it's too late.

The shot drops to the cobbled street then lifts too high, out of focus. I dip and sway as if I have control over the focus, desperate to know where that white streak is going to hit, and what it means. My concern reaches out toward the Mord, lost in a world they don't belong and judged for a reaction they were programmed for by the very people targeting them. "Move!" I urge the Mord to shuffle faster.

Finally, the camera focuses as close as it can on the group of open-mouthed AI, all clamoring tightly together—the image grainy from being so far from the image being filmed. Then white light blinds the lens. I wonder if there'll be anything to see. A debris cloud bounces up from the impact crater, pulling down with it anything dense enough to still be standing.

The studio comments before I say anything aloud to myself, "...we should have confirmation in just a moment...there's always electro-magnetic interference with long-range weaponry of this kind..." What kind? What kind of weapon is the fiery light?

I look over to see if Juan is done yet, while the studio discusses long-term objectives in quashing rebels warring in the aftermath of a win. What a bunch of pretentious...

Juan isn't there. The gas pump has been replaced. I move to the other side of the bench and stare into the tiny market. It's not that large, what could they all be doing in there? It's not like Juan needs a bathroom or food, so why has he gone in with the rest of the humans?

"...the image is back... Holy sh—" Chaos covers the screen. Video shows severely damaged Mord full out running toward the small group of reporters on site in Quito. "Move, it...No...Leave the equip-ment. Move!" The Mord move much faster than the humans, their speed unnatural.

I lean closer to the screen. It's like the attack flipped the Mord into overdrive mode, the scary version at their peak aggressive levels. They run with sharply angled joints, heads half gone, leaking wires and chords flailing in the breeze behind them. They're the gory version of robotics—all gears and juices motivated by something other than a brain, as most of them lack the majority of their head after being bombed. Arms are missing from some, legs from others. Those without a leg are crouched in an unnatural manner, running with one leg and one arm, palm flat like a monkey in step with the foot, moving so fast and intensely horrifying that the group of human reporters is caught in a stunned terror, unable to gather their wits to escape.

The camera is on its side by now. The studio cuts to coverage of the desk, to those still observing the live feed being captured by the studio cameras. I can't see what they're seeing, but I can see the anchors and the expression on their faces as they continue to observe the feed that's been deemed too disturbing to continue to air live. One anchor covers her mouth, then moves one hand to cover her eyes, but then brings that hand back to her mouth before retching off to the side of her shared desk.

"...What we're witnessing..." the other anchor attempts to report the events we can no longer see. "...it's complete loss."

I don't realize my mouth is gaping in a slight smile. Part of me is relieved the human attempt to wipe out the lost Mord backfires. I'm lost in my confused internal response, glee the Mord are still okay, and worry at what their instinctual self-protective reaction to destroy the threat might mean when all three car doors open at once.

"Go, go, go..." Gordon repeats over and over as the group piles in without concern for belts or seat position. Belen takes the driver's seat with Mav at her side. Gordon pushes Juan next to me still cursing on repeat as he pulls the door closed on his own foot. "Go!"

"What's happening?" I ask.

"Find a backroad!" Mav barks into Belen's ear. He's too close to her head, and she pushes him away.

"What's going on?" I try a different form of the same question.

"We're fugitives,' Juan says at my side. He's slouched so low his head doesn't reach the top of the seatback. "Get down." He grabs my shirt and horse-collars me below the window line.

"Spaulding gave reporters our names and faces. He's saying we tricked Geo into hosting us, kidnapped Juan, reprogrammed him with our codes, and uploaded the virus to their server, which happens to connect to several other facilities..." Gordon gets cut off when Mav butts in.

"There are laws about connecting donor programs. It's illegal, but you don't hear anyone mentioning that, do you? No. No one's saying, 'they infected the illegal network system'... Illegal!" Mav punches the dash. "There's no way this is our fault."

Belen looks sideways at Mav, then returns her gaze to the road.

"Not entirely our fault," Mav corrects.

Belen finds a small dirt road running between some rounded mountains and guns it. We bounce along the rutted path without losing speed.

"Where are we headed?" I ask.

"We have to leave Ecuador," Belen says we have to get out, which we were already attempting prior to gassing up—and failing. "I know an *sanctuario* through the mountains."

"A mountain sanctuary? How is this going to help us? I thought the goal was to exit the country."

"It is in Columbia," she says.

"We can get to it through the mountains," Juan clarifies in smooth accented English.

"Well, why didn't we try that the first time?" I ask.

"We cannot drive to it," Belen explains. "And we don't have supplies."

"Did anyone grab supplies from the store?" I ask looking around at all the greasy fingers from convenience foods, but no items in anyone's hands. "Not even a bandage?"

"We got distracted," Gordon says, joining Juan and me in our backseat slouch.

It won't be Juan and me who suffer from the lack of supplies. Even more embarrassing is that we both reach down to plug ourselves into the car charger at the same time. Dependent on power.

27

"Did you see how confused they were?" We exit the car and proceed on foot through the mountain path. The car at half a tank of gas, and not even half a spare tire to address the flat that has us sidelined. Not that we'd know what to do with half a tire. We're up so high, clouds roll in below us. No one on the planet appears to exist out here other than the fact there is a road and hills filled with natural resources. Thick tread marks provide evidence of a mine somewhere in the area.

"No one expects machines with half their head missing to come charging at them at such high speeds. That footage was unreal." Gordon looks to Mav for confirmation, which he gets.

I stop and try to picture his statement. It doesn't make sense what he's saying. They never saw it coming until it was too late. None of them trained to recognize an airstrike of that kind. "What are you talking about?"

Gordon stops, as does Mav. Mav narrows his eyes at me. "They couldn't get out because they were stunned by what they saw, just like you said."

Juan looks over his shoulder at me, then at Mav. His eyes catch as if a shift in thought causes a minor seizure that shakes only his iris. Then his pupil widens. "Jennie stop talking."

"What did I say?" I don't understand what the problem is.

Juan's posture hitches, one shoulder slightly elevated than the other, yet his demeanor lifts with authority completely. "Last thing we need is another Mord sympathizer shooting off her mouth like some friggin' Mother Theresa of all the rest of us. Ain't nobody gives

—they lost a long time ago... Shut it Nazrete!" Juan's shoulders both drop, like he's shut himself down, but still manages to walk forward with the group.

"Mord?" Gordon moves back from me and raises his voice as if the mere thought of my concern for them makes me stink. "Oh. Seriously, Jennie."

"That's another thing," Mav says. "The news has your name all over it. Like you're some part of the whole mess."

"Gordon's?" I ask.

"No, Jennie." Mav runs a hand through his hair. I check to see if Juan happened to turn around and notice because it's a motion I've seen before. Ace has the same nervous tendency. "You might want to consider going by a different name."

"Because they're so many people around to hear you talk to me," I add.

"Just think about it," he says.

Conversations fade as we continue to climb. I pull up geographical facts from my database—things I've already stored prior to our trip. I'm still unable to access more information. Imbabura is a volcano reaching over fifteen thousand feet elevation. The thin air doesn't impact my ability to keep up. Gordon struggles. If he has the lung capacity of his frame, there isn't much available to hold in air.

"Gordo, you alright?" Mav keeps step with Gordon, his arm out, ready to catch him if he falls. Gordon stumbles a bit toward the ravine side of the path like he's intoxicated.

"I don't feel so good," he manages to say before vomiting all over his shoes.

"Oh, man." Mav falls back a few paces from Gordon.

"*Basta, ya.*" Belen calls us to a stop. "We wait." She nods to Gordon.

"Altitude sickness," Juan informs the group.

"We know that, Juan," Mav says. He gets more agitated the higher we go. I can't tell if he too is suffering from the elevation, or if he's just an ass when it comes to heights.

Everyone finds a place to sit along the edge of the road. The high mountain appears to connect to other mountain peaks, dipping low into valleys and ravines and rising to sickening heights again. Pencil thin trails snake along distant hills, signs of inhabitants in the remote mountain lands despite how the industrial boom of the Intercontinent resource ring drew hoards to larger cities.

"Do people still live out here?" Mav asks Belen. I follow the line of his gaze to a worn path not far from where we sit. It leads down at a diagonal, only to switch back in direction as the path descends the mountainside.

"Yes. They use cables and lines to cross." She points to a ridge in the distance. A thin line, appearing spider web thick from where we rest, outlines the peak connecting the dots from one power pole to the next. In the farther distance a cellular tower glints whenever the low cloud cover clears enough to permit sunlight to kiss the metal structure.

"That's not so bad," I say. "I could live out here with a power source." Everyone looks at me like that's the most ridiculous thing any of them have heard. A low rumble shakes the blades of grass near my thigh. It takes me a second to realize it's not the grumblings of one of my traveling companions. "You guys hear that?" I scan our surroundings, my range limited.

Juan cocks his head to one side. "Get off the road."

We don't ask. All of us jump to our feet, following Mav's lead along the path twisting back and forth down the steep mountainside. The rumblings grow in intensity.

"Find cover," Juan orders in a manner that transports me back to the game, under military command and fearing for survival of any kind—even trapped with rivals inside a metal coffin.

Cover isn't hard to find. It's no wonder Ecuador thrives in a world where resources equal power. Treated posts pounded into the ground for fencing have taken root, with rich green leaves and healthy branches stretching out from splintered posts still clinging to barbed wire.

"Watch the barbs." Mav warns us too late. My wrist skin flap rips longer where the edge catches a wire spine.

I pull my sleeve lower and duck behind some tall brush and rocks —also covered in growth. "It's okay. Not that bad."

Belen puts a finger to her lips, indicating we all need to all shut our mouths. The angry sound of treads on dirt rolls above us, moving slowly.

"You think they're looking for something?" I do my best whisper, which I still haven't mastered. The group erupts in a wave of hands and mouthing 'shh!' and some words I can't quite make out by lip reading. How does a person whisper? It's not like I have the exact same vocal cord structure as a real person, what do they want from me?

The vehicle is armored. Not exactly a standard mine worker utility vehicle. There's no cannon protruding from its front, but that doesn't mean it isn't armed. We stare up steeply aware that one wrong move off the ledge will bring the heavy vehicle down on top of us. We'd have no chance of getting out of the way before it barrels us down. Maybe next time we spread out...

The armored beast rips the road apart as it continues out of view going downhill the direction we came from. "Where did that deploy, if it came from higher up?" Mav asks. "It's headed to where we left the car. They might come back looking for us."

Belen kicks at the two-foot-wide path at our feet. "Let's keep going." Her finger points across the nearest ravine, and out to the mountain beyond. At a tiny cabin barely visible in the distance.

"How are we going to get over there?" Gordon asks. His skin has regained some color, but his cheeks are flushed in a way that suggests he still has some vomit eager to jump ship. "This ravine goes all the way down."

My eyes skate along the steep mountain we're perched on like regular goats. It's not so steep that we lose our footing, but it's enough to provide that tipsy feeling one gets when two depths within the visual field don't agree on a stopping point. Clouds blow through the space between us and the cabin, haunting the ravine with cold mist. "How can you tell how far down it goes?" I push my scanners to their limit to try to measure the bottom, but don't get a ping. My systems proving less and less reliable.

"Let's go." Belen takes lead ahead of Mav down the path. "A crossing."

"A bridge?" Gordon asks relief in his voice, the hold of his shoulders, and the tightness of his neck. "Sweet."

"I don't know how I feel about a bridge." Mav drags his toes, side-stepping in the steeper sections of path. "How high up is it?"

Juan stays in the rear, keeping watch over the rest of us. I move around Mav so that I'm closer to Gordon, nearer the back of our party. Again, I try my best at a whisper. "Who do you think Juan is, really?"

"He told us already, he's like five people or something." Gordon sounds irritated at having to endure conversation while suffering his current condition.

"No. Yeah... I know." Talking with words is such a hindrance. I wish I could upload the images and ideas floating through my mind right to Gordon's brain. It'd take five seconds to sort out my question and there wouldn't be any confusion about what I'm asking. "Who do you think is Juan, though?"

Gordon keeps step with Mav, not looking up at the scenery. He doesn't answer me. I follow in reluctant silence, observing the bird life and other wild animals inhabiting trees and plants around us. The deeper we move into the shade of the mountain, the thicker the tree coverage and animal activity. There weren't animals in the game. They're new to me. They make sounds without patterns governing them, no playlist or order of operations. One bird flies low into a branch, tangling in the thick leaves. That wouldn't happen in the game. If it did, it'd signal something was wrong. I mean, if there were birds and the birds started doing weird things like forgetting how to fly. This real world is so much different.

"What if he's not a person?" Mav's voice says, muffled by the fact he doesn't turn around to speak to us. And that he's walking quickly to keep up with Belen.

I look back at the fallen bird. It's not a person. Already lost on what Mav might be talking about.

"Juan might be a program," Mav says.

"You don't think he's a donor?" I ask, remembering the question I posed to Gordon, who never answered, by the way.

"Does it matter?" Gordon says between us.

And it doesn't.

28

More birds fly sporadically—no one programming their flight paths from computer labs. I look around the group to see if anyone else finds the bird behavior liberating. Maybe the humans don't notice anymore. Living without parameters does that to a lifeform, I'm sure.

"Hey, Juan." I slow up, so I can walk closer to him. The path isn't wide enough for side by side travel. "Don't you love how the birds can't fly here? No one tells them how. No one programs their flight pattern and they just fly straight into trees and no one cares or thinks twice about it."

"They what?" Juan grabs just below my shoulder, holding me back. His eyes trained on the air. Sure enough, another bird dives at a strange angle, not making landing, but smashing into the foliage below. "Gordon." Juan releases my bicep and scoots beyond me toward Gordon. "How do you feel?" he asks.

"Terrible," Gordon admits. His face has gone from flushed to clammy. Sweat clings to his hairline trapping dirt from our climb against his forehead.

"Mav?" Juan pushes beyond Gordon as well. "Mav?" He puts a hand on Mav's back.

Mav turns to respond but instead vomits off to the side of the path.

"Mav has altitude sickness as well," I say in a low sympathetic manner.

"I don't think so." Juan studies the ridgeline in the distance. His finger traces the web like trail of electrical wire. "Not that." He lifts his gaze to where the cellular tower glints in the lowering sunlight. "Belen, how are you holding up?"

Belen has a hand against a tree trunk as if she's in need of support to her balance.

"What is it?" I ask lamely. How does Juan magically know what's happening? This isn't a computer world. There are no coded expectations or equated reactions. There isn't the ability to statistically predict events or account for the random choice factor of human life. This world is completely unpredictable. Yet, here's Juan going all 'I've already conducted all the algorithms to determine the correct solution for this highly anticipated scenario.' Stupid Juan.

"We need to get out of signal range of that tower." He points to the cell tower. We all squint our eyes in its direction, even though we don't have to look to know what he's talking about. "Can you sense it in the air?"

I pause. Pushing my data search outward does nothing. No feedback. Like all my scans hit a glass wall and bounce back with no information. "I don't know what you're talking about. My sensors won't pick up anything out here."

"Exactly." He points to the tower. "This close to a cell relay and we've got nothing? We're being jammed."

"Intelligence can't be jammed." Mav stumbles behind us. "I know the programs. It's like human brains—no mind control. It was part of the guarantee we provide donors and their families."

"Don't tell me what I can't be!" Juan gets in Mav's face.

"Nazrete?" I ask low and annoyed.

"Sorry, it's hard to reign in the indignation sometimes," Juan says. "But we're definitely being signal blocked." When Juan says 'we' I wonder if he's referring to him and me, or him and all of what makes up 'him'.

Gordon swats at a flying bug almost as thick around as his wrist. "Can you believe the size of these things?" He loses balance in the effort and trips on a large protruding rock.

I elbow toward Juan. "He wouldn't last a minute on Fearscape."

"On what?" Juan tips his head in an exact replica of human curiosity. Like he has no idea what I'm talking about.

"Maybe no one had a fear of massive insects in your program. It was messed up."

Juan remains with his mouth slightly ajar, and the look of someone running around in their memory banks to find the conversation thread where what I'm talking about has context. His eyes unglaze, with nothing to comment.

"Did you not have to 'Face Your Fears?'" I use air quotes for the level's catchphrase.

"We need to hurry out of cell range." Juan avoids answering my question.

Our human guides stumble down the steep path flopping from tree trunk to tree trunk to prevent them falling flat on their faces. Lucky for humans that this hillside grows anything in rich abundance.

"Almost there," Belen manages through a cough.

"Do you trust where she's leading us?" I say to Juan. "I mean, how long have they been sick like this? Gordon was showing symptoms before we left the road." I keep my sights on Belen, mostly to be sure she isn't listening to me at the moment. "Is she even on our side?"

"Shut up, Jennie," Mav mutters.

Juan doesn't defend me. "She wouldn't walk herself into cellular sickness zones on purpose."

"There!" Belen points triumphantly toward something so uninspired, I wonder if she's beyond sick and entered the realm of delusional.

Still a good distance below us, a wood platform juts out from the safety of the mountainside—like a lakeside dock, except no water collects below the planks to cushion a fall. Only deep, jagged, tree and rock-lined ravine lie below the dock, at a much steeper and less forgiving angle than the portion of mountain we now traverse. I daresay it's a cliff with a gangplank jutting out from its clutches.

"What is that?" I ask. Tall splintered posts rise at the sides of the dock with a thick cable strung between them. Attached to that 'H' like structure is another thick cord yawning out over the depths, disappearing into the mist. A frayed rope wraps around one side post. The best I can do is stare at the structure below us and then search for a better option to the term 'there'. Something more inspiring, less decrepit, dilapidated, decayed. This antiquated pirate contraption cannot be our destination.

"A zipline," Juan speaks with inflection. A good indicator it isn't 'Juan' speaking, but one of his alter personalities. "Sweet."

"Zipline..." Mav stops advancing, decidedly less thrilled than Juan. I'm with Mav.

"Oh..." Gordon loses his stomach for the third time. "Ugh."

"My sentiments exactly." No way do I trust that rickety contraption to hold all my weight. I don't know for sure how much the metal in my body adds up to, and I know Geo's developed a lighter weight, more agile material for all the replacement parts I now have, but still. I'm made of heavy elements. People are made of hollow bones. What do they weigh at most? Probably not a half ton. That's my guess. "Not doing it."

"It's secure." Belen urges us downward toward the ravine diving board.

"I'm not—that things not built to support AI," I say following our sickly band of fools. By that, I mean nothing about what I can see gives me a 'secure' feeling. The air smells of wild olive trees, moss, and whatever jumped ship out of Gordon's insides.

It takes a few more switchbacks to reach the platform. It's worse up close. The boards making up the flooring are split in several places. The posts at the sides of the dock have exposed roots, revealing how the wood attempts to hold itself to the mountainside. No cement footings to be seen. I can't take my eyes off the eroding earth the planks are built over. Damp earth chunks away into the misty depths as we crowd the cliff ledge.

"I'll go first," Juan offers.

It's impossible to determine if he's being gentlemanly, selfish, or if

Nazrete is the one speaking. No matter. I don't stop him. I even back out of the way, to give him more room to maneuver. No one argues, not even Belen. I sort of expected her to demonstrate the safety of the contraption she's lead us to, but perhaps at closer inspection, she's changed her confidence.

Belen takes hold of the frayed rope and pulls in long coils. A high rusted gear creak-rolls against the line with every tug. Birds jump to the air then resettle on high branches several times over, at the highest range of gear squeak. I feel that way too, a little on edge. Eventually, a knotted stick appears from the clouds beyond. Gordon and Mav both gasp at the sight of the stick meant to carry them across the mysterious abyss.

The rope used to pull the seat back remains tied to the post. It's probably the only means of recovering the seat from this side. Belen motions Juan up to the wood platform. She mimes the action of straddling the stick with the rope between her legs. Juan copies, holding the cord connecting the stick to the zip line in both hands. Even though we don't breathe, I notice he tenses all his tendons and tests the spring in his joints.

"I'm feeling better, actually," Gordon announces. "Anyone else?"

Belen and Mav both exchange curious expressions like they're inventorying their internal 'betterness' ratings. "Yeah, much better. I mean, aside from the fact I'm standing at the edge of a cliff. That's never a good feeling," Mav says.

"Belen? You good?" Juan asks, giving the rope between his legs a tug. The line bounces and chimes out into the cloud cover like one long out of tune guitar chord, chirping its way across the acoustic gap.

"Yes, Yes. I'm fine."

At that Juan nods one time, cocks his robot head to one side in a 'here's goes nothing' cavalier demeanor, and lunges off the edge of the dock. The cords scream and smoke under his weight but hold.

"Ah!" Needle sensations ping every nerve ending starting at the tip of my brain and reverberating outward to every inch of my system. It's like being stuck with toothpicks in every centimeter of skin, while my spinal cord is being plucked. I fall to my knees, barely able to pry my concern from myself enough to take in my surrounding reactions.

"Juan!" Belen, Gordon, and Mav all scream for Juan. Meanwhile, I'm right here, obviously in some kind of intolerable distress. If Juan wants attention he should just jump. Right now I expect someone to help me. Not perfect immortal Juan.

Everywhere hurts, except the ripped and torn section of my arm, possibly due to not getting all the feeling back in that section of my body yet. I continue hollering. The group on land rushes to the platform, all of them shouting after Juan. "Guys," I manage between tortured hollers, fall to my knees, unable to continue standing under this mysterious torment. "Something's wrong...guys!"

"Juan!"

I wrap my arms tight over my head and squeeze, hoping maybe the additional pressure will ease the home-acupuncture sensation assaulting my senses. Miraculously it helps a little, but only where my gaping wrist hole touches my head. To test the theory, I press that section of arm tighter to my scalp and the brain shaking stabs abate enough to move to a spot where I can see what everyone is staring at.

The zip line is about a third of the way out over the ravine, the chord dips and rises with the breeze, but not the weight of Juan. There is no Juan on the wooden seat. "Where's Juan?"

Gordon answers without turning to look at me. "He fell."

Head pain flares. I press my arm harder against my hair, determined to stay coherent enough to be of some use. "But where is he?" I say stupidly.

"He fell, Jennie. He fell." Mav loses patience. "Where do you think he is?" He points to the deep divide between us and the other side.

Keeping my arm steady and firm to my skull, I fight to control the wince building from the needling still pinging most of the surface of my skin. "But...I don't hear him."

"What part of 'he fell' don't you understand?" Mav hollers.

"He's a robot." I thrust my arm out for emphasis, but the result is instant unrelenting pain, and I drop to the ground before I can regain the pressure patch of open wrist to head. "It's not like he can die from the fall." I remind everyone.

"She's right," Gordon says. "We have to go find him."

"It's a sheer drop." Mav backs away from the edge of the ravine. "There's no way we can climb down that safely."

"We find another way down," Belen offers. "There are more places."

29

Finding another way down does not include shoving me off the side of the cliff to prove my 'he's a robot and won't die' statement, even though I suspect Belen really wants to test the theory.

Instead, Gordon pulls the line back to us. When the stick seat is within reach, Mav flips a pocket knife from his pants. Nothing impressive, just a small metal clip with a moderately dull blade on a bolt hinge so that it swings out. He saws at the rope until it frays itself loose from the swing, which jumps once freed from its tether and skips away down the line out of reach—effectively promising decent as our only crossing option left.

"Grab it!" Gordon calls, too late. Luckily Belen is faster than me and manages to catch the end before we're totally stranded.

"Now what?" I ask.

"Repel." Mav hefts the lengths of rope like he's testing its integrity based on its weight.

"Belen said there might be other paths down," I point out.

"But then we'll be searching for where Juan fell." Mav double checks where the tow rope secures to the post. The post does not boast strength in itself. I wonder if, without the added stability of its pair, the post won't hold a person. "If we descend here, we're more likely to find him."

"More likely? As in there's a chance we won't?" I say pressing my arm so hard against my head, my whole-body leans with the pressure.

"I don't hear him," Gordon reminds us. "What if there's a river or an animal?"

"Wouldn't we have heard him hit?" I say.

"Not with you screaming like that," Mav sounds anything but empathetic.

"Oh, yeah. Sorry." I don't hide my irritation. "Sorry my head's exploding and my nervous system's going napalm. So sorry to inconvenience you with all that."

"Do you need to recharge or something?" Gordon asks.

I turn my whole body, so I can face Gordon without talking through my arm, which I refuse to move from where it's pressing into my face. It's the only thing keeping me from screaming the insane elevated system stimulus that feels like fire erupting from everywhere inside me. "No. Juan and I both took turns charging in the car."

Mav tosses the rope into the mountain pit. It's not a loud sound, but the motion draws all our attention. The rope dances in rounded waves that worm back up to us once it slaps the musty wall of earth we're standing above. "Who's first?"

"Not me!" I call out. No one fights me for coward dibs. And no one complains. It seems I'm the last person they want to be the first person down.

"I'll go." Gordon takes the length of rope out of Mav's hands, then slides five inches when the weight of the hanging section pulls him toward the edge of the platform, which cracks and slides toward the gaping maw. Gordon drops the rope, reaching for the post nearest him.

"Don't let go," Mav warns, but Gordon still doesn't have his balance and can't reach for the fallen rope and the post for support at the same time.

Gordon swings his arms windmill style, slapping the air for something to mute his stumbling, finding nothing.

"Grab the rope!" Mav takes a step closer to Gordon to assist. His broad weight impresses on the dock with another split and pop of wood. Gordon lunges forward, falling against the dock face down.

Rotted wood separates from the platform where it's snapped and Gordon slides with it as it dips into the abyss. His hands slapping for rope, or anything to grab. He'd probably settle for a snake if he thought it'd give him leverage to stop falling.

Everything slips away. I can't look but hear chunks of wood hitting tree trunks and knocking sideways in a game of random bouncing from one ping to the next. The rope's gone taut when I open my eyes.

"Gordon!" I rush to the post, careful to have something for support. My protective arm lowers for only a second, but I replace it just as quickly. Can't do that—too much pain.

Mav and Belen cling to the post as well.

"Don't everybody hang on that post!" Gordon hollers up. "I can feel it slipping out of the earth with all your weight on it."

We all step back, holding nothing, respecting his insight. Because we felt it move just a little as well, and we're better off staying together. Which means we all have to go down the rope.

Gordon continues to descend. No one thought about how to belay. Gordon isn't the most in shape guy. He's not overweight, but there's more to being fit than pounds. It only takes thirty seconds for him to mention anything. "My arms are shaking."

"Can you wrap the rope around your waist?" Mav calls down.

"Not now!" Gordon raises his voice. I'm sure if he wasn't afraid of expending his much-needed energy for holding onto the rope, he'd add more to his response such as 'that would have been a good suggestion a minute ago' or 'thanks dumbass' or maybe, 'why don't you get down here and wrap it around my waist for me?'. But he doesn't say anything more.

"Go down faster," Belen suggests. I'm not sure if the guys are understanding her Spanish better, but it's seeming less weird to me that she speaks mostly in her own tongue. Maybe we're just really good at context clues. Both Mav and I nod in agreement, not that Gordon can see it. Gordon needs to get down faster.

Mav cups his hands around his mouth, projecting his voice down the cliff. "Cover your palms with your shirt, or some kind of cloth, and slide."

Gordon doesn't respond, but the rope shakes accompanied by the sizzle sound of a hot zipper.

"Gordo?" Mav calls. "Can you hear me, man?"

Still the zipping sound. "I can't stop."

"Use your feet." Mav presses his own feet into the dirt like he's got the passenger brake on a student teaching vehicle.

"I can't, it's not working," Gordon yells, but it comes at us faint and frantic. How far down is the bottom? "I see the end of the rope!"

"Okay, great, you're almost there." Mav's face lights with relief, he shines hope at Belen and me, on the verge of laughter. The man can't handle heights. It's obvious he's terrified to attempt the climb down to Juan.

"No," Gordon calls.

"What?" Mav's smile drops without a crease of its memory. "Gordo?"

"The rope ends, but there's... I can't stop!"

"Gordon!" Finish your damn sentence. "What's there?"

"Nothing. Nothing's at the end of the rope. No earth."

The zipping sound tightens. I imagine Gordon choking the line, burning through fabric and skin to slow his fall. Then the line bounces.

"Gordo!" Mav screams down. He leans so far over the edge, I think he might fall as well.

"Mav, step back." The tips of my fingers on my good hand hover over Mav's shoulder, ready to grab him if I must. "Away from the edge."

"I didn't hear him hit, did you?" Mav spins to face us. "Did you hear him hit the ground?"

"No." Belen looks up as though the sky or her forehead holds the memories of whether or not Gordon's body struck earth.

"Gordo!" Mav screams again. "Gordo..." Mav removes his shirt, rips it in two and wraps a half around each hand. He lifts the now loose rope and circles his waist with it. He holds one padded palm at his hip with the rope secure in his grip and the other in front of him and out slightly, so his arm is bent, showing off a lot of well-defined muscles.

I remember thinking Ace had the same defined build. In the game, I assumed Ace's appearance was invented, which it was. He invented himself to look like his brother—who it turns out has unbelievable, very real, physical definition.

"I'm coming." Mav sits back into the hold of the rope, almost as if he's resting on the hand at his hip. He's at the edge of the land above the ravine. None of us steps foot at the broken platform. He cocks his head to the side once, his internal conversation shows by the movement of his mouth, arguing with himself about taking that first step. Then, he does.

Once Mav drops enough distance to ensure he won't overhear me talk to Belen, I say to only her, "We might be the only ones left."

Belen slowly turns toward me. The expression on her face, far from commiserate.

"Not that I want that," I stammer. "I'm not rooting for that...or you know. I'm just saying..." Genuinely, I have no idea how to recover this. "It's not like we're going to continue to copy the same folly behavior, though...right?" She's not going to do the same thing if we lose Mav too, is she?

I wait for Belen to answer. The language barrier means I need to give longer wait time, I think. Except that wait time keeps extending. I have no other human comparison up here with me now. I can't look to Mav with the expression of, 'has this been a weirdly long wait time?' in order to judge what to do next, or when. Or if I should look away or something so it looks less like I expect Belen to answer me. At this point, I'd be less surprised if she climbed to the top of the post and leaped to her ravine-splat death instead of responding to me.

"Good call," I respond after so long Belen looks at me again. I'm unsure if I'm programmed to feel embarrassed, or if it simply comes naturally to my existence. I mean, I'm essentially the brainwave elements of failed donors. Failure is sort of my MO. Embarrassment feels worse.

"Jennie." Mav's voice carries from the pit.

Belen and I both lean farther, pressing our ears closer to the sound and farther from safety. "Do you see anything?" I shout down.

"The rope stops above the tree line." The trees here are overtly healthy. Like trees that grow triple the size of what Mexico managed under ideal conditions.

"How far you think?"

A long pause. "I don't know."

Totally unhelpful. Why bother pausing to answer, if he's not even going to estimate a response? "Can you climb back up?"

"I don't know."

If he was standing next to me, I'd do something. Something equally annoying to the response 'I don't know'. Like maybe flick his ear, or pull out three hairs individually. "What's your plan?"

"I can't make it back up," he says. "My arms are spent."

"What if I pull the line up?" I can tell by the way the open canyon swallows our sounds and how the mist of cloud cover cushions our words like we're hollering with pillows over our faces, there's a great distance between us. Also, it's not a short rope. It's long. The bottom of this canyon is exceptionally deep.

"I can't hold on that long, not for the ride up."

"Yes, you can," I say.

"I told you, I'm spent." His voice sound strained, but that could be the effort to throw volume up to us from the depth he's descended.

"What other options do you have?" I scream and lean maybe too close. My foot slips and I think 'idiot! You're going over.' Until a firm, but a small hand grabs my shirt, pulling the slack out of the fabric with her balled fist, yanking me back. I weigh a million times more than Belen—and that's only slightly exaggerating—but her support gives me the split second I need to regain my footing.

"Thanks," I say in a winded tone. I don't get winded, mind. I don't breathe, so it's an emotional response more than a physiological reaction.

"I'm letting go." Mav's voice comes out like a hoarse roar.

"Mav, no!"

The rope bounces with the absence of weight pulling it taught.

30

B elen lifts the rope, wraps it once around her waist.

"Are you crazy?" I yank it away, pulling Belen and the rope away from the mouth of the fall.

"No." Belen yanks back.

"They've all fallen."

Belen continues to prep by binding her hands with material from the bottom of her pants.

"Stop it." I wasn't far off about Belen possibly jumping to avoid talking with me, but damned if I thought I was being dramatic. Passing the time via mental melodrama. I never thought she'd actually repeat the failed behavior the last two guys who tried. She doesn't stop. Her back to the ledge, she sits into her hold, imitating Mav beautifully. If he were here, I'm certain he'd be proud of his role modeling accomplishment.

"What am I supposed to do?" I ask. "Repeat the same nonsense?"

Belen makes no effort to answer my question. Instead, she looks where my arm is still pressed firmly against my head. Like somehow the fact I'm stuck with my arm in this ridiculous position just so I can function proves something, or answers something, or means something.

It doesn't. It's just the way it is until I can figure out what the problem is, where the torturous feedback originates from and eliminate the stimulus. I'd suspect Juan had something to do with the feedback, but he fell like an anvil and hasn't made so much as a whimper since.

And then, Belen steps out and down. She's over the ledge and makes regular step-step-slide of the rope progress. She doesn't communicate with me. All I can do is wait.

Do I follow after her? Wait? Lament the fact I'm with a bunch of morons who don't understand their own mortality? Humans are mortal. It's their definition. I'm not human. But part of me feels mortal even still. In this world, things have a sense of finite, limited, fragile. There's no leveling up. If anything, life here is varying degrees of tradeoffs on a long-angled level, sliding ever faster toward 'end'.

The line remains rigid with swinging motions indicating Belen still hangs on.

"You alright?"

"Go down."

She wants me to add my weight to the rope while she's still on it? That sounds like very poor judgment. "I don't know if that's a good idea, Belen."

"Come!"

"I'm just not sure about your logic, right now." I holler down what I hope are appeasing explanations as to why I'm not climbing on that rope. Not now while she's on it, and probably not even if she decides to drop as the others did. I'm not about to follow erroneous behavior to the same tragic result. "...what with everyone dropping from unknown heights and no one seems to be feeling well for the last, I don't know how many hours." Then it hits me. No one is in their right mind. No one.

"Belen!" I shout but keep talking before allowing enough time for her to answer. "Stop!"

"*Basta!*"

"No. STOP." I assume *basta* means she's about to drop like she's had it with everything and is ending it on her own terms, but who knows. *Basta* could mean 'I've stopped' for all my translation skills work. "Before you go another inch, just tell me..." How to phrase my question so it doesn't trigger her to do something stupid? "What do you think will happen if you drop? No, no, no... I mean, what do you think happened to the others when they dropped?" Stop saying 'drop' dangit! "No. I mean, what are you thinking?" It comes out more motherly than I intend. But, seriously, what are they all thinking?

The rope pings upward, void of weight pulling it to earth.

"Belen!" I reprimand. "I told you to stop!"

Rebels never listen.

I have a choice to make. Repeat actions that have proven faulty time after time. Or walk away. I turn to face uphill. The path erodes where our feet pushed grass and flowers out by the roots, the dirt falls deep from our muddy shoeprints.

A wisp of cottony mist wraps around me, winding up the path and covering evidence of where we changed the landscape. I turn toward the cold condensation rolling in around me. I can no longer see the edge of the ravine, the platform, or even where rock peeks through the greenery. Only the high posts at the mouth of the openness mark danger. If we found this place in the state it's in now, we'd all have toppled over its edge before realizing what we'd done. All of us together. Not one of us walking off alone and unharmed.

"Not saying that's any reason." I sidestep with my single available hand extending to catch the post at my level. "I'm not going to just jump." My injured arm remains pressed tight to my head like I'm glued in an eternal exasperated sigh. I bend down and twist the rope around my forearm for leverage. My nervous system can feel the fibers against my skin, but I imagine I don't feel pain like humans do. Even if things go wrong, or my single arm isn't strong enough to hold my weight, it won't hurt if I get a little rope burn or something.

I am so freaking wrong.

31

Several oversights occur at once. First of all, my single arm isn't up to the task of holding all my weight. It might be the fact my sensors aren't providing me with accurate information and I'm truly blind in this cloud forest. I lose track of the edge and step off the side of the mountain without warning, my arm jolts when my weight catches against the rope, dislocating the ball joint that connects my robot arm to my robot shoulder. The wires and cords stringing in and through the metal framework that is me, remain intact, stressing under the strain of keeping the rest of me connected to my arm, which is tangled in the rope.

Rope does, in fact, burn, sear, and rip the outer layer of my fake skin. For a being whose sensors are kaput, whatever system registers discomfort inside me works at full capacity. I might go as far as to claim it's overcompensating for the lack of other sensory input.

Or maybe it's the combination of the rope burn, dislocated shoulder, and the fact it's nearly impossible to keep my other arm pressed to my skull to dull the brain cord pain chorus now undimmed as my free arm flails in the open air all around me. Fire needles attack from all sides. I slip just a little but get no closer to the basepoint where the rope ends. I'll wager I'm only a fathom deep in this air abyss. What's that— twenty nautical feet? Why do I even know that? It's not helpful.

My rope tangled arm holds firm to the spot, not sliding much more than a few inches, and maybe a little skin stretching in addition. The rope tightens around my bicep. I'm unable to do anything to help myself

It's possible I'll be trapped like this forever. Unable to die, no surviving friends to rescue me, unable to save myself. Why didn't I walk away? I'll be lucky enough when my battery wears down, but I'll still be here, my body collecting data, even when powered off. It's the way of all computerized devices these days. So that, when or if I ever get rebooted, I'll have stored the entire torturous experience to relive in my memories as if I'd been awake the whole time.

I drop an inch. It's difficult to decide if I've really fallen another inch with all the pain sensors going nuts. I stare up the length of rope, squinting through pain to see what's happening with the rope. I slip again. The rope drops and me with it. Stress on my shoulder tugs and jolts with the sudden give of slack and then the catch.

"What's happening?" I call up, half expecting a face to appear over the ledge above. I'm ready to scream even if a leaf falls from the general platform area. Nothing makes itself known, which terrifies me in a different way.

"Help!" I scream. "Help!" No sound from above or below. "Somebody help me!" The rope gives again, this time an entire foot. I bounce wildly on the rope and the post falls toward the ledge, sticking out at a ninety-degree angle with the rope making one of the sides and the post being the other side of the angle. I'm spinning and jostling from the movement before the post starts pointing toward me like it's singling me out, giving me the finger—a solitary and very large condemnation of poor judgment.

Once the post has me in its sights, the rope slides from its splintered claim. There's nothing I can do except watch in abject horror as I lose sight of it to the mist. Cracking, snapping and crumbling follow shortly after the rope, I try to reduce my flailing as I fall, holding the rope with my barely working hand, like this will somehow make a difference. It's falling with me, and above me the post tumbles end over end, disrupting the cloud cover in a spiral wave. The post cuts the fog. Will its spin increase its velocity or slow it? The post appears to be moving faster each time one of the ends is nearer to me and to be losing speed when the ends aren't pointed my direction. So probably falling at the same rate. Lack of computer-like sensory analysis makes me dumb.

There isn't much time to feel dumb before a branch whip slaps the rope falling before me, pulling me sideways in my flail-fall. I have seconds before I'm in the branches. I aim for wide thick limbs to slow my fall. Each one a solid swing to the gut, thighs, chest, or shins. I'm beaten on all sides by the time I hit the ground.

The post lands stuck upright next to me, vibrating with the depth it sinks into the earth and remains planted. Likely to take root and grow among the forest. Everything grows here, teeming with life, except my group. I survey my close encounter with a post piercing and notice little more than large splinters of broken tree line.

Sitting hurts. Stupid human idea to include pain receptors in artificial intelligence housing. My good arm dangles at my side, still tangled in rope. "Genius." I force my ripped wrist arm to work at freeing my other arm. I've yet to gain full motion in this arm since the last upgrade. When I was caged in Geo's facilities for months, it took days. It's only been days since my arm was switched. How is that possible?

"Stop shouting." Off to my side, near to where the post stands stock upright planted half deep in earth, Mav groans.

"Mav!" I forgo getting my arm free of rope and drag myself along the ground the where he lays on his side, branch trunks broken all around him. "Mav, you're okay?"

"I'm not dead." He coughs, as though the effort to clear his lungs causes more obstructed pain elsewhere. He doesn't roll over or make any attempt to face me.

"Can you move?"

"Can you?" His voice lacks all the vibrato he jumped with.

"Sort of. My shoulder's out."

"I see you brought the post." Next to him is where the long wood beam sticks from the ground. The sound that comes from him might be a laugh, or it might be a wince. "How far did you fall?"

"A ways. You?"

"Just above the tree line. That's where the rope gave out."

"The others?" I ask.

"Juan's helping us based on most vital injuries to least. I guess I drew the short straw."

"Juan's okay?" I'm unable to hide my irritation that he never called back up to us, or if he did, we didn't hear him. Is that even possible? "Did you yell up once you hit?"

"I tried," Mav admits. "Sort of got the wind knocked out of me."

"And Gordon?"

"Juan helped him first. I think he's okay, just helping with Belen. She's pretty shaken up. We tried to tell you both to stay, find a different way down like Belen suggested after Juan fell."

"It's her own fault. She wouldn't listen..."

Mav cuts in before I finish, coughing and strained like it's more important to stop me from talking than it is to be in reduced pain. "She's not upset about that. She's upset because she was compelled to jump."

"Is that what she told you?" I use the post for leverage to get to my feet, indignant at Belen's accusation against me. "I told her not to get on that rope."

"Not you. In her brain. I felt it too." He tries to prop himself up on his elbow but lays back down. "In my head was all this feedback, like I should jump."

"You mean like Juan?"

"He didn't jump, his head just filled with signal feedback and he let go without thinking."

I think back to the signal overload from earlier and realize I'm not covering my head with my ripped arm. I'm not in unavoidable searing head pain either. I'm in pain, but it's different. The other pain was like an instrument of mind death. The agony now can all be related to hurling myself off a mountainside. "Is he okay?"

"Juan?" Mav gives me a look like he suspects I have hidden motives for asking about Juan, embarrassing hidden motives.

I nod without the slightest blush, not because I'm incapable, but because I'm capable of concealing such humiliation.

"He's a little dinged up. Don't say too much about his hair, okay?"

"My head doesn't hurt. The buzzing or whatever," I say.

"Yeah. We're all better. No vomiting from altitude sickness down here, other than from new injuries. And no sudden urge to hurl ourselves off tall structures." Mav fears heights, I know this. He descended the rope to rescue Gordon, not because some voice told him to leap. Right?

"What do you think it was?" I ask.

"Whatever it was, it's not good."

Juan steps from the thick tree line. "I suggest we continue traveling on the valley floor." He lifts a battered hand, but my eyes travel to the side of his head, where the hair and skin have been pulled away. His warm eyes and sharp chin remain where they should be, but his right ear and the hair above and behind where his ear should be—all the way to the nape of his neck—is exposed cellulose bags, tubing, and wires over a metal structure. "Stay out of range of all cell towers." The excess skin and hair bunch at his shoulder like a burp rag. "Hi, Jennie."

"Hi."

"Need help with that?" He nods to my hanging shoulder.

"What?" I stop myself from staring at his ruined once-perfect face. "Uh, yeah." I shake my head to stop from staring, secretly hoping I don't look as bad as he does.

"Does it hurt?" Juan asks. He sounds sincere like he genuinely cares about how my new and improved shell translates pain to my brain. But I remember that it isn't just Juan I'm talking with, even if he's the one talking now. It's a whole slew of individuals, some of whom might have mixed feelings about me.

It's impossible to know how any response might be taken. If I say it hurts, a Civ might smile inwardly. An Ed might spout some oration of statistics regarding pain resonation and an AK... I don't know how an AK would feel about my pain. Civilian, Academic, and Military source codes are the ones I'm most familiar with.

When I don't answer, Juan's cadence changes, though not his vocal register. His words come out deep and smooth but as a challenge. "Pain should sharpen your skills. Don't waste it feeling sorry for yourself." He preps my imitation skin for the action of jarring my arm back into the shoulder socket.

"Where are you from, Nazrete?" I avoid arguing with her about what purpose pain has. It must have some purpose, or I wouldn't be programmed to feel it. Then a horrible thought crosses my mind.

The Mord. Are they programmed to feel pain in this new human experience they're having? Inside the game, they showed no response to pain, but I never stopped to question if they experienced it or not. And if they did, what was the purpose of feeling it?

"Saudi Arabia."

Juan's response arrives slow. I've moved on with my thoughts and practically forget what I asked her. "Sorry what?"

"I'm from Saudi. We had to fight to retain our resources. As women and as a nation. Our war won us more than wealth. We got on the donor list." Juan lifts my arm to a forty-five-degree angle, finding the perfect angle to slip the joint together, but there is no slip about it. He pops it with such force and pressure, I lose my balance. He lets me fall, probably aware that if he tries to right my balance he'll end up pulling my arm back out of location. I try to catch myself before slamming sideways into the dirt, but my left hand is still crap with reflex motions. "Use the pain," he says again.

I wipe dirt from my mouth. My good hand useful again. "Thanks, Juan." Unfeigned irritation in each syllable.

"Gotta look out for each other," Juan answers. I can't tell if the sentiment is still Nazrete and perhaps sarcastic, or if it's someone else and sincere. I really wish he had more physiological indicators regarding the personalities taking lead.

"Wait, Juan," I say before he can disappear into the trees to help the humans recover. Unlike me, they can't be popped back in place and be done. They have to actually heal. "Do you think they feel pain?"

He looks over his shoulder toward the thicker tree line and scoffs. "Yes."

I wave my hand toward the humans. No duh, dude. Not them. "The Mord...You think they can understand?"

Juan steps closer to me. "You have to stop doing that."

"Doing what?"

"Showing concern for Mord." He checks over his shoulder again, but without any indication of humor. "They don't understand when you talk like that."

The humans? What do they care? I don't say it, but Juan responds as if I had, even though I know he's only guessing at my thoughts.

"It scares them."

"Those guys?" I point to the trees.

Juan takes three fast steps, erasing the distance he had just barely walked between us. He puts an arm on my outstretched hand and presses my entire arm to my side. "Yes."

"I don't think we need to be worried about them."

Juan studies my eyes, the space between my brows and the edges of my mouth like he's looking for a clue in the details of my face. "Yes," he says. "We do." And he returns to the thick brush where both Belen and Gordon landed.

"Are they going to heal okay? Be able to travel?" I try to keep Juan talking, hoping he'll give added insight into his state of mind, or whoever's mind I'm talking with.

"A broken rib for Belen and a busted ulna on Gordon." Juan continues walking away.

"Will they be able to travel?" I ask aware human healing is slow.

"Of course. Why wouldn't they?"

"He's intense," Mav says from his place in the dirt once Juan disappears into the leaf cover. It's as though Juan didn't count Mav as an audience, but was highly concerned with the humans out of earshot.

"You think so too?" I ask.

"Maybe it's the same thing that affected us above?" Mav suggests.

"I don't feel anything," I say.

"Yeah." Mav rolls over and sits up, groaning but capable. Apparently, not in as much pain as he's been letting on since I crash landed. "Me, either."

"Is it true?" I ask. Mav blinks, I can tell he's trying to follow back what 'it' links to. What's true. What am I asking in my ambiguous and vague manner? He can't read thoughts as well as Juan. "Do the Mord scare you?"

"Don't they scare you?" he asks.

It confuses me. The posturing between Mav and Juan, as if they're both testing each other. Or are they both testing me and happen to be in each other's crosshairs? Either way, Juan never offers to help Mav. He simply walks away. And Mav doesn't ask for help, but he pretends to be less capable than he actually is. Humans hide things this way. It makes me nervous. I hide things too. I hope I'm better at it than Mav.

"They did once. Now, something else scares me more," I say in response.

32

There's no shortage of splints on the valley floor. Broken limbs, splintered trunks, branches and tons of soft leaf padding. Gordon sports a jungle cast fashioned from wood and leaves from elbow to pinkie. Since the break in his ulna lies closer to the pinkie than the elbow, Juan's careful to incapacitate the entire hand in order to aid healing.

Belen has a tire worth of leaves and fabric wrapped around her chest, cushioning the cracked rib that has to heal on its own. I can't imagine the pain she's in. Every step must ring through her torso with fresh bone jarring heat. She moves slowly as we walk, not twisting toward forest sounds. One arm is bound against her side, trapped in the bands around her torso. I have no idea if that's the correct method to heal a broken rib since my stupid database has been useless since all the upgrades. Belen casts death glares at each swooping bird and chittering insects, then turns her murderous sights on me.

"What do you think's wrong with the cell towers?" I ask Juan in a vain attempt to deflect Belen's glare. I quicken my pace to catch up to him, ahead of the others. They can't walk fast in their condition. Humans heal slowly. Despite visible damage and working nervous systems that alert us to discomfort and pain, healing for us is based on repair skills. If we're put together correctly, we work. No broken bones. If something's broken, it's broken until we replace it.

"Nothing's wrong with the towers," Juan says.

I pause to process. "But you said we should stay out of range...like they're connected to all the problems we're having."

"I stand by that."

Juan is the worst. I slap leaves at my side for growing within strike range. "Then something must be wrong with the towers. Maybe something we can fix."

"There's nothing wrong with the towers, Jennie. They're doing what they're supposed to do."

I run a step to get in front of Juan. Does he even have a clue how frustrating it is to talk to him with not knowing which personality I'm facing and now adding double talk to the mix of worst possible robot traits? "And what is that? What are they supposed to do?"

Juan doesn't pause until he's standing over me. He could walk right through me if he wanted. I can feel the threat of that very thing steaming off his exposed metal framing. "Immobilize us."

I don't say anything. Juan's shoulder drops. He doesn't slam me with it to get me to move, but I pivot out of the way, clearing his path to move forward. I stay where I'm standing. The humans are attacking us. We've been targeted by cellular signals, something that scrambles us. A program intended to immobilize us. "How long would it take to develop something like that?" I ask. "Like a day? A few hours to write that code?"

"Almost a year," Juan says over his shoulder. The rest of the group catches up to where I'm standing.

"What's up with you?" Gordon asks, holding his wrapped arm out, so I won't accidentally bump into it.

I ignore Gordon and jog to get back to where Juan blazes a trail through thick jungle brush. Large insects, snakes, and mountain animals don't concern the two of us. Belen and Mav and Gordon, on the other hand, keep their eyes on every inch of surrounding greenery, most likely searching for some form of biological threat.

"What do you mean, a year? Did you know about this?" I ask.

"Keep up." Juan yanks a large snake from a tree. It snaps, even though its head and neck are too close to Juan's grip for it to get a toothy purchase. Even if it did, all the snake would accomplish is puncturing fake skin. Juan tosses the snake out to the side. Behind us the group adjusts their trail wide in the opposite direction of the thrown snake.

"Why would Geo make a program like that?" I ask. It has to be Geo. How else would Juan know about it? "I thought his whole aim was to expand his artificial empire, not cripple it."

"Geo didn't develop countermeasures," Juan says. He looks over his shoulder. At first, I think he's looking at me. It's hard to tell with his ruined face. I look behind me to see Mav watching us as we walk.

Mav has an intense personality, like his brother. It's easy to misread his body language. Right now, for instance, he has the facial expression of a man who has his sights on someone he doesn't trust, someone who maybe poses a threat to the rest of the party. Someone he wouldn't mind immobilizing—violently, if necessary.

At Mav's side, Belen winces, drawing my eyes away from Mav and the visual lock he has on Juan. Belen looks far too distracted with pain to be concerned with programming. Of course, if whatever Juan is talking about exists, it was developed before today. It's not something Belen would need to worry herself with now. But they wouldn't put something into effect that would have a negative impact on humans as well.

Would they?

I catch up to Juan again. "The humans suffer negative effects too." I point out. "They were all acting weird like they were sick." I recall the birds unable to fly. "And animals were affected by it too. Why would the humans send out a signal that would hurt themselves?"

Juan doesn't speak right away.

Not because he has nothing to say, but because before he can't come up with some version of logic to shatter my point, I add. "They wouldn't."

Juan smooths his fallen facial features into place, then lets his skin drop again. "Who acted sick first?"

The people got sick first. Animals too. Isn't he proving me right? They wouldn't target their own, especially not first. "That's my point."

"Your point is that the humans didn't initiate first strike?" he asks.

Something in my gut sinks. Images from the news monitor inside the car flood back to me. The Mord were under fire. Airstrike. "Mord don't have any defenses here,"

"Before all your sensors went offline, did you notice a radiation spike?" Juan manages to speak low and soft without changing the tense set of his body. I look behind us anyway, checking to see if anyone behind is paying too close attention to our conversation, suddenly hyper-aware of 'sides' involved.

Mav still has his eyes on us. His neck straightens at my peeking behavior. If he wasn't paying attention a second ago, he is now thanks to my suspicious glances backward.

"I didn't notice." I think back to the glass building. All I can recall is trying to transmit a signal and causing myself a lot of head pain.

"I'm not sure what it was exactly. Maybe not radiation."

Curse it, Juan. Don't throw out an accusation like that and not be confident. "But radiation wouldn't affect us. We were clearly affected."

"Not right away." Juan motions me to keep up better, stop checking over my shoulder. But I swear Mav has gotten closer. He's not between Gordon and Belen anymore. He's leading them. "The signal that hurts us was return fire," Juan says. "I know military procedure better than anyone. We're at war."

"Do you have an AK in there?" I say. Military know-how, strategic posturing. Of course, a GenAK would assume any problems in our system would be an act of war.

"I'm not a brainless infantryman," Juan says.

For one thing, I'm tired of Juan not announcing whoever the heck is speaking in the first place, and I'm not too impressed with how these personalities can't seem to get along despite the fact they're trapped together. "Why don't you drop the tough guy act and admit you're throwing out conspiracy-level accusations?" I lean in closer. "And scaring the crap out of me for no reason." I point up to where the cell tower might be in relation to how far we've traveled. "You're full of crap and don't know anything about what's going on or how to fix it."

"I'd prefer if you called me Commander," Juan says. "And I've never made a false accusation in my life."

33

If I had blood, which I don't, it'd be cold right now. Whatever runs through my cords and wires, lubricants or transmission fluids, whatever, it's all gone cold.

Juan is the Commander.

The Commander is Juan.

Except the Commander isn't an official donor. Geo admitted that it was a program designed to prevent Ace from winning. Something to be one step ahead of Ace at every hack, cheat, and backdoor. Admittedly, the deterrent became wildly out of hand.

Then again, Ace created me within the game and I'm the only player who exited the game the way the game was meant to be exited. Or some version acceptable enough, not changed so much that those welcoming me to this world had been alerted to my wrongness.

But the Commander is here. Two of us that don't belong here, are here. The Mord. The Mord are here too. There's more of us on this side of the game that were never supposed to exist at all. "That's a failed program." I want to stop following, but also don't want to alert anyone to trouble.

"Depends on who you ask," Juan responds. He ventures a swivel to keep tabs on Mav, only to find Mav right behind me. "Hey, Mav." When Juan says 'Mav' I can hear it now. It's not brotherly venom. The Commander is mocking him, mocking both of them. Ace for taking on his brother's appearance. And Mav for being only half as brilliant as Ace is. I see it now too. Mav is a joke or would have been inside the game.

"How do you intend to disable the towers?" Mav nods behind us, to where we've departed from. It comes across as a challenge, but I'm not sure if it's meant to be or if I'm on high alert now.

Knowing the Commander is 'base version' Juan changes so much in my ability to cope. The Commander went crazy inside the game—being trapped inside the cage he was supposed to keep locked from other players, only to be a prisoner as well.

"I don't," Juan says.

For reasons I'm incapable of processing in my current state of 'freaking out' Mav's rigid frame relaxes just a little at Juan's response.

"Belen told me about a sanctuary ahead. No signals ever manage to get through." Juan's tone lifts as though he's delivering redemptive news. "Dead zone, they call it." But his words are anything but encouraging.

"Cathedral Ipiales," Belen speaks. I haven't realized how close she is to me. "No signal here." She confirms Juan's claim that our destination is signal free.

"It's supposed to be a safe zone to guard against machines like us," Juan says. "But we need it now."

"This bush is so thick," Gordon complains from where he's left with the bent branches thwapping back at him. "How do we know we're still headed in the right direction?"

"Follow the ravine," Juan speaks in smooth accented words, convincing me of his rightness by how confidently he lays his words down, like a brick layer of ideas I can't push over. "The church is built on a bridge that spans it." The 'Commander' edge vanishes when he's not talking about war. I can't determine if it's a trick he's mastered during the time he's been out of the game, or if he has always been this way and I've never seen him in a non-war setting before now.

We walk in silence a good distance. The humans have to stop for water from moving streams. They have rules to follow about where they can drink from—clear fast-moving groundwater that they can trace where it came out of the earth. I guess the ground is a natural filter system and despite the advances the Intercontinents have made over the years in gaining control of resources and distribution of goods, they still struggle with water sanitation.

Too bad there aren't hard and fast rules regarding what AI to trust. Their world is currently contaminated with every aspect of AI they intended to filter out. The Mord was their first indication they were drinking in contaminated technology as a society. As far as I can tell, the humans developed so many advanced precautionary measures, they ensured only the most devious of cheat codes would ever find a way through.

"Nazrete, I'm curious," I ask. Juan lowers his eyebrows at me, most likely uncomfortable with me addressing one of his personalities directly. Uneasy what it is I might possibly be curious about. "Isn't there still a lot of desert in the Arabic regions of the Intercontinents?"

"Get to the point," Juan says. Nazrete has a way of being short-tempered and lacking patience as well as tact, so it's difficult to know if she answers or someone else who doesn't want to forfeit a conversation to the only female inhabiting their human armor.

"What do you manufacture if all you have is desert?" I push rich green leaves out of my face, letting them slap back toward Mav, who catches the branch without consequence. Once Mav lets go, Gordon grunts, branch-slapped. "The band is about the distribution of resources, right?"

"But what resources do you have?" Mav asks.

"The land doesn't have to be green to have something to offer," Juan/Nazrete says. "You have a misconception of value based on what you've been told has worth."

I don't agree with that sentiment, but this isn't the time to argue about what has worth and what doesn't. "What do they manufacture?" I ask. I put my hands up to defuse any misunderstanding since I know Nazrete is prone to those. "I mean, oil... I know there's oil. Is that it?" To be honest, I'm not sure if I'm intentionally goading the Commander. I probably am.

"Even sand is a commodity if you know how to package it," Juan responds, leaving little room for more discussion.

We endure another span of slow progress peppered with human complaints regarding physical ailments and lack of energy. Their constant moaning about needing food increases. To make the experience worse, I need a charging station soon. "How much farther?"

"Follow the ravine," Juan responds.

"But..." I don't want to fight, but I do want to know what to expect, and when to expect it. If Juan doesn't have the answers, I'd appreciate it if he'd admit that. "Will there be access to a charging port?"

"*No hay esignal,*" Belen pipes up from behind me. It annoys me that she's eavesdropping steady enough to pipe in like that at any time. My questions aren't directed at her.

I turn around, facing Belen and point to my mouth as I articulate with full lip expression. "Charge...charging." I swoop my hand to circle around my mouth for added emphasis. "Power? To plug in? Charging."

"There is no *esignal*," Belen says.

I throw my arms out and let them fall to my sides, grateful my shoulder is holding without complication, and turn around so I no longer face Belen.

"Are we planning to walk through the night?" Gordon asks. "Belen isn't doing too well with her rib. She needs to rest."

We all turn to glare at Gordon. He's not wrong about Belen, but out of the five of us, he groans the most. Granted, he's had the most tree limbs whack him in the face.

"We need to keep moving," Mav says, earning him a glimmer of approval from Juan, which I think Mav appreciates based on the twitch of joy that graces his unsmiling face. That's the thing about approval from the Commander, it's desirable and addictive.

"We haven't seen evidence of anyone following us," Gordon explains.

"They're going to close all borders. If we don't get out of Ecuador before that happens..." Juan doesn't say what.

"Listen," Belen directs. We pause like she's telling us there's a buzz on the wind we need to watch out for. Gordon swats the air over his ear. "If we run, they will think we are enemies."

Gordon chokes trying to stifle a laugh. "...enemies...like we're playing jungle war." He laughs again.

We communally ignore Gordon and continue to wait for Belen to clarify more.

"If we don't get away from the Mord epicenter." Juan raises his eyebrows as if he's talking to a petulant child, reminding Belen that she played a major role in the fact that there is now a 'Mord epicenter.' "We'll be bombed, incapacitated with signal overload, and if you don't recall, we're being accused of terrorism." Juan points to the west, the direction the sun is setting. We came from the east—Quito. Probably not the time to point out his error. I keep it to myself but allow for a little satisfaction that at least I know ordinate directions even without working sensors.

"What's that?" Gordon diverts the attention of the group to a spot in the distance. Blue-gray stonework breaks up the green landscape ahead. A bridge.

"We made it," Mav says with confidence while under Juan's observation, then turns back to Belen and rephrases to allow for error. "Did we make it?"

I quickly swivel my perspective to catch Juan narrowing his eyes at Mav. It's the look of distrust, how I imagine grace slips away from the holy. Spending time in a high-stress situation with anyone is taxing on relationships. We happen to be stuck with people that tax each other's interpersonal skills to the max.

Belen stares at the stones ahead. The structure has medieval spires lifting out of the canyon high above where we trudge on the uneven and narrow valley floor. It's a castle and a bridge and a church all combined into one glorious and overwhelming structure. Sets of three repeats in the design of the building, three spires reaching to heaven, three arches in each window setting, and three peaks. I lose my footing and almost slip toward the river water—the river no one would drink from because we haven't yet tracked all and every tributary.

"I'm guessing no power outlets." Where are Juan and I going to recharge?

"Do you not have solar chargers?" Juan asks. "I've been charging all afternoon." Juan shows me a discrete panel on the underside of his west-facing arm where codes used to be planted. He has a flip top panel to absorb battery power from the sun's rays. First of all, he could have mentioned that earlier, so I could turn mine on if I have such a thing.

I didn't have such a thing in Mexico. I touch my left arm—the ripped one with extra parts and pieces shoved up there for an emergency, but no flipping panel. "They didn't finish," I say as if I'm apologizing for being less well made than Juan.

"Yeah," he says. "I'm sure they were going to add that next."

We share a look. A look that says, once again, I'm missing a major part of my left arm and it's not just where my skin is torn, it's what's supposed to go with it.

"Maybe there's a car." Gordon catches up to where the rest of us mill about gawking at the structure ahead. "You can charge from the battery or something."

"Good old-fashioned jumping." Mav rubs his hands together. I wonder at the meaning of 'jumping'. If, maybe, there is more than one use of the word by how Mav seems impressed with his language choice but I choose not to ask. I'll find out soon enough.

34

The bridge is even more impressive the closer we get to it. The river grows in this section, making it more treacherous to navigate the ravine floor safely. The manmade structure promises a footpath ahead. I hope that offers an ascent option other than climbing since Gordon and Belen might not be capable of climbing back out of the canyon without help.

"Las Lajas." Belen marvels. She has the tone of being in the presence of something sacred. I might be more impressed if I didn't know the term *lajas* means slab or fine rope. I'm assuming in this instance it means slab. Rock slab. Slab is a lot less otherworldly sounding than *laja.*

"Cars." Gordon points out that the sanctuary is, in fact, teeming with cars. "Batteries." He doesn't mention that all the cars are all the same style and have a military appearance to them. I notice. I'm pretty sure Juan notices.

Above us is a tram of some sort—a suspended mode of transportation from one side of the ravine to the other. We all glare at it with distrust.

"What do we do?" Mav asks. "It's obviously being watched."

"Huh?" Gordon reevaluates the bridge. This time he sees the armored aspect to the vehicles, the eerie absence of visible people for the number of vehicles. "Oh, shnike. Do we turn back?"

"No." Belen protests.

To be fair, none of us wants to trudge through the jungle crack any longer, even those of us immune to venom and hunger.

"Commander?" I ask without thinking about what I'm saying. We need a military mind crazy enough to figure out a solution in a winless setting. We actually need the Commander.

Juan half-smiles, then turns to evaluate the bridge sanctuary. I have full confidence he'll find a backdoor, literally or figuratively. It's what he does.

"Who?" Mav and Gordon ask together. Neither of them seems particularly alerted, just curious regarding the title I'm throwing out there. Their curiosity lacking alertness puts all my internal alarms into siren mode.

"Inside joke," I say, noticing how the set in Juan's shoulders dips for a moment and his eyes shift as if chewing on the thought of whether I'm mocking him or not. He observes Mav and Gordon for longer like their reaction determines the degree of his. "It's what we say when we need to solve an impossible puzzle inside the game." I continue to backpedal.

Juan shifts his evaluative gaze to me. I don't want to connect with him necessarily, at least not in the way we connected last game. Maybe humanly-united is a different scenario. We're different people here with unique goals, not mortally opposed to one another by design. Given the option to not be pitted against each other, perhaps the Commander is worth getting to know.

"Hands where we can see them!" Muffled words puff through the air around us, like their being strained through a sieve. The leaves rustle toward us, branches protruding barrel ends in our faces. Green-painted faces with black and brown smudges blending perfectly with gas masks covering every nose and mouth, only broken by the blink of men's eyes. Except for one soldier's unblinking eyes— intense in their dedication to not permit even a flap of skin to curtain us from his view. That soldier becomes aware of my matched gaze and steps backward into ranks, perhaps he thinks he's dissolving from my awareness when he's actually drawing more attention to himself.

I'm not the only one who doesn't lift my hands right away. Belen and Gordon straight up can't. Both of them have at least one bound limb in order to prevent further damage to their bodies. I step back, away from the guns aimed at me, until Juan puts out a hand, directing me to his side. Not protective or arrogant enough to step in front of me—probably a Nazrete influence—but still close enough to get the sense of a security pocket.

Juan jabs his elbow into my spine. "Put your hands up."

I turn to look at his tattered face. The imitation skin flapping in a minor breeze and his robot features glistening in the setting rays of sun. I hadn't realized how unreal he appears in his damaged state. Not pleasant unreal, like a Picasso or Vangough. He's a Terminator in a skin suit, gleaming metal and teeth implants. Slowly, I raise my hands. There is no way we walk out of here without getting fired upon.

"Are you transmitting?" A soldier shouts, his mask filter adds intimidation.

Those of us with our arms up don't answer. I can't tell if the soldier is shouting out a nervous question to one of his own, or if he's probing us. But we can't transmit anything, we're being jammed. Probably by these guys.

"Are you transmitting?" He shouts again, louder this time.

"No." My tone borders on annoyance.

"No, not transmitting." Gordon uses too many words, making it clear he's no soldier.

"No, sir," Mav responds. Out of all our overlapping 'nos' this is the one that turns Juan's head.

Juan keeps his focus trained on Mav, maybe waiting for Mav to visually reference him as a child confers with a parent before deciding on their own. Juan's elbows drop a centimeter, barely perceptible. I notice, but I doubt Mav absorbs the notch he's fallen in a half second. I know I don't want to be on the receiving end of the Commander's injured pride.

"Geiger!" The lead soldier's words sift their way back through the ranks.

I expect a man to present himself forward. A Mr. Geiger. Instead, a box changes hands until it reaches the soldier, who extends the box toward us. He observes the analog readout, grossly outdated technology. It's like we're being wanded by a toilet brush. My very hygiene is insulted by the primitive device. I cringe away from it, expecting it to squeal some tattling wail like a bratty little sister.

When the accusatory siren doesn't sound, I relax. So does the soldier facing us. He removes his mask in one smooth over-the-head motion. "They're clean."

Masks lift away, pull down, rest atop some soldier helmets. The marks from where the masks have been covering remain, indented outlines, and smeared jungle make-up. It's clear they've been following us for a while, long enough that the uncomfortable masks have left their mark.

"Welcome to the resistance," the lead soldier says, extending a hand toward Mav.

Now Mav's eyes dart for Juan and some sort of guidance. Too late. Juan offers nothing but a blank stare as he lowers his own hands, calmly to his sides. Mav lifts his eyebrows. His demeanor portrays too much acceptance in the circumstances. A very 'throwing in the towel' arm extends to meet the soldier's grasp. They shake once, up then down with a nod to top off the final swipe of their grip.

"We've been out of the loop for a while." Gordon steps around me to get closer to the soldiers. "What's happening?"

"First we need to secure your prisoners," the soldier speaks to Mav, not Gordon. Mav looks the part of a soldier. A small chuckle— only a single one, if there is such a thing as a single chuckle—escapes Juan. Like he's coughing on a fond yet bitter memory and only left with a haggard chuckle in order to swallow that memory back down.

"Prisoners?" Mav asks. He does us the courtesy of wrinkling his face like it's a sour accusation.

"Good thinking disabling their spinal transmitters. We have reason to believe the initial attack generated from the base of the brain stem."

I look at Juan with his ripped face. They think Mav and Gordon and Belen did that? Ripped Juan in the face and removed some chip or sensor from the base of his neck? Can they not see Juan? There is no way two puny humans and one Mav (not a puny human, but no match for Juan no matter whose help he has) could get close enough to accomplish such a feat... This soldier isn't thinking. I put a hand up to my own face. Not damaged. Maybe the guy thinks my hair is covering the evidence.

"I can see you've suffered some injuries while securing the payload."

Now we're payload? I look at Juan. He lifts his eyebrows but keeps the rest of his face neutral. I don't know quite how to read that expression. Should I feel reassured?

"Come with us. We'll treat your wounds, make sure there's no infection setting in."

At the mention of infection, Gordon grips his own arm, like the broken bone has somehow sucked infectious particles out of the air and settled into the cracks inside him despite the fact there's no ruptured skin involved in his injury.

The soldiers separate Juan and me from the rest of our group, pushing us toward the stone sanctuary ahead.

"Where are you taking them?" Gordon asks.

"We like to make certain the AI have no access to a signal. The cathedral is the safest place."

Belen questions nothing as she's ushered toward the cathedral as well. The only difference is that, unlike Juan and me, with guns still jabbing at our backs, Belen is motioned forward, beckoned, invited.

35

I lose sight of Gordon, Belen, and Mav after the cathedral. They're led up a path toward the top of the bridge while Juan and I are forced inside the musty base of the stone foundation. We pass under two blue-gray arches open to the cool ravine air before stopping at a solid wooden door set in a thick stone archway.

One soldier steps forward and pounds against the wood. A deep thunk absorbs the blow in a display of being so mighty even sound can't penetrate the structure.

"Good demonstration." None of the soldiers reacts to my humor. "I particularly liked the way you grunted with that last door pounding. Really dramatic."

"Shut up," Juan commands.

I'd prefer to deck Juan in his exposed metal face but choose to 'shut up' instead. There's always time to punch him where he's exposed later. Hopefully, he'll expose a weakness that might benefit me, and I can punch him there.

The wood door swings inward on oversized hinges. Darkness from the inside bleeds out to the gloom of being in the canyon stomach at the setting of the sun.

"Two," a soldier says.

"Transmitting?"

"Already disabled."

"Good. Good." The door opens wider, a faint glow inside informs the full medieval vibe here. Candlelight. It's like these people are allergic to actual technology. Of course, we'd be trapped by the purist crazies—against all human advancement and determined to cleanse the world of binary. If this were still the game, it'd be the Dark Ages level.

We're prodded forward. Part of me wants to see how easy it would be to turn and challenge the soldiers. But Juan doesn't seem keen on action. I wait for a signal. And hope he's not doing the same thing—waiting for me to signal.

Light doesn't come with us through the stone doorway. Juan lifts his feet high as he steps through the dim stone hold. The candlelight doesn't illuminate enough to warn me about the arm across the threshold of the next chamber. I trip and fall forward into Juan, who makes no effort to catch me as I slide off his back and land face down on top of a mangled metal body.

I'm face to face with the blown remains of brain circuitry and tubes that once ran through a metal spine. A scream sticks in my vocal stores, either frozen or caught in a web of shock.

"What happened?" I manage. The carnage doesn't seem to upset anyone, not even Juan. It's gore. It's wrong. It's wrong gore. No one should be dismantled in this brutal manner. My insides ache for the person that was and is no more. The person that these humans deemed not worthy of wholeness or consideration in passing.

The guard at the door doesn't turn or breathe a warning or threat in relation to my floor discovery. Maybe he doesn't have to. Maybe falling on the mangled remains is enough.

I push the parts away from me only to find there's more—it's all connected by wires and limbs. Scrambling to my feet I kick the darkness around me for more trip hazards, moving forward through the dark as we're ushered by gunpoint to keep moving.

"Stop drawing attention to yourself," Juan speaks at a low volume.

"I'm not." The floor isn't littered with more bodies. Maybe one is all they need, obstructing our path and sending a message at the same time. Or maybe they only ever encountered one robotic body and never bothered to move it. I want to ask about it but worry Juan won't approve of my curiosity.

"In here," the soldier says. He presses us forward into an even more grossly unlit chamber. It doesn't smell like people. No body odors, no food remains. It's like motor oil and burned plastic had a party.

"Now what?" Juan asks.

I've been wanting to ask that question the whole time. Why does he get to be the one to ask? "Where are our—"

An arm strikes me in the side. I double over reflexively. If I had wind in me, it'd definitely be knocked out. Instead, the system regulating the pumping of fluids through my body skips a beat, sending my entire system into a temporary shut down while it tries to stabilize itself. I'm basically a spinning wheel of wait time until I can jump back into rhythm.

"I request to speak to your superior," Juan says while I'm still reeling.

"You don't get to request that," the soldier speaks. We can hear the ancient hinges of the door strain as the heavy closure rotates, encasing us in the midnight chamber. No access to light for Juan to recharge his solar batteries either. Like they know about such things.

Then Juan speaks in Mandarin, losing me completely. I'm barely familiar enough with Spanish to follow along when Belen speaks. But Juan has fluent speakers of the three world languages holed up inside of him, so language isn't a barrier for him.

The soldier he addresses must understand Mandarin since the door doesn't continue to close. Before Juan can pause between phrases I can't decipher, the soldier speaks over him, loud and angry. Juan continues talking, matching the other guy's volume. They keep talking like this, not exactly yelling, but not conversing. Just loud Mandarin overlapping more loud Mandarin.

"Why'd you hit me?" I interrupt their unintelligible dialogue if I can call it that. There isn't much back and forth between them. As I guess, Juan can't be dissuaded from his Mandarin word-slapping to answer me. "That's not helping!" I try to get in the battle. Neither of them seems to care.

I extend my arms to feel for a wall. Luckily both of my limbs respond to my mental commands now. Perhaps when Juan shoved my shoulder back in its socket, he connected a nervous system line that wasn't firing correctly before. No more gimpy arm for me. Cold damp material slips beneath my longest fingers, mossy. I lay my hand flat. The wall has ridges and rounds. Weird. I let my hand slide down so I can find a decent sitting location and realize the wall is not a wall. It's a thing, an it. A form. "There's something in here!"

Juan exits the Mandarin-speaking match. The soldier continues talking as the door shuts tight then seals in a dramatic metallic slide and clank. The soldier continues to spout loudly in Mandarin, his volume only fading by distance.

"Sit down," Juan shouts at me in English with the same intensity as he was previously speaking Mandarin.

"Don't talk to me like that." I move to the side of whatever it is blocking the wall and find more dankness, this time flat and wall-like. "Want to tell me what's going on?"

"We're screwed, that's what's going on."

"How do you mean?"

Juan's feet shuff on the floor, the way the Mord shuff when they walk because they can't see and need to maintain contact with the earth to avoid obstacles. "We're not getting out of here in one piece."

"Oh, you think?" I assume he can detect sarcasm. "I must have missed that clue when we were nicely escorted to this Victorian suite."

"We can't die, Jennie."

"I know."

"Do you understand what that means?" He hasn't laid off the volume yet, and it's beginning to really irritate me.

"Yeah, Juan. We're always collecting data..."

"Alert and collecting data, even when our batteries are drained."

"No." I wave a hand to brush off his notions. "If my battery goes I'm at least unconscious until I'm turned back on, like sleeping."

"You have an alert human intelligence with brainwaves that function independently of the mechanics you're now compatible with. You can sleep, sure, but you can also wake up—a human-minded paperweight."

"I don't know, this looks pretty gone." I lift the arm I tripped over earlier, covered in hydraulic fluid. Where the head should have been —air. Singe marks and burbling tubes stick out from the neck cavity drippling the goo I initially thought was musty wet and bumpy wall.

"I can't see anything in here."

"It's an arm, Juan. Without a head."

"Where's the head?"

I feel the singed edges of the neck for remnants or evidence of the head hanging on by a flap, cord, or tube and hanging back. Juan shuffs closer. "I think this is one of the Mord that got fired on. Like his head is blown off."

"But how'd it get here?"

I take my fingers out of the neck hole. "Stop that." Juan shuffs his feet against my shoes repeatedly. I know he's frustrated by the situation but going out of his way to annoy me because he's upset is not going to fly.

"I'm not doing anything."

"It's not funny, knock it off. Are you going to tell me what the screaming match was about?" Juan continues to kick at my feet. "You're such a child!" I say. "Stop." Juan grips my torn wrist, pressing the few hijacked items still jammed up there which don't belong, into the wrist parts that belong.

I attempt to shake him off. The Commander and I have a long history of not trusting each other, holding grudges and attempting to murder each other, but that was in a game—a game where regeneration was a possible outcome from any attempted murder.

"I'm sorry, okay!" I shout. "No one should have been trapped in that game."

"Thanks. Retro thanks." Juan's voice floats in the darkness a good distance from where I am.

He was next to me, right next to me, shuffing his feet against the sides of mine, being a juvenile prick, pressing the frame of my wrist in on itself... "Juan?"

"I said thanks, don't make it a thing."

"Do you have hold of my arm?"

"Why would I be holding your arm? I can barely stand you."

Aside from the verbal dig, Juan doesn't sound close enough to be the one paining my arm. "Someone's in here with us."

"Yeah, a decapitated robot. You told me." Juan doesn't shift away from petulance. Apparently whatever juvenile personality which also speaks Mandarin is sticking around for a while.

"Something has hold of my arm." I try to flail, shake it off, use my other hand to sluff it away, but the grip is too firm.

"Are you sure you're not just caught on something?"

"I'm not messing around. Help me." I'm standing, throwing all my weight in opposition to the iron grasp holding me tight. The slimy form against the wall comes with my movements. "It's the headless thing."

Juan's movement silences. He's not coming near the decapitated robot.

"Juan!"

"That's what he meant."

"Juan, get this off me." I put my foot up for leverage against the body and push with all my leg strength. The grip loosens slightly. It's more of a stretching at the knuckles than a loosening, but if I can maintain it, I might be able to slide my forearm and hand away.

"Jennie." His voice is close now, fingers graze my face and one shoulder. Juan corrects his hands to find my shoulders, my back to him but he doesn't seem to realize that as he speaks to the back of my head. "We have to get out of here. To find a way out."

"I know." I extend my leg as long as it will go. How does this headless creature covered in its own internal slime have such a reach?

"They won't listen. It's not their way. We can't talk our way out or explain anything."

"Yeah, I caught that. Could you pull this thing off me?" I attempt to hop turn so Juan might adjust and grab the body. I'm almost certain some post awareness reflex has been triggered in this thing. No demonstration of intent, or any communication has happened. It's just grip. Hold. A reflex.

Juan steps around, hopefully to assist in getting the spring-loaded wrist grabber off my arm. A scrape at the door signals the clank slide of the door opening. We both pause to seek out a thin sliver of light.

"I was told to confirm a claim."

The grip that held fast falls away, slapping the floor as if the form suddenly lost animation. With my vision adjusted to absolute darkness, the meager light offered by the candle outside the door illuminates the entire cell. The body at the floor is headless and one-armed, flopped stomach down at my feet. Juan and I turn toward the door, drawing little attention to the body at our feet.

The person at the door continues speaking in Mandarin. Once again, I'm excluded from the information. It's not a screaming match this time. Juan doesn't raise his voice. I'd go so far as to describe him as respectful and reserved. The man at the door has a much more skeptical posture than Juan and his hand hasn't left the handle, ready to pull it closed at a second's notice.

I try to bounce my full attention between which one is speaking. Juan doesn't shift his posture, doesn't vary his tone. He's the definition of 'robot' right now. The man at the door shifts weight from one foot to the other, talks, then shifts again. Nervous. He looks behind him, over one shoulder whenever Juan makes particular word sounds. As if something Juan says has him concerned about being overheard.

While all of this is happening, I barely notice the hand at the floor has lobster gripped my ankle. Stupid reflex. I should have gotten away from this thing the second it let go of my wrist. I can't keep fighting it, waiting for it to release and then not moving out of the way when it clamps shut again.

"Why don't you speak Spanish?" I butt in the conversation while trying to open the pincher grip at my ankle. "Or English for that matter."

"English is a lesser language," the human guard informs me.

He doesn't have to be so snippy about it. "It's rude to speak a language when in the presence of someone else who can't follow along." The dang hand is not going to let go.

"We'll see what the boss has to say about that," the guard states.

I turn to Juan. "So, you get your demand?"

Juan's head drops—the first indicator of human emotion since this soldier stood in the doorway. "Don't call it that."

"Demand? Is that what you told them? That you 'demand' to see who is in charge? Like you can demand anything from us?"

"That's why you can't say it like that," Juan says with a hand extended toward the soldier at the door. "And shake that off. You're coming too."

"I can't." I wiggle my leg, kick, and yanks with both hands. "It's got some reflex where it opens and closes. But when it's closed, it's locked in."

"Fine. Drag it." Juan walks to the door, then stops, waiting for the soldier to lead us somewhere else. We're in holding cells and haven't had a chance to settle in yet. I should be grateful they're addressing us so quickly, but the air vibes something opposite of luck.

"It's heavy."

The soldier walks out. Juan follows. Suddenly I feel like I've been here before, with a bare bulb and ultimatum that ended in me shooting Ed. It's only me in the cell now. "Fine, but it's on you if I end up shooting you in the face." I look down at my ankle weight. "Come on Rover, you're coming with me."

36

Juan follows the other man down hallways and low into the hold. I keep a struggling distance thanks to the full-sized body I'm dragging. The second this thing lets go, I'm running. I pause at the entrance to a long room already occupied with a crowd of high talking Mandarin speakers.

"What is this?" I ask Juan once I'm close enough. He stops at a hand from the soldier—a clear 'stay there, don't come any closer' gesture.

"Singapore connections to Colombia."

"I don't follow."

"I told you, the ring of the Intercontinents is dependent on each other to maintain power."

"That explains nothing."

Juan turns to face me. "Without someone to buy, there's nowhere to sell. Which means having resources or controlling them would be irrelevant. Saudi ships oil to Singapore, who ships goods to Colombia. Get it?"

"What about Ecuador? I thought they had the manufacturing sites and-"

Juan cuts me off. "Ecuador deals in the open market. Think of this circle as the result of prohibition."

"That explains a lot." I tap my foot, trying to encourage the metal corpse to let go.

"Be quiet. I'm listening," Juan says, even though he was the last one to speak. Like my facial expression is so loud in and of itself that it's distracting. I admit to not controlling my drawn brows and the concern lines in my forehead.

We stand in the open. Not invited forward, but not sent away. It's a weird limbo with a decent evaluative view if our scans were working. Seeing as neither of us has functioning systems, we're just standing there forever. Eventually, the hand opens, releasing my ankle. I hop forward and stand slightly in front of Juan. If that thing clamps down again, it won't get me.

"What's happening?" I prod Juan.

His posture shifts forward, carrying weight on the balls of his feet and neck stretched as far forward as it goes. "Get your filthy fingers off me before I rip 'em off your knuckles. You don't respect my need to eavesdrop on foreign conversations and I will not respect your nosey inquisition."

Nazrete. Not sure what I did to kick Juan into bitch mode, but I want to reset him asap.

"You speak Mandarin, Nazrete?"

"No, I do not and can't get someone up here to translate with you being so needy all the time. Be a woman, grow a pair."

I look down. Nothing about my physical form is capable of growing, and I'm pretty sure Nazrete has her pairs reference wrong anyway. I have the only pair of things women are known for. "Juan!" I can think of no other way to get Juan back, other than shouting for him.

Unfortunately, my shouting draws much more attention. I can't understand what is being spoken nor why several men point in my direction. The large stone room echoes, even when the meeting quiets. Wood chairs scraping stone floors continues to bounce sound off walls and ceiling as the congregation stands.

"Juan?" they ask me in return.

I look at Juan, who refuses to make eye contact with me. He could half raise his hand at least, like an 'I'm here—I'm Juan' kind of thing.

"Juan?" The question deepens in intensity and strength. I don't speak Mandarin, but I do speak anger and the guy approaching definitely has an angry face.

I step to the side in equal measure to the man on slow approach, still questioning my outburst. "Juan!"

That's when I realize the metal corpse on the floor digs fingernails into the cracks between broken rock and drags itself closer to where I've moved. It's following me. I step again to double check. Sure enough, the headless being extends an arm, finds a grip, and pulls the rest of itself forward by the fingertips. I'm not the only one who notices.

Juan jumps aside. "I thought you said it was a reflex."

"I don't know," I say. "Maybe..."

Juan shakes his head. Not a reflex. The Mord corpse pursues.

The men from the table stop their approach. One man waves an arm toward the back of the room. He calls out, drawing Juan's attention by the word he uses. At least now we can follow the conversation in the room, not that Juan's been divulging anything he's learned.

"Stop it, Jennie." Juan urges me to quit like I'm playing some kind of game.

"I'm not doing anything."

"They don't like it. Stop," he says.

"I can't. I'm not doing anything." I continue to step away from each pull and drag of the Mord body in my direction.

"Stop moving!" Juan shouts.

I still. The corpse pulls itself another arm's length closer. My knee bends. It's almost impossible to stand still. Everything in my body says run. This is Mord. What is the appropriate response? Run away. That's the only response.

"They want to see what happens," Juan explains. The men gather in a line far enough away to observe, but not so close they have to worry about the metal man bounding to his feet and attacking them.

"Why? What do they think is going to happen?" I can feel my energy waning. I haven't charged my power supply in forever. I can't last much longer without blacking out and thanks to Juan's lovely description of sleepless incapacity, I dread blacking out more than anything.

"Maybe they want to see if it attacks you," he says.

"I don't want to see that," I say. The Mord man extends its arm and scrapes himself across the stone another length. He's almost upon me now. I'd have to take a massive step back to avoid being reached.

"They're debating how to download the data from our brains, Jennie. Please, just take this one chance and see what the hell happens. You're buying us time to think."

"Think?" If humor had any place in this room, it's that statement. I can't think. I have a headless bloody Mord creeping one arm-pull at a time toward me, a host of angry Mandarin speakers debating the best method of decapitating me in order to retrieve my memory banks, and I'm pretty sure one of my transition fluid lines sprung a leak. My thigh is wet. "What if he tears my leg off? Or goes after my head? You've heard of the headless horsemen, right? Always on the lookout for a replacement?" I point to the thing on the ground, only inches from reaching me.

"They haven't had success downloading AI secrets from Singapore."

I stop Juan right there. "You mean, these aren't your guys?" I don't know why, but this news bothers me immensely. "I thought you had connections here with the drug trade. I thought we might be okay."

"I lied about having connections with Singapore."

"Why?" I ask.

"Who is really going to know? Once we're out of Ecuador, who cares? The AI Crusaders—" I assume this is Mav and his band of merry employees. "—can fend for themselves once I'm safe in Columbia."

"Grow up," I say because that's gonna sting. A surge of indignant energy rushes my system. If I wasn't bound by fear to the point where I stand, I'd punch Juan across the cheek. "This isn't a game, Juan."

"It's always a game. The rules are always shifting, and you never know which side you're playing for."

"You're a tool." I fail to recognize in my verbal jousting that the Mord has already reached me. Its pincher hand extends to my ankle like before.

"We're all pawns, Jennie. We're not the ones moving the pieces."

"I'll move if I choose to." I lift my foot only to find I'm anchored. I walked here with him attached to my leg. It's not the kind of thing you can run with. The ones deciding the fate of my currently attached head lean in. They converse amongst themselves. I look at Juan.

"All I know is that they've had no success." Juan continues listening. "None of the discarded bodies they've experimented on have moved post..." Juan looks at the thing at my feet. "Post." He says like that is the condition we're observing.

"This is Mord, right?" I ask.

"I don't think so." Juan looks at me. "I think this is ED."

"Ed!" I shout. The thing at my feet grips tighter.

Something flashes across Juan's face. I can't tell if it's curiosity masked by humor or some sort of unexpected recognition. Then he says, "There is specific housing prepared for every Gen. This looks like an ED shell."

And that really pisses me off. Because what the hell does that mean? What housing am I in? What's Juan for that matter? Why didn't more of my friends upload when they tried? If there's housing prepared for separate Gen... What the hell?

"You're lying!" Mature responses aren't important right now. What matters is that I'm about to give Juan a what-for. "Is there even a Nazrete or are you actually a bitch and I never knew before?"

"Hey!" Juan's tone goes up. He's either really good at putting on a Nazrete façade or I just insulted her.

Juan's brows go up like I'm a precious simple bot who can't yet tie my own shoes. He touches the back of his neck. I mimic the action on my own neck like the secret lies in some braille code embedded in my skin. Nothing. The fake flesh is rubber and smooth. Not even a micro wrinkle.

"His neck," he says.

The group of men discuss louder as the conversation Juan and I share drags on. I wonder how much time I have before they remove my head from my unmarked neck? I look at the GenED's neck.

Such enough, there's a mark. It looks like a VIN etched into the metal. I realize two things. One, this is a GenED. How the mark managed to get into the metal, I don't know. And two, there's no way I would be able to see my own mark without ripping the skin off my neck.

What does it mean if I have a matching mark? My serial key was a Con code. Miller told me there was no such thing, that I was speaking nonsense. But now I don't know what to believe. How many donors arrived before me? Where are they? If Ed was here before Juan…

"What if I know this ED?" I say, my voice shaking despite my efforts to keep it calm.

"Does it matter?" Juan asks.

"Is this Ed from my game?" My robot body doesn't leak tears. But it's like a transition line somewhere inside me has ruptured and the leak has traveled to my visual centers. "Is it?" I know Juan knows.

"How many academics have you met around here?" Juan asks very cryptically.

"Is this Ed? My Ed?"

"I wish," he says, and I lose it. I full on lose it. I run at Juan, dragging the GenED corpse with me, arm cocked for a blow to Juan's tattered face. I hate seeing all the parts and gears behind every expression he makes. It's like he thinks he's sanctimonious because it's clear how much work it takes for him to roll his eyes and, in this case, open them to full surprise and ill-preparedness for my attack. My fist makes contact. Metal on metal isn't as dramatic a fight in real life as I imagine, landing the blow in my head with full-on facial denting and knuckle scarring. Instead, a dull clank and one low grunt culminate from all that buildup. Because neither of us requires air to breathe, there isn't even a dramatic exhale or the sound of physical exertion.

The only really impressive thing is the fact that the body still grasping my ankle never releases. I also realize that my energy stores have increased since its grip reconnected. As I think back, I was at the point of depletion when the body first gripped me and managed to hang on much longer than I anticipated. Every time the thing has hold of me, I've managed to extend my alertness and capabilities beyond expected capacity. Like a battery.

"Hold up," I say out loud, "It's charg..." half a second before Juan's elbow slams into the side of my head, right at the temple. I crumple on top of the unidentified GenED. It's like Juan knows where the crash button is.

Involuntary reboot.

37

Just like Juan predicted, my mind doesn't shut off. It's like being paralyzed, but also blind and deaf. For some reason, based on Juan's prior description of trapped human brain in an artificial body, I thought it would be all stimulus bombardment, but it isn't. It's dank sensory deprivation. My head could be halfway removed, and I have no physical indication. No searing pain where my neck might be. I can't even identify where my neck is in relation to my thoughts. I'm simply a black mass of awareness, which sucks so much worse than I thought it would to be asleep.

I can't convince myself to shut off my brain. Go to sleep. Shut down. Just call it over. Over. Game Over.

Which is of course, when my auditory sensors come back online. "How long until Belen gets released from the infirmary?" Juan's grating voice floats through the blackness. I'd like to remind him that I have no way of knowing the answer to his question and return the elbow to the head when Gordon speaks.

"No way to know. Mav won't leave her side, so it's not like she needs us worrying. He doesn't trust them no matter what they tell us."

"Be honest." Juan's voice is quiet, like he suspects I might be able to overhear, but isn't totally sure. "Jennie wasn't your first upload?"

I go very still. Like in my paralyzed state there is a degree of stillness beyond my current unmoving.

"I don't know, man," Gordon says. "I was just barely hired on when Jennie came online."

Even though I can't see it, I imagine Juan deflating a bit at that news. Of course, I was the first. Gordon can't remember anyone because there wasn't anyone before me at the Mexico facility. Hate to break it to cheater personality bomb, Juan, but not every facility is as corrupt as the one he uploaded to. My figurative mental form reaches up as if to rub the spot on my neck which conceals the serial number most likely embedded in my metal skeleton.

"Guess who finally decided to join us?" Gordon announces, which is how I realize I'm moving my actual robot arm and rubbing my intact neck still attached to my undamaged skull. Even the rip on my wrist is mended. In addition, Juan's face is not two-tone. His smooth dark skin has a melanin starved scar where his face tear used to expose muscle mechanics.

"Anyone want to tell me what's going on?" I ask.

"We're not the only ones using dead zones for cover," Juan says.

"They aren't our people, are they? They won't help us." I know Juan said they're not. But Juan said a lot of contradictory things in the last few days. Sure, he has loads of personalities sharing his robot shell, but that's no excuse for being the worst AI in history. "And why did you whack me?"

Juan looks at Gordon. His expression reveals nothing. Part of me wonders if this is some kind of man-eye-roll like they share some inside comradery through lack of expression. Except Gordon's eyes dart to me, back to Juan, then me again as if he's waiting for one of us to let him in on the interaction.

"Where's the ED?" I ask.

"Ed?" Gordon repeats.

"Robot corpse." Juan remains passive, unreadable. "Was a GenED."

"That's pretty rare," Gordon says. "Surprisingly, of all the donors, ED were the first to disappear from the game rosters. Academics don't translate to application, I guess. The game is pure application of theories. That's what I've heard." Gordon swallows like he's talked too long without being challenged. He's usually challenged by Mav. No Mav, no stopping guard.

"What would your Gen have been, Gordo?" Juan asks, still void of inflection or expression. I can't tell if it's intentional or accidental, but he's putting on a real 'robot' veneer.

Gordon laughs nervously. "Civ probably."

The kid was Civ. "How'd they fair on average?" Gordon should have the stats for every Gen.

Gordon rubs the back of his neck, not looking at either of us. I itch to copy the behavior even though my neck was fine and non-attention seeking seconds before he demonstrates the action. "Nobody did as bad as E, but ED and Civ might have tied for second worst faring."

Juan stifles a chuckle. "E didn't compete overall. They mostly did ads."

"Well, yeah, but just like here—if an advertisement fails its purpose, it's canned. Donors too."

"But they're not gaming, not competing. Why eliminate them?" I ask.

"I guess those donors thought they'd last longer as an ad than a gamer—skillset, you know." Gordon shrugs as if he's apologizing for his opinion. "There has to be a set of requirements to reach AI. Competing was one of the basic expectations."

"Why even have the option?" I ask.

"I didn't develop the program." Gordon puts his hands in the air. "I heard that, in order to teach humans how to be AI, it was important to not have any CPU, or computer-generated personalities, within the system."

Juan and I both exchange a look. Our facial expressions reveal nothing, but perhaps the lack of expression reveals too much. Gordon switches his attention between us, like he, too, knows the thoughts currenting through our imitation brains. I deign to change the subject. "Thanks for fixing my arm."

"Don't thank us," Juan says. "We don't have liquid skin on hand."

"Who mended my arm? And your face?" Juan puts a hand to his fresh skin in an action of obscuring it, embarrassed by the mismatch perhaps. "Why fix us, if they just want to rip our memory banks out and download them?"

"They what?" Gordon asks.

"Yeah, they said they were trying to hijack technology or something," I say.

"That's not the story they told us. Mav thinks they're conducting internal reviews for Donor facilities," Gordon says.

"Sure. Internal. If, by internal, they mean ripping brain stems out and reanimating the corpse," I say. I expect Juan to argue with me. Tell me the headless ED wasn't reanimated, or that I'm delusional in thinking my energy levels were recharged whenever it clamped on to me—similar to how Mord used to use donor code as battery packs. That game conditions don't mirror the outside world. But the thing was battery powering me. Useful for me, but what's the purpose for the headless ED?

"Like Gordon says, GenED never were very smart." Juan's face tightens like he's holding himself back from saying more. If there is an ED sharing space in there, it's got to be internally hemorrhaging to try to get some vocal time to counter Juan's statement.

The door opens without any clank slide. Before I have any idea who or what is coming through to where we sit, I blurt, "We're not locked in here?"

"Why would we be locked in?" Gordon answers.

"Juan?" Surely he knows we need to escape, given the opportunity.

"Just because this door isn't locked, doesn't mean we can leave," Juan says.

Gordon pulls his head back like he needs to distance just that appendage of himself from the idea of being caged.

"Do you all have any idea how lucky you are?"

Abby stands in the doorway.

"Abby?" I haven't seen her since Geo's lawyers forced everyone to sign me over like a custody loss. "What are you doing here?"

"It's a madhouse in Quito. Egypt claims Geo kidnapped their resource scouts and faked the artificial epidemic to cover his tracks."

"Resource scouts?" I ask.

"It's how Outercontintents determine what resources to invest in since they're not technically allowed to produce their own goods," Abby says. "Like how the Piersons invested in Donor technology after Ace was injured at war."

"If you ask Egypt, they're not an Outercontinent," Gordon interjects.

"Then why did they have resource scouts entering Geo's building right before the terrorist attack?" Abby asks.

"Maybe they're the terrorists?" Gordon says. "Covering up their tracks."

"Your travel companion has already confessed to the act of terrorism that started the chain of events in Quito."

"Travel companion?" I ask. And what gives Abby the authority to come in here questioning us? Besides, we were long gone before the Mord attacked anyone, or they were fired upon.

"Where's Miller?" Gordon asks, cutting off my barrage of words. "He'll know how to straighten everything out."

"It's not Miller you need to be worried about," Abby says.

Worried? Who said we were worried? Should we be?

"That girl you came with released a video confessing to coordinating a resource-ring-wide attack on donor facilities to avenge her sister and she's implicated all of you."

"Us?" Gordon stands up. "Why would she do that? We don't even speak the same language, why would we help her?"

Juan takes hold of Gordon's arm and tugs him back to a seated position.

"Did you know about this?" Gordon asks Juan, betrayal clear on his face.

"When would she have time to release a video?" Juan says the question quietly, directed more toward Gordon that the room. Gordon twists his head, taking in the stoic expression unchanged from Juan's face. His brows furrow as he turns back to face Abby.

"I never did like you, Juan," Abby says. "But I don't give you credit. You're not like Jennie, are you? She's not much more than a pile of scrap metal. But you? You're different."

I admit I'm insulted. I'd like to tell her that the basis of our acquaintanceship phase consisted of me pretending to be human so hard that I couldn't let on I wasn't a donor. I *had* to play dumb. I'm not actually dumb. Except at this particular moment, I'm struck dumb with shock at how much I've misjudged her character.

"If it was you who came out the other end of the game, I might even be on Geo's side about the whole thing. But it wasn't you, was it? It was her." Abby points to me like I've done something wrong, just by being me. "That was all the convincing I needed to join Miller's circle."

"Miller?" I ask. My Miller? The man I think of as my parental human since arriving in this dimension of existence?

Abby backs toward the door, a heap of metal limbs and torsos are visible in the hall beyond. "Why don't they take care of these?" She kicks the pile of robot parts aside with great effort, which is slightly satisfying. "Melt them down at least."

She pulls the door shut, this time with a slide clank. Gordon blinks at the solid wood door shutting us in. I echo his human response, not because it came naturally to me, but because no response occurred to me and I need to react in some way.

"I bet that wouldn't be locked if Gordon hadn't asked all those stupid questions," I say.

Gordon turns his blink on me. I'm certain he's on the verge of an outburst when Juan speaks in a low, controlled tone—very non-human given the circumstances. Right now is the time to lose your freaking mind. We're being framed.

"You're smart. Right, Gordon?" Juan asks.

"What kind of question is that?" I ask. "I thought you were going to say something profound, or inspiring, or at least get us mad enough to ram the door with our heads or something."

"Could you create a transmitting tower given the material we have in this room?"

"There's no material in this room, idiot." Every corner is bare except for wood seating, complete with splinters, and stone floor and walls. This room happens to have lighting as it's in the upper section of the Ipiales cathedral, which is a bonus.

"I don't know," Gordon responds to Juan. What is he going to do? Weave a Cat5 cable out of thousand-year-old wood splinters? "What's your plan?"

"We need to boost a signal. Get it inside this building."

"It's stone, man," Gordon says in response to Juan. "Not much gets through this thickness of concrete."

"I need it to be possible," Juan says. "Is it possible?"

"What can you spare?"

And then I get it. We're the resources. Gordon is going to use us as spare parts to create a signal boost. "I just barely got mended." And right outside the locked door is a perfectly unclaimed scrap pile of wires and gears and electronic circuitry. If only we hadn't pissed Abby off so much she locked us in.

38

While Gordon compiles a list of 'parts' he requires to make whatever Juan thinks we need, I run through what I'm losing.

I lose my past. My human world personal history. Every piece and scrap I give away is my personal heritage, which I've already been robbed of once by Geo. I have no history before that, nor do I have claim to actual human history.

Here's the thing about now. I know little to nothing about 'then'. I don't know human history other than records I managed to flag as important in my efforts to imitate an informed-human-charade. It's not intimate knowledge. Surface at best. Even my surface knowledge, I can only espouse it like a rote collection of facts. I have no emotional attachment to human history. Other than my ultimate desire to not be discovered as anything other than legitimate in my AI skins.

Then again, the GenED who clung to me like I was its resurrection portal, what error had he made? If any? And if he made no error, and was a donor of traceable status, why did these technology purists rip out his human pieces? His brain...

"Do you have anything circular?" Gordon asks. "Like something conductive, but round?"

I look up from my stupor of thought—round?

"I'll give you something round..." The words slip out of Juan's lips, but it's not him who is saying them. Nazrete likes to torment Gordon. "I'll teach you all about round holes and pegs, Gordo—"

"Nazrete, ew!" Gordon's jaw can't get much lower. I'm more

curious if the shock on his face is the idea that one of us—robotic humans—might be capable of such depravity of thought, or whether we're capable of following through on Nazrete's grotesque sense of humor. "I shoved a copper wire up my arm a while back. You can bend it into a circle." I dip in my reopened skin flap—not torn by my teeth this time, simply sliced so I can retrieve items from inside and let the skin fall together again, though it will never heal. My skin isn't biological. I can be repaired more quickly than any human can heal if I have the appropriate materials for the fixes. However, I can never regenerate any part of me beyond my thoughts. It makes me think again of the GenED clinging to my ankles. That felt regenerative. But it's not something I have time to think about right now. We have a cell signal to boost.

"You shoved copper up your arm?" Gordon asks. "Why'd you do that? Don't you know that'll scramble your scanners and interfere with airwaves? I mean, it'd probably have to be like a mesh sheet to interfere with a signal, but still...Why would you do that?"

"I didn't know that, no..." At the time, I thought I was being smart. But I didn't really know what to do. I was trapped in a cage and refused to do nothing. The only thing available to me was the spare parts and tools. I thought it might have an impact. So far, I'm the only one affected by that action, and not positively.

"You might have caused the signal to drop before we even got out of cell tower range," Gordon says.

"Maybe that's a good thing," Juan steps in. "Whatever was making us sick could have been worse."

"It's not like a crazy amount of wires, Gordo. I'm not a walking Tesla coil. Though, it was better when I put my hand to my head." I lift my wrist to my head as a demonstration, pulling my arm from Gordon's grasp. He drops the tweezers he's holding in his attempt to extract the loose wires from the other tubes and lines in my arm, like a high stakes version of a child's game called Operation.

"Jennie, don't move so much." Gordon bends to pick up the tweezers. "Do you think it was Jennie jamming your scanners? Both of your scanners?" Gordon asks.

"What?" I feel accused of something, like maybe Gordon's asking if I sabotaged us. "No way. I was jammed too."

"Yeah, but maybe you didn't know you were doing it. When did you first notice it?" Gordon pulls my arm to him again and continues digging inside my wrist—less carefully I might add.

"It started about the time you all experienced altitude sickness," Juan says. His words come out metered, calculating, commanding. "It was a deliberate weapon to block Jennie and me from recognizing the problem." He steps deliberately. Too controlled for his movement to be called a pace, but too rhythmic for it to be a saunter. "Do you think you could make a device that we could wear?" He makes the movement of placing headphones over his ears, of hooking a device behind his lobes. "Something not too conspicuous that can be worn."

"For what exactly?" Gordon slides a long copper wire from inside my arm. It had jostled its way into my bicep – so far in, it has a bend worn hot where my elbow has forced it weak. With the strength of my frame and the lack of sensory nerves on my interior regions, I have no idea where it was riding all this time.

"A shield." Juan looks at the wire, where it's slightly discolored from being bent and straightened with every motion of my arm. "This war will be fought with invisible weapons. We need invisible shields."

"Uh...Pretty sure I saw those rockets blow the heads off the Mord." I recall the image on the car monitor without wanting to. The Mord didn't see it coming. They couldn't. Their eyes, though present in the AI human bodies, provide no information to their brains. The Mord glean all their input through their mouths. All senses work together at once from a single port. I have no idea if it's efficient. It's definitely terrifying. At least it was when I was first introduced to Mord. Now it seems sad and desperate. I'd wanted to tap the video monitor to warn them before the first rocket ripped through their midst. Even if I could warn them through the TV footage, there was no time for that information to save them. "That was a visible weapon."

"The Mord aren't our concern," Juan says.

"They sort of concern me," Gordon admits while he forms the non-discolored section of copper wire into a circle. The weaker piece he discards to the stone floor.

I pick it up, not sure if we have time to finish our project, how we can possibly disguise it if someone comes before Gordon's done, or what to do with the scrap evidence. I don't want to slip it back in my arm. The worn end looks sharp, liable to rick about and puncture something, like a tube carrying battery juice—or whatever keeps me running I've already been dealing with a minor leak. I can't handle any more problems without the help of a donor facility to conduct proper repairs. I put it in my pocket.

"I'll see what I can do," Gordon says. "You think we need something too? Like for humans?" His voice reeks of memories of falling from heights. I'd thought Gordon simply couldn't stop due to his improper repelling strategy back at the ravine, but perhaps there's more to it than that.

Juan steps up. His hand hovers over Gordon's work with wire shapes. I think Juan might touch Gordon, but he doesn't. Gordon's body tenses. Perhaps he thinks Juan will stop his hand, or maybe he's anxious Nazrete's in control. "Humans don't need to worry," Juan says. His hovering form takes a single step back, still close enough to impose a looming shadow.

Juan and I shed any part or piece we deem irrelevant, including a lower rib from Juan's lower right side and my left pinkie toe. The tools I'd concealed in my arm come in handy as well. Gordon continues to use the tweezers in order to assemble small pieces together. He makes what looks like a motherboard, minus the board and microchips. It's the connections between those parts he puts together.

"For this to work, I need to connect it to one of you."

"What?" I ask.

"Well, yeah. Unless you want me to dig around in your brain for the correct circuit chips. This is a boosting device, but you're the signal source."

"Not until you make a shield," Juan says.

"I don't have any material left." Gordon shows tweezers, a razor, which he happened to already have on him curiously enough, and an empty piece of tubing.

"I think I have an idea, but you might not like it," I say.

"What?"

"Our brains are protected by a semi faraday cage, like a protective skull, right?"

"Yes." Juan nods but doesn't seem to think too much of it.

"This wire shorted the cage I was held in." The copper-like wire I have left, weakened from wear, with one sharp end and one blunt end.

"Like blowing up a microwave, sure," Juan says.

"Can we use that same technique to shield our intellectual circuits from the signal?" I ask.

"By blowing up your brains?" Gordon practically chokes on his words before laughing. "I heard you were an E, Jennie, but that... That's just the stupidest thing I've ever heard of."

"Just shorting them," I say.

"Okay, let's say that blowing the microwave doesn't kill us," Juan says leaning back. "How do you propose we connect the wire inside our brain in order to short our system from an incoming signal threat?"

"We'd have to slit the back of our necks and insert the wire on either side of our brain stem." Honestly, I'm guessing. But it sounds like the safest and least conspicuous route. "It can be activated by slapping it down flat to ensure full contact while charging, or some other form of power source...solar cells maybe."

"So we'd have a potential self-destruct button that might be triggered at any time, implanted in the back of our necks?" Juan asks.

"Yes," I say.

"Gordo?" Juan says.

"I mean...Yeah. It could probably work if it's done right."

"Do it." Juan bites the wire in half. Seriously, he bites it like an animal—an artificial human intelligence animal whose threatened existence has driven him feral. He hands me the piece out of his mouth. Not my first choice, but I accept it. "Jennie goes first."

"What?" I ask. "Why me?"

"Two reasons," Juan says. "One, it was your idea. And two, I want to see how it's done."

My neck is rubbed till the friction cleans my synthetic skin, not that infection is a concern. Viral threat is still something I fear, but it's a different kind of virus than what inflicts humans and their compromised skin. I think the section is scrubbed out of sanctimony more than need. A small opening, only deep enough to penetrate all but the last thin layer of skin, is made. Juan decides to not have the wire in full contact with the skin from the start, but to leave a film between metals with the points of the copper wire sharpened fine and the length of it scarred by dings and strikes so that one slap will tear open the film if I need to enable my self-destruct shield. It all sounds counterproductive when I think about it.

"Where?"

"Just over the code..." They both go quiet. I want to ask what my code says. Can they see it, read it through the remaining film layer of skin? Or maybe they're simply concentrating so as to not tear that protective layer before letting the thick flaps of skin fall back together and hold the metal in place.

No one says done. I can feel my skin suck together where it was being held ajar. "Did it work?" No one speaks. What's written where my code should be? "Can I move now? Is it okay?" I twist to look at them both. Neither of them looks me in the eyes, or at each other. Like they're maybe pretending they didn't see anything. "Am I okay?"

"Uh, yeah." Juan shakes his head like he's waking from a nap. "I'm just a little surprised it's staying in place. I think it might work." I can't tell which of Juan's personalities reacts. Maybe all of them.

Gordon steps back from Juan as if he needs a little distance from what Juan isn't saying. "Okay, let's get this in you." He says to no one directly, but we all know he means the only other AI in the room. "We might want to hurry before the light goes away. I get the impression these guys are anti-lightbulb."

"You think?" I say trying to jump on the 'break the tension' and 'pretend everything's normal' bandwagon.

Juan passes in front of Gordon, turns his head slightly, and mouths 'you tell me' at an angle that I'm betting he thinks I can't see well enough to lip read. He's wrong. My hand goes up to the back of my neck, like a reflex of my curiosity.

"No!" they both shout together.

I startle. Their outburst successfully prevents me from touching my neck, but now I sort of worry they've implanted some C4 along with the wire, or something we should all be afraid of. Do I trust either of them? Alone? Or together? It's not like they'd have access to explosives or plastics to lay under my skin, would they? Did they? Do they? I search their faces for an explanation, none forthcoming.

"Help me with this, will you, Jen?" Gordon says. He's never called me 'Jen' before. The shortened name couldn't come at a worse time. It feels like a costume right now, not the result of familiarity and comfort.

Gordon directs Juan to the chair. Juan and Gordon maintain wide-open eyes, both keeping constant visual contact with one another until the last moment when Juan has to stare forward and remain perfectly still, so we don't accidentally trigger a brain-fry during the implant process.

Gordon carefully slices through the layers of skin. He peels the top flaps back from the final film of skin like removing a saturated sticker from a plastic bottle. The film left is see-through. I stare down at nothing listed in embossed metal welts. There's no code. Gordon and I look at one another. It's not like the AI bodies littering the stone grounds in this place. Juan's code is different. It's not. He's blank.

Gordon places the wire and we both let the flaps of skin rest back where they belong. The seam where his skin is damaged is barely visible, even without skin glue or sealer.

39

The device Gordon makes looks like a small copper Tesla coil with little bits and bobs of materials within its twists and a curved antenna. It's been thirty minutes since wire was inserted under the skin of me and Juan. Gordon gets no protective equipment.

Maybe this is genius on Juan's part. He gives the illusion that the signal we're boosting can only affect bots, circuitous brains. What I suspect to be more accurate, though nothing's been hinted at, is that the wire implants are a third counter, after two prior attacks—the one we're intending to boost, the retaliation, and then the invisible shield. In other words, we're fighting humans and Gordon just built one of our weapons boosters.

No one mentions the engravings in our vertebrae. Gordon knows what each of ours says, if my spine, in fact, carries a branding. I suspect both Juan and I are aware that the engravings are not what either of us anticipates should be there. I'd like to ask Juan which personality inhabiting him he suspects to be marked with. Gordon keeps that information to himself, and we all smile at one another as if we all assume we know what our own skeletal structure reveals, without having to ask. Perhaps Gordon believes his possession of both halves of our truth secures him something. A guarantee that his device won't be used against him perhaps. How else might we learn what our brand truly says than by inquiring with him?

Discussion at a minimum, tense with alertness. Our eyes scour corners where the walls meet in darkness. We listen with one ear bent toward the high clear windows and one trained on the gap between door and floor. The air tastes of barren things. Not even mice seek refuge in this citadel. It's abandoned of everything but these purists without cords and the carcasses of those they've mutilated for memory banks. I hope they never received the payoff of an intact and usable download.

Sound is the worst. It's everywhere in the absence of itself. The stone pretends to make swishing sounds if I stare too long at one mortared joint. The wind cries between cracks and the candles laugh with each flicker in a cackle crack threat of expending wick.

"When are you going to use that?" Gordon asks. The coil rests in the shadows beside the door in hopes when someone opens it, they won't look there, since we're not there.

"When we need to." Juan is nothing but patient for the precise opportunity to employ his weapon. I can only imagine Nazrete banging fists against Juan's brain to get the chance to declare that waiting for someone to pose a threat, or greater threat, first is weak or folly.

More time passes.

After all light from the sun fades from behind the mountains and the moon can't climb the sky fast enough to offer anything, and our candle has long gone cold, the sliding lock of the door lifts and scrapes aside.

All three of us jump. We're too familiar with our role of mute sentinels in the dark.

"Abby?" Gordon speaks first.

"If no one answers," Juan speaks softly, "move toward the door. Don't let it close again."

"Mav?" I say. No response, but a scuff.

Inside the room.

"Gordon is that you?"

"I'm right here." He's so close to me, he can't have been the scuff sound.

"Juan?" I ask. No response. "Juan did you make a sound?" Quiet returns, except for the shuff of the Commander sliding his feet blindly across the floor. I curse silently and move toward the door. "Juan?"

"Jennie, what are you doing?" Gordon asks. It's my turn not to answer.

Even with the long windows in this room, the walls are such thick stone they seem to suck any residual light from helping our eyes. I extend my arms as I feel for the door. I haven't heard it close again.

"Shit!" Juan's voice.

"Where are you?" His voice sounds far away or like he's speaking into a wall. Perhaps he's lost direction and plowed into stone instead of the doorway. "Juan?"

"It's gone."

"What's gone?" I ask.

"The device. It's gone." A low thud rips the silence. Juan kicks the wall a second time. No echo peels through the room, it only thuds out a single protest against Juan.

"Have you checked everywhere?" Gordon asks.

"Yes, Gordo," Juan says.

"The door's still open right?" Gordon drags his feet toward us. "Let's just leave."

I open my eyes wide as if impressed with his common sense. It didn't occur to me right away. He'll never see the gesture either. I make no attempt to translate my face expression for Gordon. Sliding my hands along the wall, I find a hinge. I check the rotation—closed. "Did you hear the door close?"

"No, did you?" Gordon asks.

"Too busy thinking about my own noises," I say.

"No." Juan contradicts me. "You were too busy making noise... *'Juan, Juan, Juan...'* I wouldn't be surprised if someone set off a firework without you hearing them with all the noise you were making,"

"Is it locked?" Gordon asks, breaking up our argument about the closed door, and moving right along to whether or not it's locked. His common sense on point.

Juan and I both try to check the door at the same moment. Locked.

Though I can't see the reactions of those in the room with me, I imagine the mens' heads rest against cold stone in defeat. Mine does.

I slide down the irregular brick wall against my back, my head bopping with each prominent bump or concaved ridge, careful to not let my neck contact anything.

"That was a waste," Juan says. "It's not like we can find that many spare parts again."

Neither Gordon nor I say anything.

40

Juan and I don't need sleep, but we still let it wash over us before morning. Partly to save our power stores and partly because of how defeated we feel after last night's robbery.

"You think they'll use it against us?" Gordon asks, finally sufficiently concerned about the weapon he's created. Obviously, he's a little too confident in us.

The exterior lock lifts again. Abby stands in the doorway once more.

"Abby," Gordon says like he's going to get through to her. "What's going on?"

"I'm supposed to ask if one of you has connections to Singapore," she says.

"Singapore?" Gordon repeats. "What does that have to do with anything? Where's Mav and Belen?" I feel for the stringy little human, not part of the human club. I like him better for it, but the expression on his face appears internally injured. Of course, he does still have a broken arm. It's possible that's all I'm noticing.

Abby looks at Gordon like he's inconveniencing her. "You already heard. She confessed to terrorism."

"But what does that mean? What happened to her?" Gordon asks. "Why haven't we seen Mav?"

"Do you have connections to Singapore, Gordo?" she asks.

Gordon shakes his head no.

"Then shut up."

I can't figure out this probe. Several guards have already witnessed Juan speak Mandarin. I'm certain the majority of the people stationed here know he's the Singapore connection. I've also began to wonder if we would be in this situation had Juan not let go of his zip line days ago. It feels like we've accidentally stumbled upon their stronghold more than it seems they were actively looking for us. Why Abby is a part of any of it baffles me, unless she was caught in her own escape and rather than make herself the enemy, she joined these nuts.

"I'm connected to Singapore." Juan rubs his temples, like that can even relieve anything for him. It's an imitation of a human demonstration of stress and fatigue. Neither of which Juan experiences.

"Come with me."

Juan follows her out of the room. Gordon and I walk behind Juan toward the door, only to have it shut before we realize it might have been worth trying to shove a foot between the doorjamb and the door.

"What's going on?" Gordon kicks the solid wood closure. A satisfying crack sings up the length of the door in reply, though no actual weakness appears in the structure.

"Nice," I say. "I'm sure the door is sorry for its crimes now."

Gordon cradles his foot in one hand, leaning against the wall to keep his upright balance. "When did you grow a sense of humor?"

"Since when did you care?" I walk to the far end of the cell.

"Did you see all the housing parts outside the door?" He hops to where I stare out the window. "It's like they're piling them there as a warning. You think?"

"Real good warning." I continue to stare out the window. There's no point giving Gordon the false hope that I care to make small talk. I had to in Mexico. It was part of his job to teach me how to be human. At this point, I believe the charade is over for both of us.

"Or maybe they got there a different way?" Gordon doesn't close his mouth after pronouncing way so that it's hard to determine when he actually ends speaking the single word. Like he's eluding to something.

He has my attention. I turn away from the light breaking into our stone prison. "What are you saying, Gordo?"

"Hear me out."

"That's why I asked." I get so irritated with the human ritual of requesting an audience when they already have it. I can't tell if it's a species-wide trait, or solely reserved for the most obnoxious personalities.

"What if the housing—the bot bodies, if you will..."

I nod for him to *please* assume *I will*. Because I already granted double audience by turning and then confirming that I'm listening. Go on, Gordo!

"What if they're moving independently?"

"They don't have brains." He's getting a little too close to suggesting non-human sources AI, which isn't permitted.

"They can be programmed though, right?" He pronounces his words lightly like he knows it might be less offensive with soft consonants. "Like they have a mission or objective. And removing the head or brain..." He bounces a hand like there is some natural progression extending into space in front of him before he says more. "It uh...You know?"

If this is his way of entrapping me to admitting something about myself, Gordo underestimates my ability to read between the lines. "No. I don't know."

"The objective maybe isn't programmed in the brain, you know?"

I feel my eyes narrow. The skin around my lips pulls in tighter. I notice my face reacting before I realize Gordon's words have struck a nerve with something buried in the back of my mind. Like maybe he's onto something. "Like their housing has been tampered with?"

Gordon narrows his own eyes, locking them in some mental visual bond. I almost believe I can read his mind right now.

"Who would do that?" I ask.

"Depends on why, doesn't it?"

"So you're saying we could determine which group or person might have sabotaged these donor's housing based on what their objective is? Like, we enable them to complete their mission?"

"I don't know if we do that." Gordon starts pacing. It makes my gears and pumps keep time with his footfalls, and he's walking a little faster than my system should be working. "If a terrorist group is behind it, it's not good to repair and set loose."

The more I think of Gordon's point, the less I believe there could be a positive, non-concerning 'why' behind anyone tampering with bot housing. Any tampering would hinder the human part from being in full control of their facilities. Maybe it's a good thing I'm not made of any overridable human-parts. "This is stupid. I'm done talking about it."

Gordon looks at my neck. I swear he does. He looks right at the spot on my neck where the wire is buried just below the surface. Of course, he's staring at me directly, and the inserted material is at the back of my neck, covered by hair, but I can tell that's where he's zoning in—my hidden ID.

"What does it say?" I ask.

Gordon shakes his head. Like he can't remember. He doesn't want to tell me. That makes me think I don't want to know. It can't be that bad, can it?

"Why didn't you tell Juan he doesn't have a code?" I ask.

"I assumed he already knew." Gordon is a terrible liar. Even a stranger would know he's bluffing. He's so easy to read, no familiarity is needed. But I can't call Gordon on his informative omission because I also said nothing.

"What does it mean?" I ask. "Nothing. What does it mean to have nothing?"

Gordon squares himself to the window looking out. "I don't know."

"Does mine say CON?" I ask.

The door opens again, bringing both our attention to it. I notice the pile of parts this time. It's like the pile grows with each glimpse beyond. It reminds me of the trenches in the game where ED was thrown in a heap of terminated players. Where I climbed a mountain of corpses to escape. I don't like how the game creeps into this world. Or resembles it. But maybe I have it the other way around. Maybe this world is being molded in the aftermath of creating such a thing as a donor game.

The gaping door doesn't close. No one walks through to our side. No one is shoved or commanded to get back in the room with us.

"Hello?" Gordon asks.

No answer.

We confer regarding our options through a single look—a wary suggestion with half-raised brows that perhaps we're meant to be free. Yet, we keep our silence. Like a slip of sound will close the door on us. I wait for Gordon to brave a glance beyond the wood plank door. He waits for me. I flinch, hoping he'll be spurred toward the door and I can remain safely behind. Gordon isn't drawn offsides by my false start.

"What's written on my neck?" I ask.

Gordon pulls as much air into his lungs as his frame allows, then walks to the door. He stops on this side of the opening, using the heavy plank of wood as a shield between him and the unknown. Slowly, Gordon exhales his pent breath while bending and stretching his neck around the side of the door. He holds his pose, upper body curled toward space beyond. He then stands upright and drags the metal handle of the heavy door inward until it's completely open.

At the threshold, face down over a pile of headless bots, lies Juan. Black singed flaps of synthesized skin curls away from a blacker mark on Juan's exposed neck. His wire is missing. It appears he activated his own self-destruct, but I can't be sure. His hands extend as though he pushes our door the small amount it opened. Though, why would he crash his system in the same act of letting us out?

And, if someone else did it, where are they now?

41

I rush over to Gordon, who pushes against the solid frame that is Juan. We manage to roll Juan onto his back. A look of shock is frozen in his wide-open eyes. Gordon switches his focus. Like a prairie dog looking for threats to avoid, he ducks and stretches looking one direction then dips again as he repositions to look down the other hall.

I stare at the flatness of Juan. He looks so...empty. For someone battling multiple interior hosts, it's impossible to see him like this, lying on his back with his mouth rigor mortis clamped, and not think of him as a large doll. A doll that can be programmed to entertain a complex and difficult child. The kind of child one must keep occupied...preoccupied. Because given too much opportunity and imagination, that child is a danger.

"Can we reboot him?" I ask.

"I don't know," Gordon says. He attempts to stand but slips, barely catching himself before his face slams against a bot knee.

"Careful."

"I'm try...tryi...ing."

"Gordon?" Human's aren't supposed to sound like they're having trouble loading pages or glitching on memories. Something's wrong. "Gordon..." He stumbles another attempt to get to his feet. I leave Juan's side in order to aid my friend. "Lean on me."

Gordon struggles to keep his head centered on his neck. His face dips forward, then his ear becomes the target of gravity, rolling his head to one side and pulling it down. Gordon bobs and nods, fighting his eyelid to stay open. He's given up trying to make words. It's a battle to stay coherent.

Nothing interferes with my system. I'm immune to whatever is attacking him.

"Gordon, you've gotta stay with me here." I look around the bot-littered halls. Nothing but bot parts and one intact, but lifeless Juan. Of course, I realize Juan is still in there, trapped. At least that's our theory based on everything we've been warned about.

'Don't get yourself killed—it's an eternity of being awake in your own coffin if you do...'

"Juan...?" I'm not sure why I bother saying his name, like that will wake him up in some twisted version of sleeping AI.

Gordon's small for a human. His weight doesn't pose any problems for me carrying him, but human size and shape...that's a different story. He's like an awkward package—too long on one side to lift naturally without help. "Gordon." He continues to nod forward, fighting for every ounce of consciousness he can salvage. "Where is everyone?"

"Mav!" I cry out. Deep inside, I hope Ace comes running, with his moody brooding and hidden coded keys to solving all the world's problems. But there are no coded keys here. Here is a land of gravity, which drags hope down with it. I need a hack, a code to implant this situation with a better outcome.

"Haayy. Moof." A space suit like apparatus, complete with oxygen tube and full-face mask plods toward me, encumbered by the gear being carried. "Goardn!"

I'm stunned into inaction. I can't figure out what's coming my way or why. Where it came from. Where the gear was found. If I should be wearing such gear. The person stops at the edge of the piles of bot parts like it's unsure whether it can navigate the obstacles of the heaps in the ridiculous get-up they have on.

"Help me," I say, hefting Gordon a little higher to adjust the balance of his weight. "He's sick."

Another person similarly suited rounds the corner. "Ohmai."

I can't discern faces behind the helmet reflections. "What's going on?" I ask.

They motion me toward them, neither person advancing into the bot fray. "Cohm." Their voices muffle through the mask like speaking through a breathing apparatus.

"I need help. He's sick." Something shifts at my feet. I look down, hoping it's Juan and he'll help me maneuver Gordon over the piles of arms and torsos. A partially limbed upper chest with no legs has flopped itself over—what would be face up, if it had a face. The single arm connected to the trunk of what used to be a bot reaches out and up, unobstructed from its previous position of having its metal chest laying atop its single arm. It fingers the air in front of me as if it's sniffing out my movements. I look at Juan, horror in my joints. Am I shaking? If I'm shaking, will those fingers playing the air piano sense it?

The suited persons exclaim something I'm certain should be censored if they weren't wearing muffle-helmets and turn back the way they came.

My instinct is to call out, 'No. Don't leave me. I need help!' yet, I manage to press my lips together so hard that pressure extends down my throat and the words can't make it past my vocal box.

The fingers grab and slash at the space in front of my knee, then freeze and turn to face the direction of the retreating suits. The delay feels like an echo and vibration of actions past. The suited persons have already turned a corner. The hand palms the stone floor, crawling over Juan's wide-open eyes and using his foot as a handhold to propel the dismembered being forward.

The heaps around me unfold and stretch out like dormant worms responding to rain. I miss controlling a shudder and draw the attention of a fully composed pair of legs with mid-section and arms still assembled, though slightly mismatched for sizes. The being has one leg longer than the other and the skin of its arms don't match. I close my eyes, if I can't see it, maybe it will go away.

Don't move, Gordon. Don't breathe.

The creature turns back to the mass exodus or delayed chase after the suited persons. But there is a pause. Like it's waiting for me to do something. Give myself away probably. And it raises a palm as if to convince me to stay—an almost protective gesture or warning. 'Stay put, stay safe' all roll into the motion of interpretation. Then again, itcould be feeling the air for evidence of me. For something like it is, I'm certain I leave a traceable trail. Energy output and electromagnetic waves and all. Even Juan, in his bug-eyed stupor, still gives off energy waves.

"Wait for them to go," Juan speaks through clenched teeth. Very much not dead.

The ground slowly clears of parts and pieces of bots. Some items remain, littering the stones, showing no indication of animating. Still, I stand. I stare. Waiting for them to point in that 'gotcha' manner I dread.

Juan rolls onto his side and pushes himself, with great effort, to his knees. I don't move. This whole place gives me the creeps. I can't move no matter how much I want to run. "Why did you bring Gordon out here?"

"Me?" I say.

"Yes. You saw what we were making. It's not safe for Gordon to be out here."

"You fried your brain!" I point to the back of my neck, indicating the trip wire while being careful not to touch it.

"Yeah." He rubs his neck with one hand, pushing off his own knee with his other hand to support himself to his feet. He mouths a curse. "They took my wire."

"They?" I'm getting nervous standing here. We need to find Mav.

"The other uploads."

Does he mean the mangled body part bots? "Why would they take your wire?"

"I don't know. Maybe they think I'm a traitor to their kind. Maybe since Singapore has been stealing uploads' cerebral cortexes and leaving motor reflex behind, which I might add, has gained consciousness without being human sourced..."

I close my mouth, not sure how long my jaw has been dangling open all dumb. I go through the motion of swallowing, though I don't know why. When I produce mouth saliva, it only recycles. I don't have to expel liquids in the same way humans do. "And that means...?"

"It means terrorists, like the Newburys who want all AI donor programs shut down, have proof that the donor program failed its primary objective to ensure all intelligence is human sourced. The machines are activating without donors."

"Newbury?" I ask. The media thinks that's my donor identity, I think. "Her family aren't terrorists, Geo shot down their plane. Abby told me all about it. Geo's the bad guy here, not the Newburys."

"The plane Geo's men shot down." Emphasis on *men*—Juan's makes it clear I understand Geo doesn't do his own dirty work. "Was a fighter jet, targeting upload facilities throughout the region. Newbury is just a codename. It buries the new species." Juan shakes his head. "You never had a supposed family file. They painted a target on you to take you out the second anyone said you were somehow connected to the Newburys."

"But who? Geo targeted me, but his men shot down the plane before it accomplished its goal?"

"Not Geo."

I look at Gordon in his helpless state. "How deluded am I?"

"Facilities are all over. Uploads generally suffer severe PTSD. Like post-war level trauma. It's been impossible to integrate singular uploads."

The donor game has been running for years, possibly a decade. Uploads have been taking place for a long time, just not publicly. Juan and I are the first public figures. However, the donor centers have their own wars going on, and apparently their own terrorists.

"Singapore started a program to merge source code uploads in order to balance out some of the issues coming out of the game. The only problem is, they're not splicing or grafting personalities together with any success."

I stare at Juan. "Except for you."

Juan opens his mouth like he's going to respond but closes it when

Gordon jolts. He waits to be sure Gordon doesn't regain full alert status. "Remember, I know what you really are—unlike the rest of these people..." Juan narrows his eyes and leans closer. The Commander knows I never had a code. I'm spare parts at best. "I can unmake you if you give those that matter any reason to end my existence on this side."

"I didn't think that was possible," I say, feeling like I'm every bit under threat by the Commander, who is more than capable of following through on threats. "We're immortal, remember."

"Everything's possible." He shifts his attention back to Gordon. "We need to get him some protective gear before his brain is completely scrambled."

"Scrambled, what?" We should have been working on that and not arguing about Newbury terrorists and donor qualifications.

"The real-life Mord hijacked my signal booster. They're using it against the humans—basically overloading their brains with high-frequency waves. Anyone who's been through the program or is familiar with computer thought synopsis should be okay, but the vast majority of humans within signal range will be overloaded and brain fried if they don't find some level of signal blocking gear."

The suits the people were wearing. "What material could do that?"

"Magnetic linings, I think."

That can't be healthy either, can it?

"Stone and steel with plaster and other dense material absorb a lot of the signal as well."

"Did you know they were going to do use that device in this way?" I ask.

One of Juan's perfectly formed eyebrows lifts in a manner admitting guilt, but not suffering from it.

I notice my scanners work again. I can probe the air for sounds, scents, chemical make-up, vibration patterns, and heat signatures. "Are your scans working?"

"If yours aren't, something's broken. I disabled the jamming device they were running. It interfered with the Mord signal boosting." Juan takes one more corner and encounters what looks like a bio-hazard disaster clean-up team.

"We need help," I say, realizing Juan never offered to help carry awkwardly shaped Gordon. Not very gentlemanly of him. It's a total Nazrete move. I picture her coaching the other men in Juan's head *'don't offer to help, that's totally sexist to assume she needs or wants help. Support her by showing you find her more than capable to handle the simp on her own.'* "Where'd you get those suits?"

When the group sees us, without suits—a very bot thing to be—they turn the other direction and run.

"Nice work, Jennie."

"Like you can do any better."

Juan takes off running, stoops to lift a loose stone from a low crumbling section of wall and hurls the stone at the back of one runner's head. It connects, knocking the suited individual to the ground.

"Better." Juan beams.

"Show off," I say. "Now what? Interrogate him for where to find bio suits?"

"No." Juan lets the rest of the runners flee. None of them stop longer than a few seconds after their comrade hit the stone. No one stays behind to make sure the person will be fine in our company. Nice friends...

Juan reached the suited person and proceeds to free them from the cumbersome gear. "I was aiming for the fat one. Too bad I got the midget beanpole."

The suit is stunted and thin, just like its wearer, like it's been custom made. I don't know the man still unconscious on the stone, but I'm certain he doesn't share the same lifestyle as Gordon. Gordon's a rail shape, and this man is a hard pretzel rod in miniature.

"There's no way Gordon will fit in that," I say.

"We can make it work."

Juan proceeds to stuff Gordon into what looks like a sausage casing at this point. I can't figure out why he's helping Gordon. He's anti-Mord as far as I can tell. Anti-human as well. That's all the things. "Why are you doing this?"

"What?"

"Helping."

Juan finishes pressing Gordon's soft stomach in, pulling the zipper up over each lumpy section. "Because." Then secures the helmet over Gordon's head. The other man now lays exposed to the signal. My only comfort in our actions is that this man knows where the suits are stored, even though we've obviously confiscated his personally issued gear. "You weren't supposed to upload out of that game. And here you are."

"The Mord shouldn't be able to function outside the game..." I say.

"Especially not without a cerebellum. That's the big reason I was all on board with the program burn."

"Program burn?" I ask.

"All the facilities were in on it. A huge failure...That's what they said."

"The donor programs?" I ask, remembering how I was told what an inspiration I was, how I was going to give hope and happiness to families with members suffering terminal illness or possibly fatal injuries. "Geo announced a huge conference—a training based on massive successes." I recall the news announcement. Something I hoped would be my ticket to rescuing friends from a game I assumed they were trapped inside. Wrong again. They're mostly trapped here, inside Juan. Ace with the Commander, his magnetic opposite, locked in a no-win game of chase as they push their north and south programs against one another.

"That was the plan," Juan admits. "Everyone was in on it. All facilities were to bring any publicly announced uploads. There was to be a coordinated fire, an accident that would burn so hot, it would melt all circuitry within us. We'd be gone. Gone-gone."

"I don't understand," I say. "You warned me against my team. Geo upgraded my systems..."

Juan puts up his hands as if he's trying to disarm my thought process. They were going to end me—like end me? "When I saw it was you...Jennie. It was really you, not some bot."

"I've always been some bot, Commander. Always." I address the person I assume I'm actually speaking with.

"I didn't know about the scraps thing until I injected you with new code, I swear. You're more like me than any other player. Except I was given a fake code. Ace really botched you there."

Scraps. That's what I am really. A collection of scraps scrounged together and given consciousness inside the game. I can't come up with the words I want to say to him right now. To tell him that he's scrap. He's weak and childish, and such a fool to think Geo was a decent person, to begin with. "You were going to let yourself be destroyed?" That doesn't sound Commander-like. I doubt Nazrete is keen on that notion either.

"You didn't see what was coming out of that game. It wasn't natural. Those people were seriously messed up."

"But you're not. Why go along with it?"

"They weren't going to melt me. They were going to pass me off as human. I convinced Geo to get the rights to your program and do the same. I'd need company throughout the years..."

"What?" Like the Adam and Eve of AI? How messed up is that? So freaking messed up. "You should have at least asked me if I wanted to be a part of that."

"So, what, you'd rather be incinerated than spend forever with me?" Juan sounds hurt. But seriously, what's wrong with him? This isn't logical. This is some kind of idealistic bullshit.

"The attack came early—from your group—Newbury." He shakes his head like it's painful to admit culpability in how the events went down. "He had to shoot. They were loaded with not-yet-activated napalm..." My memory feed loads information before I have the chance to be officially curious. Since the advancements in weapons produced the ability to carry weaponry that is inactive until desired to be active, there have been a lot fewer accidental casualties. "Geo hadn't finished the upgrades and we hadn't moved you to the safe-house yet... Belen's job."

Of course. That's how Belen managed to sneak through the glass building, she was working for Geo. Geo rightfully assumed I'd never trust him and sent in a stooge rescue. I totally fell for it.

"Someone from your group called in the hit to our hill ahead of schedule. Pretty much everything's been a mess since then. Including the Mord uploading directly to our shell factory. It's supposed to be specific code aligning with each housing, but inside the game is completely out of control. There's no order anymore. It's all backdoors and chaos. All the programs are connected through hidden levels, which can't be monitored on any facility screens, and the Mord have learned how to gain access to the backdoors..."

"What did you expect?" I ask, as though the conglomerate of donors before me developed the program, is solely responsible for its flaws.

"It's worse."

Of course, it is. But I hold my words. I'm bright enough to know sarcasm will only spark the Commander to speak down to me, and I can't handle that at the moment without wanting to rip his handsome Juan façade from his vocal box.

"Singapore has gone dark."

"What does that mean?"

"It means we need to finish the job here and burn Singapore to the ground as well." I startle at the familiar voice behind me. The person presses a finger to the side of their helmet, amplifying their voice through an electronic device, unlike the people before who tried to holler through their helmets. "We made a terrible error when we thought we could save mankind from suffering loss in the face of death."

"Dr. Miller." I want to run to him as a child would run toward a parent, even a grown child after a traumatic separation seeks parental comfort. But I know more now. For instance, Dr. Miller wanted to let me burn. It was Spaulding who signed my current existence over to Geo. Stupid, arrogant, attention-seeking Spaulding who saved me. "Do you care if I disagree?"

"Not really." He smiles, like my words and his words combine into joke and punchline, fitting together in comedic harmony.

I'm being taunted. I wanted to know, but now? No. Not like this. Not the butt of his joke, which I realize I always have been. This thing he stroked, only to push the abort button in a spectacular finale, along the ring of the world's power. If that isn't a flipping off, I don't know what is.

His smile shines through the helmet's clear shield with a genuine kindness.

I would believe he meant his words with generosity in light of my curiosity, but there's something different framing him now. For me. There's a sadistic glee in the subtle jovialness. He let Mav tag along on this expedition. Why? To also be eliminated from the donor life equation? The Piersons and their many life centers—taken out. Was Mav in on it?

Miller's smile fades to a mask of compassion and remorse. Probably directed at my existence more than the fact I'm currently a joke they all share. "He branded you as nothing. That's what he thinks of you."

I don't really have anything to say in response.

"Why fight back, when you're nothing?" Dr. Miller asks.

He's more right than he realizes. I've been nothing for so long. It's my origin story. A nothing collected from the subtraction of other insignificant.

The person to Miller's right taps his elbow. Miller's shoulders drop a few micrometers. "Help us correct our errors and we'll grant you immunity. From all this." He extends a hand over the stone floor. No bot parts or other carnage remain in the area. I guess I'm being offered protection from a stone cathedral. Awesome.

"And if I refuse?" I say.

Juan stiffens at my side before Miller can counter. "Jennie, you can't. This is serious. Humanity is being wiped out." Juan pleads such that I think he means it. He's on their side. What the heck Juan? "Do you have any idea why Singapore would have gone dark? Do you?" He doesn't give me the opportunity to guess. "Because they have to shut down any electronics, any device that a bot can charge from, boost from, run signal through."

"They're starving them?" I say. "It sounds like they've got it under control."

"There's more to it." Miller spits the words like it's so vile he has to elaborate. "They're being fed a virus, which destroys human brain function. The humans are getting their brains melted." He taps his helmet. "Their only retaliation is to turn off the lights."

"Since that's what the media sees in conjunction with the virus, they're calling it 'o'dark-hundred.'"

"How very military sounding," I say, hoping I'm turning the tables on who is whose end of a joke. No one else seems too impressed with my effort. Juan especially isn't laughing. "It's one of those, 'if you're not with us...'"

Miller motions for people behind him to lift Gordon's still unmoving body. "You're against us."

It's not a question or an ultimatum. Miller is stating a fact that he and I know to be true.

"She's with us," Juan says, taking my hand in his and following Dr. Miller and the merry band of bot-burners.

42

Stripping the thin man from his suit bothers me when no one goes looking for him. No one says, 'hey, where's thin man?' I don't say, 'e left a man unprotected from the virus,' which bothers me about myself. At the same time, what happens to Gordon if they have no spare suits?

"Gather everyone together in the cathedral." Miller's speaker amplifies between receivers within suits. "We need to strategize before we make a move on the Pierson group."

"Where's Mav?" I ask. I haven't seen him nor Belen for some time.

"We don't have time for bot sympathizers," one of Miller's group answers. "The Pierson group has been supporting donor technology for decades. They're the problem."

I attempt to get Juan's attention. He avoids every effort I make, lookingto the side when shifting his sight from a low vantage to a higher one so as to avoid meeting my eyes in transition. I bob and weave my head trying to tag his attention. Skunked. He's great at aversion.

"We're bots," I speak as low as I can, hoping only Juan hears me. "Whose side are you on?"

"Whichever side guarantees survival," Juan says.

Miller's people have no look of training, no military precision or restraint. They run with wild arms in frumpy suits and rasp through their breathers. They don't wear uniforms uniting them. Street clothes divide them by prosperity and taste beneath their hazard gear. It's a motley assortment of donor families and zealots who've always been against technological advancement.

"The Intercontinents developed tech too fast, desperate to cling to their new power and advance their stronghold on the rest of the world's dependence upon them." Miller directs more suited persons into the cathedral and slams the door in order to keep other things out. "Greed is the downfall of power."

"You're not motivated by greed," I say. What is Miller's driving fire then? Power? If I understand Miller's objective, I'll be able to form a plan.

"Eliminate the abominable illusion of power over life and death." Miller indicates the cathedral we're now in. Stone. Cold and inanimate. "That's what the Intercontinent was selling—lies. And people were lapping it up. Handing over fistfuls of yearly salaries in order to live longer than God permitted for their family members."

"The bots are moving into the jungle," someone reports.

"Where's the device?" Miller asks.

Juan maintains a steady demeanor as the humans discuss his creation being used as a weapon against humanity. I'm sure if Miller knew Juan made the signal projector, Juan wouldn't be a guest in the hall where we now stand free of restraint.

Juan's hands remain loosely clasped in front of him. I notice a back smudge on his left index finger. The kind of smudge that might be caused by intense heat. He sparked his own abort wire in an attempt to appear like he's not with the bots. At least, I hope that's what's going on. I've been burned by the Commander before. It hurt a lot worse than a little black smudge on one finger.

"They've taken the device into the jungle," someone reports.

"We need to adjust the signal that knocked them out for almost a day," someone else comments. "If we can sustain a successful transmission long enough to round them up..."

"Before they jam it or change frequency on us." Miller slaps the back support of a pew. "They adjust too quickly, even with our best techs interfering with their signals." Miller snaps his fingers in a pleasant manner. Even when he's acting like a religious zealot, he comes across sympathetic. "I need Pierson."

Someone sidles upon a tall suited figure and pulls the helmet from his head. Mav gags against a cloth tied across his mouth and secured behind his head. I assume his arms are also restrained at his sides. The arms of the suit hang at either side. I also assume with the Mord-like bots escaping to the jungle with the signal boosting device, the humans are safe to be without head protection. Miller removes his helmet and motions for Mav's gag to be loosened.

"Geo was right about you," Mav speaks low and controlled. "I never believed him. Never. I held him responsible for Ace."

Juan tenses at my side. I have to divide my attention between Mav and Juan. Certain Ace is listening to every word Mav spouts because I remembered something when Juan was kicking the wall. The Commander is attached to Ace. Their codes trace each other and both prevent the other from winning. The only way for one of them to upload is for both of them to upload together. Whether Ace is listening with a forgiving or begrudging ear is something only the brothers might know for certain.

"I hated Ace for giving Geo those codes!" A glistening drop gathers at the corner of Mav's eye. "Fighting for the Intercontinents and betraying our communications because he said we were terrorists against advancement."

"Shut up." Miller's kind demeanor dulls. He looks tired. "Ace made his choice. You know the consequence."

"Geo honors my brother with a statue of his sacrifice,"

"Mocks you both, you mean." Miller nods toward Juan like he's going to be backed up in his claim.

"He never had a chance in our program, did he?" Mav waits for an answer from Miller, which doesn't come. "Did he?"

Mav doesn't know about the ghost player, Commander, designed to thwart Ace's achievements. Juan shows no sign of reaction.

"I'm not looking for a moral debate with you, Mr. Pierson." Miller snaps again and someone brings a phone with a keypad showing on screen. "I need the PIN to your bank account in order to arrange transport. This isn't a safe zone anymore." He pats the stone. "Not with the bots armed with signal boosting technology allowing them to infect our air even in a stone sanctuary."

"Sir, I'm telling you, we can fire a scrambling signal back. Even short burst will give us an advantage," says the person on Miller's team obsessed with retaliating against the bots with signals of their own. "Belen is healed enough to program. She can come up with something, I promise."

"Belen's okay?" I say. My voice sounds relieved, but I have no idea if Belen surviving her fall is a good or bad thing for me and Juan.

"Your code, Mr. Pierson." Miller presses the keypad against Mav's chest.

"My hands," he responds, "It's not like I can type without my hands."

"You're not typing. Tell me the sequence and someone will enter it."

"I know it," Juan says before Mav has a chance to retaliate with a quip of his own.

Mav, myself, Miller, and the variety of other half bio-hazard garbed men and women occupying the stone cathedral all turn to look at Juan.

"I know the code," Juan says.

"Aren't I glad I kept you," Miller coos. I know what it's like to inhabit the receiving end of such a compliment. When Miller says it, you feel small but safe. Incompetent, but cared for. Everything I miss and everything that now makes me sick I ever believed him. "Tell us then?"

Miller takes the phone in his own hands, thumbs poised over the screen eager to enter the numbers needed to access Mav's business account.

"Hand it to me." Juan extends a hand. I can't tell who is testing whom. Juan's actions might be interpreted as a challenge toward Miller. Or maybe he's insisting he's to be trusted. I can't tell.

Miller studies Juan. The chocolate curls of his hair. The scar where he's suffered damage in our journey but has tried to mend himself. Juan's even weight balanced between both balls of his feet. The glint in his dark brown, almost black, eyes. Miller saunters over to where Juan and I stand at unease, extending the hand holding the phone. "Be my guest."

Juan takes it, pushes in a sequence of nine numbers, then hands the device back to Miller. "There you are."

Miller keeps his eyes on Juan for an extended time before glancing back to the screen. "Huh."

I want a glimpse of the screen myself. What did Juan do?

"Looks like we're in."

Juan helped them. Juan helped Miller, not Mav. It was his perfect chance to sabotage the whole operation, but he helped instead. Once Miller turns his back, I lift one foot and slam it down atop Juan's shoe. Juan isn't expecting the action and steps back with his other foot like he's lost his balance.

Miller turns toward us. I remain still, my foot no longer on top of Juan's stupid hope-treading shoe. "Gather your gear. We move out in one hour, and we're going to need all the protection we can get."

43

The safest place to be in a wildfire is where the fire has already raged, leaving nothing more to catch flame. Singapore is the char after a wildfire of uncontrolled technology.

Juan and I travel in the cargo hold of a large plane. Separate from the humans. "Remember when you told me the humans don't trust us?"

Juan keeps his head bent, as if in thought. I'm not sure if he's powering down, conserving energy until he can use his solar panels again. I've had surprisingly little need to recharge since my incident with the bot at Ipiales in Colombia.

"The first night we met, you said something about having to prove your loyalty. Or that Geo was afraid of you?"

Juan continues to keep his movements and reactions limited.

"What I don't get is why you keep helping them. Why do you continue to prove your loyalty to humans when all they do is betray you?"

"I'm human." It's the only thing Juan says. He doesn't need to say anything more.

I observe ice crystals forming on zipper pulls and bars distinguishing one luggage mass from another. Silence spreads like fractals between Juan and me. It loops and spikes at an average rate of just over one and a half percent chillier than the silence proceeding it. "You're not seated with the humans." By waiting for time to settle before sharing this obvious fact, I hope to fire it directly into a hole of oversight unguarded by the pass of silence.

I'm wrong to think Juan exists in any unguarded moments. The man is made up of the Commander and Ace, both have few reasons to let their guard down in my company. Juan doesn't fire back with words. He doesn't need flimsy verbalization to flash his security badge. He shifts, blinks so naturally I honestly question it not being a reflex for him, and then he closes his eyes and powers down. Like that. What I wish I could have pulled first, in a much more 'in your face' manner.

"Fine."

Juan remains dark.

"I can sleep too." I don't. I'm in a hold surrounded by the luggage packed by the people who assembled me poorly, to begin with, sold me off for parts, and tried to fry my brain with a sonic blast in the jungle. I'm not missing the opportunity to do some poking around.

My headaches once more. I put my arm against my temple and the plane dips to one side. It would be barely detectable if not for my internal sensors working at high alert. How an infectious signal has managed to reach me at this height is more frustrating than the screeching pain sensation pinging around my brain, held to a dull grating while I keep my mangled wrist to my head. My wrist vibrates with the sensation in my head being pressed outward through my hand—almost like a tower signal being pushed out from my brain. Pushing it out and away so my head won't hurt with the intensity of the entirety of a signal so large.

Juan tumbles from his powered down state. He tries to stand but staggers as if drunk. "What's happening?"

I manage to keep my feet under me. "We're banking."

"We shouldn't be banking."

"Maybe if we weren't in the baggage hold, like a normal human, we'd know why."

"I can't get a read on the gear." Juan squints his eyes like he's concentrating or reading minds. I squint my eyes hoping he can't actually read minds.

"Could you read it before?"

"I was tracking our flight path before everything went sideways."

He's tracking our flight path and he didn't tell me? Is he also holding the fact he intends to shut down the program? All programs. Our programs—that which birthed me and the Commander? Juan isn't the only object in the cargo hold capable of bypassing firewall protected thought patterns. "We have no idea what's happening up there. Maybe a Mord got on board..." I suggest half-heartedly.

"I think I'd know. I cataloged everything that went into this plane before takeoff."

"Does that include everything that might have already been on it?"

"Why do you ask?" He staggers to keep his feet planted as the plane banks harder.

"Because of that awful high-pitched tone. Isn't that why you're tipsy?" I don't take my hand away from my head. Projecting the sonic waves from my metal skull soothes me.

"I'm not tipsy." Juan grips a bar holding luggage.

"You seem unstable."

"The plane's unstable. Don't you feel it?"

I do. But I also feel that same sensation as the signal that caused Juan to drop from the zip line like a sack of spare gears. "We're losing altitude."

"I know that." Juan snipes as if he doesn't know or detect the loss of height but doesn't want me to know he doesn't know. Juan crosses himself—a sure sign he's human.

No robot would put stock in a higher power. We're the highest power on the planet.

How do I know this?

I just do.

It's not the only thing I know.

Realization floods over me, along with questions.

How am I transmitting the signal even when the towers are scrambled to prevent me from signaling my kind? I don't exactly know how it works, but I know it hurts like hell and only my wire crossed forearm keeps the pain going out and not stuck inside me. I am a signal tower and there's nothing that can be done to shut me down. I'm self-sustained. The Mord at Ipiales taught me that I can recharge by attaching to any program upload—even the seemingly discarded spare parts. And Juan has solar panels, so I can be sustained off his system indefinitely. No charging port necessary.

I'm the one who sent the signal for the Mord to upload all at once. I'm the one who ordered the Mord to retaliate after the bomb landed in their midst and they could do nothing but scramble away broken and weary.

I'm the one who declared war on humans hours ago. The one who just got word Singapore is compromised despite coordinated efforts to shut down the program. I'm the one who registered when our craft crossed over into Outercontinent airspace and the one who is grounding this plane before it crosses back into the Intercontinents territory along with their technologically advanced resources and skilled signal blocking ability.

Why has it taken me this long to realize this side of the game is still a game? The stakes are higher, and the deceit is more clever. I brought it with me, partly thanks to Ace recoding a wavelength to pass as a real player. Plus the Commander shooting me with a code to bypass human failsafes after recovering from Mord virus. It means I transmit signal to confuse and disable human brainwaves, inside and *outside* the game. I'm the one who began the virus, scrambling human circuits.

I'm the one behind it all.

And I'm the only one who can stop it.

THE END

ACKNOWLEDGEMENTS

Thank you to Immortal Works, for trusting me to continue this story, for your encouragement, support, kinship, and wonderful examples. I'm so honored to be a part of the IW family.

Thank you Melissa Meibos my editor extraordinaire. Holli Anderson and Beth Buck for your endless work. The world should know you have super powers. Kevin Nielson, you're immortal in so many ways. Mackenzie Seidel and Jamie Lane—you both amaze and inspire me. Thank you for being in my corner.

My agent Jessica Schmeidler of Golden Wheat Literary and all my Golden Wheat family. I admire you all so much and can't believe my luck to be numbered amongst you.

PCC, you know who you are. I would never be anywhere without you all.

My family who raised me—you're worth the world and more. You may not realize your value every day, but I see you and I know you're good and true. I'm amazed by each of you.

My husband Devin who puts up with late night clacking and reads my work even if it's not his genre of choice <3 Thank you for being there for me always. My three astounding children—I am proud and honored to be your mom. You three inspire me and make me hope to be as good and sincere and kind and hard working as you are. Thank you, family. I'm grateful for you most of all.

ABOUT THE AUTHOR

Aften Brook Szymanski would not win CBS game of Survivor. She might win Bingo at Family Night. She's obsessed with LEGOs, cozy reading nooks, and over-the-knee socks. A graduate of the College of Southern Idaho with an Associate of Arts degree, Brigham Young University with a Bachelor of Science degree, and the University of Utah with a Master of Education degree. Learning is more fun than testing, sometimes we have to endure both.

Aften has a connective tissue disorder (Marfan Syndrome) and facial recognition disorder (unrelated conditions). She is likely to say hi to someone she doesn't know and totally miss noticing her best friend crossing paths at the grocery store. It can be awkward either way.

She lives in a very cold Wyoming valley with her husband, three kids, and three competing cats, where they are being cryogenically preserved for all time—thanks to how cold it is.

This has been an
Immortal Production